THE MYSTERY OF THE HASTY ARROW

MORE WILDSIDE CLASSICS

THE MYSTERY OF THE HASTY ARROW

ANNA KATHARINE GREEN

WILDSIDE PRESS

THE MYSTERY OF THE HASTY ARROW

This edition published in 2006 by Wildside Press, LLC.
www.wildsidepress.com

BOOK I

A PROBLEM OF THE FIRST ORDER

I

"LET SOME ONE SPEAK!"

The hour of noon had just struck, and the few visitors still lingering among the curiosities of the great museum were suddenly startled by the sight of one of the attendants running down the broad, central staircase, loudly shouting:

"Close the doors! Let no one out! An accident has occurred, and nobody's to leave the building."

There was but one person near either of the doors, and as he chanced to be a man closely connected with the museum,—being, in fact, one of its most active directors,—he immediately turned about and in obedience to a gesture made by the attendant, ran up the marble steps, followed by some dozen others.

At the top they all turned, as by common consent, toward the left-hand gallery, where in the section marked II, a tableau greeted them which few of them will ever forget.

I say "tableau" because the few persons concerned in it stood as in a picture, absolutely motionless and silent as the dead. Sense, if not feeling, was benumbed in them all, as in another moment it was benumbed in the breasts of these new arrivals. Tragedy was there in its most terrible, its most pathetic, aspect. The pathos was given by the victim,—a young and pretty girl lying face upward on the tessellated floor with an arrow in her breast and death stamped unmistakably on every feature,—the terror by the look and attitude of the woman they saw kneeling over her—a remarkable woman, no longer young, but of a presence to hold the attention, even if the circumstances had been of a far less tragic nature. Her hand was on the arrow but she had made no movement to withdraw it, and her eyes, fixed upon space, showed depths of horror hardly to be explained even by the suddenness and startling character of the untoward fatality of which she had just been made the unhappy witness.

The director, whose name was Roberts, thought as he paused on the edge of the crowd that he had never seen a countenance upon which woe had stamped so deep a mark; and greatly moved by it, he was about to seek some explanation of a scene to which appearances gave so little clue, when the tall but stooping figure of the Curator entered, and he found himself relieved from a task whose seriousness he had no difficulty in measuring.

To those who knew William Jewett well, it was evident that he had been called from some task which still occupied his thoughts and for the moment somewhat bewildered his understanding. But as he was a conscientious man and quite capable of taking the lead when once roused to the exigencies of an occasion, Mr. Roberts felt a certain interest in watching the slow awakening of this self-absorbed man to the awful circumstances which in one instant had clouded the museum in an atmosphere of mysterious horror.

When the full realization came,—which was not till a way had been made for him to the side of the stricken woman crouching over the dead child,—the energy which transformed his countenance and gave character to his usually bent and inconspicuous figure was all if not more than the anxious director expected.

Finding that his attempts to meet the older woman's eye only prolonged the suspense, the Curator addressed her quietly, and in sympathetic tones inquired whose child this was and how so dreadful a thing had happened.

She did not answer. She did not even look his way. With a rapid glance into the faces about him, ending in one of deep compassion directed toward herself, he repeated his question.

Still no response—still that heavy silence, that absolute immobility of face and limb. If her faculty of hearing was dulled, possibly she would yield to that of touch. Stooping, he laid his hand on her arm.

This roused her. Slowly her eyes lost their fixed stare and took on a more human light. A shudder shook her frame, and gazing down into the countenance of the young girl lying at her feet, she broke into moans of such fathomless despair as wrung the hearts of all about her.

It was a scene to test the nerve of any man. To one of the Curator's sympathetic temperament it was well-nigh unendurable. Turning to those nearest, he begged for an explanation of what they saw before them:

"Some one here must be able to tell me. Let that some one speak."

At this the quietest and least conspicuous person present, a young man heavily spectacled and of student-like appearance, advanced a step and said:

"I was the first person to come in here after this poor young lady fell. I was looking at coins just beyond the partition there, when I heard a gasping cry. I had not heard her fall—I fear I was very much preoccupied in my search for an especial coin I had been told I should find here—but I did hear the cry she gave, and startled by the sound, left the section where I was and entered this one, only to see just what you are seeing now."

The Curator pointed at the two women.

"This? The one woman kneeling over the other with her hand on the arrow?"

"Yes, sir."

A change took place in the Curator's expression. Involuntarily his eyes rose to the walls hung closely with Indian relics, among which was a quiver in which all could see arrows similar to the one now in the breast of the young girl lying dead before them.

"This woman must be made to speak," he said in answer to the low murmur which followed this discovery. "If there is a doctor present—"

Waiting, but receiving no response, he withdrew his hand from the woman's arm and laid it on the arrow.

This roused her completely. Loosing her own grasp upon the shaft, she cried, with sudden realization of the people pressing about her:

"I could not draw it. That causes death, they say. Wait! she may still be alive. She may have a word to speak."

She was bending to listen. It was hardly a favorable moment for further questioning, but the Curator in his anxiety could not refrain from saying:

"Who is she? What is her name and what is yours?"

"Her name?" repeated the woman, rising to face him again. "How should I know? I was passing through this gallery and had just stopped to take a look into the court when this young girl bounded by me from behind and flinging up her arms, fell with a deep sigh to the floor. I saw an arrow in her breast, and—"

Emotion choked her, and when some one asked if the girl was a stranger to her, she simply bowed her head; then, letting her gaze pass from face to face till it had completed the circle of those about her, she said in her former mechanical way:

"My name is Ermentrude Taylor. I came to look at the bronzes. I should like to go now."

But the crowd which had formed about her was too compact to allow her to pass. Besides, the director, Mr. Roberts, had something to say first. Working his way forward, he waited till he had attracted her attention and then remarked in his most considerate manner:

"You will pardon these importunities, Mrs. Taylor. I am a director of this museum, and if Mr. Jewett will excuse me,"—here he bowed to the Curator,—"I should like to inquire from what direction the arrow came which ended this young girl's life?"

For a moment she stood aghast, fixing him with her eye as though to ask whither this inquiry tended. Then with an air of intention which was not without some strange element of fear, she allowed her glance to travel across the court till it rested upon the row of connected arches facing them from the opposite gallery.

"Ah," said he, putting her look into words, "you think the arrow came from the other side of the building. Did you see anyone over there,—in the gallery, I mean,—at or before the instant of this young girl's fall?"

She shook her head.

"Did any of *you*?" he urged, with his eyes on the crowd. "Some one must have been looking that way."

But no answer came, and the silence was fast becoming oppressive when these words, whispered by one woman to another, roused them anew and sent every glance again to the walls—even hers for whose benefit this remark had possibly been made:

"But there are no arrows over there. All the arrows are here."

She was right. They were here, quiver after quiver of them; nor were they all beyond reach. As the woman thus significantly assailed noted this and saw with what suspicion others noted it also, a decided change took place in her aspect.

"I should like to sit down," she murmured. Possibly she was afraid she might fall.

As some one brought a chair, she spoke, but very tremulously, to the director:

"Are there no arrows in the rooms over there?"

"I am quite sure not."

"And no bows?"

"None."

"If—if anyone had been seen in the gallery—"

"No one was."

"You are sure of that?"

"You heard the question asked. It brought no answer."

"But—but these galleries are visible from below. Some one may have been looking up from the court and—"

"If there was any such person in the building, he would have been here by this time. People don't hold back such information."

"Then—then—" she stammered, her eyes taking on a hunted look, "you conclude—these people conclude *what*?"

"Madam,"—the word came coldly, stinging her into drawing herself to her full height,—"it is not for me to conclude in a case like this. That is the business of the police."

At this word, with its suggestion of crime, her air of conscious power vanished in sudden collapse. Possibly she had seen the significant gesture with which the Curator pointed out a quiver from which one of the arrows was missing. That this was so, was shown by her next question:

"But where is the bow? Look about on the floor. You will find none. How can an arrow be shot without a bow?"

"It cannot be," came from some one at her back. "But it can be driven home like a dagger if the hand wielding it is sufficiently powerful."

A cry left her lips; she seemed to listen as for some echo; then in a wild abandonment which ignored person and place she flung herself again at the dead girl's side, and before the astonished people surrounding her could intervene, she had caught up the body in her arms, and bending over it, whispered word after word into the poor child's closed ear.

II

IN ROOM B

Five minutes later the Curator was at the phone calling up Police Headquarters. A death had occurred at the museum. Would they send over a capable detective?

"What kind of death?" was the harsh reply. "We don't send detectives in cases of heart-failure or simple accident. Is it an accident?"

"No—no—hardly. It looks more like an insane woman's attack upon a harmless stranger. It's the oddest sort of an affair, and we feel very helpless. No common officer will do. We have one of that kind in the building. What we want is a man of brains; he will need them."

A muffled sound at the other end—then a different voice asking some half-dozen comprehensive questions—which, having been answered to the best of the Curator's ability, were followed by the welcome assurance that a man on whose experience he could rely would be at the museum doors within five minutes.

With an air of relief Mr. Jewett stepped again into the court, and repelling with hasty gestures the importunities of the small group of men and women who had lacked the courage to follow the more adventurous ones upstairs, crossed to where the doorman stood on guard over the main entrance.

"Locked?" he asked.

"Yes, sir. Such were the orders. Didn't you give them?"

"No, but I should have done so, had I known. No one's to go out, and no one's to come in but the detective whom I am expecting any moment."

They had not long to wait. Before their suspense had reached fever-point, a tap was heard on the great door. It was opened, and a young man stepped in.

"Coast clear?" he sang out with a humorous twist of his jaw as he noted the Curator's evident chagrin at his meager and unsatisfactory appearance. "Oh, I'm not your man," he added as his eye ran over the whole place with a look which seemed to take in every detail in an instant. "Mr. Gryce is in the automobile. Wait till I help him up."

He was gone before the Curator could utter a word, only to reappear in a few minutes with a man in his wake whom the former at first blush thought to be as much past the age where experience makes for efficiency as the other seemed to be short of it.

But this impression, if impression it were, was of short duration. No sooner had this physically weak but extremely wise old man entered upon the scene than his mental power became evident to every person there. Timorous hearts regained their composure, and the Curator—who in his ten years of service had never felt the burden of his position so acutely as in the last ten minutes—showed his relief by a volubility quite unnatural to him under ordinary conditions. As he conducted the detectives across the court, he talked not of the victim, as might reasonably be expected, but of the woman who had been found leaning over her with her hand on the arrow.

"We think her some escaped lunatic," he remarked. "Only a demented woman would act as she does. First she denied all knowledge of the girl. Then when she was made to see that the arrow sticking in the girl's breast had been taken from a quiver hanging within arm's reach on the wall and used as lances are used, she fell a-moaning and crying, and began to whisper in the poor child's senseless ear."

"A common woman? One of a low-down type?"

"Not at all. A lady, and an impressive one, at that. You seldom see her equal. That's what has upset us so. The crime and the criminal do not seem to fit."

The detective blinked. Then suddenly he seemed to grow an inch taller.

"Where is she now?" he asked.

"In Room B, away from the crowd. She is not alone. A young lady detained with the rest of the people here is keeping her company, to say nothing of an officer we have put on guard."

"And the victim?"

"Lies where she fell, in Section II on the upper floor. There was no call to move her. She was dead when we came upon the scene. She does not look to be more than sixteen years old."

"Let's go up. But wait—can we see that section from here?"

They were standing at the foot of the great staircase connecting the two floors. Above them, stretching away on either side, ran the two famous, highly ornamented galleries, with their row of long, low arches indicating the five compartments into which they were severally divided. Pointing to the second one on the southern side, the Curator replied:

"That's it—the one where you see the Apache relics hanging high on the rear wall. We shall have to shift those to some other place just as soon as we can recover from this horror. I don't want the finest spot in the whole museum made a Mecca for the morbid and the curious."

The remark fell upon unheeding ears. Detective Gryce was looking, not in the direction named, but in the one directly opposite to it.

"I see," he quietly observed, "that there is a clear view across. Was there no one in the right-hand gallery to see what went on in the left?"

"Not that I have heard of. It's the dullest hour of the day, and not only this gallery but many of the rooms were entirely empty."

"I see. And now, what about the persons who were here? How many of them have you let go?"

"Not one; the doors have been opened twice only—once to admit the officer you will find on guard, and the other to let in yourself."

"Good! And how many have you here, all told?"

"I have not had time to count them, but I should say less than thirty. This includes myself, as well as two attendants."

With a thoughtful air Mr. Gryce turned in the direction of the few persons he could see huddled together around one of the central statues.

"Where are the others?" he asked.

"Upstairs—in and about the place where the poor child lies."

"They must be got out of there. Sweetwater!"

The young man who had entered with him was at his side in an instant.

"Clear the galleries. Then take down the name and address of every person in the building."

"Yes, sir."

Before the last word had left his lips, the busy fellow was halfway up the marble steps. "Lightning," some of his pals called him, perhaps because he was as noiseless as he was quick. Meanwhile the senior detective had drawn the Curator to one side.

"We'll take a look at these people as they come down. I have been said to be able to spot a witness with my eyes shut. Let's see what I can do with my eyes open."

"Young and old, rich and poor," murmured the Curator as some dozen persons appeared at the top of the staircase.

"Yes," sighed the detective, noting each one carefully as he or she filed down, "we sha'n't make much out of this experiment. Not one of them avoids our looks. Emotion enough, but not of the right sort. Well, we'll leave them to Sweetwater. Our business is above."

The Curator offered his arm. The old man made a move to take it—then drew himself up with an air of quiet confidence.

"Many thanks," said he, "but I can go alone. Rheumatism is my trouble, but these mild days loosen its grip upon my poor old muscles." He did not say that the prospect of an interesting inquiry had much the same effect, but the Curator suspected it, possibly because he was feeling just a little bit spry himself.

Steeled as such experienced officers necessarily are to death in all its phases, it was with no common emotion that the aged detective entered the presence of the dead girl and took his first look at this latest victim of mental or moral aberration. So young! so innocent! so fair! A schoolgirl, or little more, of a class certainly above the average, whether judged from the contour of her features or the niceties of her dress. With no evidences of great wealth about her, there was yet something in the cut of her garments and the careful attention to each detail which bespoke not only natural but cultivated taste. On her breast just above the spot where the cruel dart had entered, a fresh and blooming nosegay still exhaled its perfume—a tragic detail accentuating the pathos of a death so sudden that the joy with which she had pinned on this simple adornment seemed to linger about her yet.

The detective, with no words for this touching spectacle, stretched out his hand and with a reverent and fatherly touch pressed down the lids over the unseeing eyes. This office done to the innocent dead, he asked if anything had been found to establish the young girl's identity.

"Surely," he observed, "she was not without a purse or handbag. All young ladies carry them."

For answer the officer on guard thrust his hand into one of his capacious pockets, and drawing out a neat little bag of knitted beads, passed it over to the detective with the laconic remark:

"Nothing doing."

And so it proved. It held only a pocket handkerchief—embroidered but without a monogram—and a memorandum-book without an entry.

"A blind alley, if ever there was one," muttered Mr. Gryce; and ordering the policeman to replace the bag as nearly as possible on the spot from which it had been taken, he proceeded with the Curator to Room B.

Prepared to encounter a woman of disordered mind, the appearance presented by Mrs. Taylor at his entrance greatly astonished Mr. Gryce. There was a calmness in her attitude which one would scarcely expect to see in a woman whom mania had just driven into crime. Surely lunacy does not show such self-restraint; nor does lunacy awaken any such feelings of awe as followed a prolonged scrutiny of her set but determined features. Only grief of the most intense and sacred character could account for the aspect she presented, and as the man to whom the tragedies of life were of daily occurrence took in this mystery with all its incongruities, he realized, not without a sense of professional pleasure, no doubt, that he had before him an affair calling for the old-time judgment which, for forty or more years, had made his record famous in the police annals of the metropolis.

She was seated with no one near her but a young lady whom sympathetic interest had drawn to her side. Mr. Roberts stood in one of the windows, and not far from him a man in the museum uniform.

At the authoritative advance of the old detective, the woman, whose eye he had caught, attempted to struggle to her feet, but desisted after a moment of hopeless effort, and sank back in her chair. There was no pretense in this. Though gifted with a strong frame, emotion had so weakened her that she was simply unable to stand. Quite convinced of this, and affected in spite of himself by her look of lofty patience, Mr. Gryce prefaced his questions with an apology—quite an unusual proceeding for him.

Whether or no she heard it, he could not tell; but she was quite ready to answer when he asked her name and then her place of residence—saying in response to the latter query:

"I live at the Calderon, a family hotel in Sixty-seventh Street. My name"—here she paused for a second to moisten her lips—"is Taylor—Ermentrude Taylor.... Nothing else," she speedily added in a tone which drew every eye her way. Then more evenly: "You will find the name on the hotel's books."

"Wife or widow?"

"Widow."

What a voice! how it reached every heart, waking strange sympathies there! As the word fell, not a person in the room but stirred uneasily. Even she herself started at its sound; and moved, perhaps, by the depth of silence which followed, she added in suppressed tones:

"A widow within the hour. That's why you see me still in colors, but crushed as you behold—killed! killed!"

That settled it. There was no mistaking her condition after an expression of this kind. The Curator and Mr. Gryce exchanged glances, and Mr. Roberts, stepping from his corner, betrayed the effect which her words had produced on him, by whispering in the detective's ear:

"What you need is an alienist."

Had she heard? It would seem so from the quick way she roused and exclaimed with indignant emphasis:

"You do not understand me! I see that I must drink my bitter cup to the dregs. This is what I mean: My husband was living this morning—living up to the hour when the clock in this building struck twelve. I knew it from the joyous hopes with which my breast was filled. But with the stroke of noon the blow fell. I was bending above the poor child who had fallen so suddenly at my feet, when the vision came, and I saw him gazing at me from a distance so remote—across a desert so immeasurable—that nothing but death could create such a removal or make of him the ghastly silhouette I saw. He is dead. At that moment I felt his soul pass; and so I say that I am a widow."

Ravings? No, the calm certainty of her tone, the grief, touching depths so profound it had no need of words, showed the confidence she felt in the warning she believed herself to have received. Though probably not a single person present put any faith in occultism in any of its forms, there was a general movement of sympathy which led Mr. Gryce to pass the matter by without any attempt at controversy, and return to the question in hand. With a decided modification of manner, he therefore asked her to relate how she came to be kneeling over the injured girl with her hand upon the arrow.

"Let me have a moment in which to recover myself," she prayed, covering her eyes with her hand. Then, while all waited, she gave a low cry, "I suffer; I suffer!" and leaped to her feet, only to sink back again inert and powerless. But only for an instant: with that one burst of extreme feeling she recovered her self-control, answering with apparent calmness the detective's question:

"I was passing through the gallery as any other visitor might, when a young lady rushed by me—stopped short—threw up her arms and fell backward to the floor, pierced to the heart by an arrow. In a moment I was on my knees at her side with hand outstretched to withdraw this dreadful arrow. But I was afraid—I had heard that this sometimes causes death, and while I was hesitating, that vision came, engulfing everything. I could think of nothing else."

She was near collapsing again; but being a woman of great nerve, she fought her weakness and waited patiently for the next question. It was different, without doubt, from any she had expected.

"Then you positively deny any active connection with the strange death of this young girl?"

A pause, as if to take in what he meant. Then slowly, impressively, came the answer:

"I do."

"Did you see the person who shot the arrow?"

"No."

"From what direction would it have had to come to strike her as it did?"

"From the opposite balcony."

"Did you see anyone there?"

"No."

"But you heard the arrow?"

"Heard?"

"An arrow shot from a bow makes a whizzing sound as it flies. Didn't you hear that?"

"I don't know." She looked troubled and uncertain. "I don't remember. I was expecting no such thing—I was not prepared. The sight of an arrow—a killing arrow—in that innocent breast overcame me with inexpressible grief and horror. If the vision of my husband had not followed, I might remember more. As it is, I have told all I can. Won't you excuse me? I should like to go. I am not fit to remain. I want to return home—to hear from my husband—to learn by letter or telegram whether he is indeed dead."

Mr. Gryce had let her finish. An inquiry so unofficial might easily await the moods of such a witness. Not till the last word had been followed by what some there afterward called a hungry silence, did he make use of his prerogative to say:

"I shall be pleased to release you and will do so just as soon as I can. But I must put one or two more questions. Were you interested in the Indian relics you had come among? Did you handle any of them in passing?"

"No. I had no interest. I like glass, bronzes, china—I hate weapons. I shall hate them eternally after this." And she began to shudder.

The detective, with a quick bend of his head, approached her ear with the whispered remark:

"I am told that when your attention was drawn to these weapons, you fell on your knees and murmured something into the dead girl's ears. How do you explain that?"

"I was giving her messages to my husband. I felt—strange as it may seem to you—that they had fled the earth together—and I wanted him to know that I would be constant, and other foolish things you will not wish me to repeat here. Is that all you wish to know?"

Mr. Gryce bowed, and cast a quizzical glance in the direction of the Curator. Certainly for oddity this case transcended any he had had in years. With this woman eliminated from the situation, what explanation was there of the curious death he was there to investigate? As he was meditating how he could best convey to her the necessity of detaining her further, he heard a muttered exclamation from the young woman standing near her, and following the direction of her pointing finger, saw that the strange silence which had fallen upon the room had a cause. Mrs. Taylor had fainted away in her chair.

III

"I HAVE SOMETHING TO SHOW YOU"

Mr. Gryce took advantage of the momentary disturbance to slip from the room. He was followed by the Curator, who seemed more than ever anxious to talk.

"You see! Mad as a March hare!" was his hurried exclamation as the door closed behind them. "I declare I do not know which I pity more, her victim or herself. The one is freed from all her troubles; the other—Do you think we ought to have a doctor to look after her? Shall I telephone?"

"Not yet. We have much to learn before taking any decided steps." Then as he caught the look of amazement with which this unexpected suggestion of difficulties was met, he paused on his way to the stair-head to ask in a tentative way peculiarly his own: "Then you still think the girl died from a thrust given by this woman?"

"Of course. What else is there to think? You saw where the arrow came from. You saw that the only bow the place contained was hanging high and unstrung upon the wall, and you are witness to this woman's irresponsible condition of mind. The sight of those arrows well within her reach evidently aroused the homicidal mania often latent in one of her highly emotional nature; and when this fresh young girl came by, the natural result followed. I only hope I shall not be called upon to face the poor child's parents. What can I say to them? What can anybody say? Yet I do not see how we can be held responsible for so unprecedented an attack as this, do you?"

Mr. Gryce made no answer. He had turned his back toward the stair-head and was wondering if this easy explanation of a tragedy so peculiar as to have no prototype in all of the hundreds of cases he had been called upon to investigate in a long life of detective activity would satisfy all the other persons then in the building. It was his present business to find out—to search and probe among the dozen or two people he saw collected below, for the witness who had seen or had heard some slight thing as yet unrevealed which would throw a different light upon this matter. For his mind—or shall we say the almost unerring instinct of this ancient delver into human hearts?—would not accept without question this theory of sudden madness in one of Mrs. Taylor's appearance, strange and inexplicable as her conduct seemed.

Though it was quite among the possibilities that she had struck the fatal blow and in the manner mentioned, it was equally clear to his mind that she had not done it in an access of frenzy. He knew a mad eye and he knew a despairing one. Fantastic as her story certainly was, he found himself more ready to believe it than to accept any explanation of this crime which ascribed its peculiar features to the irresponsibilities of lunacy.

However, he kept his impressions to himself and in his anxiety to pursue his inquiries among the people below, was on the point of descending thither, when he found his attention arrested, and that of the Curator's as well, by the sight of a young man hastening toward them through the northern gallery. (The tragedy, as you will remember, had occurred in the southern one.) He was dressed in the uniform of the museum, and moved so quickly and in such an evident flurry of spirits that the detective instinctively asked:

"Who's that? One of your own men?"

"Yes, that's Correy, our best-informed and most-trusted attendant. Looks as if he had something to tell us. Well, Correy, what is it?" he queried as the man emerged upon the landing where they stood. "Anything new? If there is, speak out plainly. Mr. Gryce is anxious for all the evidence he can get."

With an ingenuousness rather pleasing than otherwise to the man thus presented to his notice, the young fellow stopped short and subjected the famous detective to a keen and close scrutiny before venturing to give the required information.

Was it because of the importance of what he had to communicate? It would seem so, from the suppressed excitement of his tone, as after his brief but exceedingly satisfactory survey, he jerked his finger over his shoulder in the direction from which he had come, with the short remark:

"I have something to show you."

Something! Mr. Gryce had been asking for this something only a moment before. We can imagine, then, the celerity with which he followed this new guide into the one spot of all others which possessed for him the greatest interest. For if by any chance the arrow which had done such deadly work had been sped from a bow instead of having been used as a dart, then it was from this gallery and from no other quarter of the building that it had been so sped. Any proof of this could have but the one effect of exonerating from all blame the woman who had so impressed him. He had traversed the first section and had entered the second, when the Curator joined him; together they passed into the third.

For those who have not visited this museum, a more detailed description of these galleries may be welcome. Acting as a means of communication between the row of front rooms and those at the back, they also serve to exhibit certain choice articles which call for little space, and are of a nature more or less ornamental. For this purpose they are each divided into five sections connected by arches narrower but not less decorative than those which open in a direct row upon the court. Of these sections the middle one on either side is much larger than the rest; otherwise they do not differ.

It was in the midst of this larger section that Correy now stood, awaiting their approach. There had been show-cases filled with rare exhibits in the two through which they had just passed, but in this one there was nothing to be seen but a gorgeous hanging, covering very nearly the whole wall, flanked at either end by a pedestal upholding a vase of inestimable value and correspondingly ugliness. A highly decorative arrangement, it is true, but in what lay its interest for the criminal investigator?

Correy was soon to show them. With a significant gesture toward the tapestry, he eagerly exclaimed:

"You see that? I've run by it several times since the accident sent me flying all over the building at everybody's call. But only just now, when I had a moment to myself, did I remember the door hid behind it. It's a door we no longer use, and I'd no reason for thinking it had anything to do with the killing of the young lady in the opposite gallery. But for all that I felt it would do no harm to give it a look, and running from the front, where I happened to be, I pulled out the tapestry and saw—but supposing I wait and let you see for yourselves. That will be better."

Leaving them where they stood face to face with the great hanging, he made a dive for the pedestal towering aloft at the farther end, and edging himself in behind it, drew out the tapestry from the wall, calling on them as he did so to come and look behind it. The Curator did not hesitate. He was there almost as soon as the young man himself.

But the detective was not so hasty. With a thousand things in mind, he stopped to peer along the gallery and down into the court before giving himself away to any prying eye. Satisfied that he might make the desired move with impunity, Mr. Gryce was about to turn in the desired direction when, struck by a new fact, he again stopped short.

He had noticed how the heavy tapestry shivered under Correy's clutch. Had this been observed by anyone besides himself? If by chance some person wandering about the court had been looking up—but no, the few people gathered there stood too far forward to see what was going on in this part of the gallery; and relieved from all further anxiety on this score, he joined Correy at the pedestal and at a word from him succeeded in squeezing himself around it into the small space they had left for him between the pushed-out hanging and the wall. An exclamation from the Curator, who had only waited for his coming to take his first look, added zest to his own scrutiny. It would take something more than the sight of a well-known door to give it such a tone of astonished discovery. What? Even he, with the accumulated surprises of years to give wings to his imagination, did not succeed in guessing. But when his eyes, once accustomed to the semi-darkness of the narrow space which Correy had thus opened out before him, saw not the door but what lay within its recess, he acknowledged to himself that he should have guessed—and that a dozen years before, he certainly would have done so.

It was a *bow*—not like the one hanging high in the Apache exhibit, but yet a bow strong of make and strung for use.

Here was a discovery as important as it was unexpected, eliminating Mrs. Taylor at once from the case and raising it into a mystery of the first order. By dint of long custom, Mr. Gryce succeeded in hiding his extreme satisfaction, but not the perplexity into which he was thrown by this complete change of base. The Curator appeared to be impressed in much the same way, and shook his head in a doubtful fashion when Correy asked him if he recognized the bow as belonging to the museum.

"I should have to see it nearer to answer that question with any sort of confidence," he demurred. "From such glimpses as I can get of it from here I should say that it has not been taken from any of our exhibits."

"I am sure it has not," muttered Correy. Then with a side glance at Mr. Gryce, he added: "Shall I slip in behind and get it?"

The detective, thus appealed to, hesitated a moment; then with an irrelevance perhaps natural to the occasion, he inquired where this door so conveniently hidden from the general view led to. It was the Curator who answered.

"To a twisting, breakneck staircase opening directly into my office. But this door has not been used in years. See! Here is the key to it on my own ring. There is no other. I lost the mate to it myself not long after my installation here."

The detective, working his way back around the pedestal, cast another glance up and down the gallery and over into the court. Still no spying eye, save that of the officer opposite.

"We will leave that bow where it is for the present," he decided, "a secret between us three." And motioning for Correy to let the tapestry fall, he stood watching it settle into place, till it hung quite straight again, with its one edge close to the wall and the other sweeping the floor. Had its weight been great enough to push the bow back again into its former place close against the door? Yes. No eye, however trained, would, from any bulge in the heavy tapestry, detect its presence there. He could leave the spot without fear; their secret would remain theirs until such time as they chose to disclose it.

As the three walked back the way they had come, the Curator glanced earnestly at the detective, who seemed to have fallen into a kind of anxious dream. Would it do to interrupt him with questions? Would he obtain a straight answer if he did? The old man moved heavily but the now fully alert Curator could not fail to see that it was with the heaviness of absorbed thought. Dare he disturb that thought? They had both reached the broad corridor separating the two galleries at the western end before he ventured to remark:

"This discovery alters matters, does it not? May I ask what you propose to do now? Anything in which we can help you?"

The detective may have heard him and he may not; at all events he made no reply though he continued to advance with a mechanical step until he stood again at the top of the marble steps leading down into the court. Here some of the uncertainty pervading his mind seemed to leave him, though he still looked very old and very troubled, or so the Curator thought, as pausing there, he allowed his glance to wander from the marble recesses below to the galleries on either side of him, and from these on to the seemingly empty spaces back of the high, carved railing guarding the great well. Would a younger man have served them better? It began to look so; then without warning and in a flash, as it were, the whole appearance of the octogenarian detective changed, and turning with a smile to the two men so anxiously watching him, he exclaimed with an air of quiet triumph:

"I have it. Follow and see how my plan works."

Amazed, for he looked and moved like another man,—a man in whom the almost extinguished spark of early genius had suddenly flared again into full blaze,—they hastily joined him in anticipation of they knew not what. But their enthusiasm received a check when at the moment of descent Mr. Gryce again turned back with the remark:

"I had forgotten. I have something to do first. If you will kindly see that the people down there are kept from growing too impatient, I will soon join you with Mrs. Taylor, who must not be left on this floor after we have gone below."

And with no further explanation of his purpose, he turned and proceeded without delay to Room B.

IV

A STRATEGIC MOVE

He found the unhappy woman quite recovered from her fainting spell, but still greatly depressed and not a little incoherent. He set himself to work to soothe her, for he had a request to make which called for an intelligent answer. Relieved from all suspicion of her having been an active agent in the deplorable deed he was here to investigate, he was lavish in his promises of speedy release, and seeing how much this steadied her, he turned to Mr. Roberts, who was still in the room, and then to the young lady who had been giving her a woman's care, and signified that their attentions were no longer required and that he would be glad to have them join the people below.

When the door had closed and Mr. Gryce found himself for the first time alone with Mrs. Taylor, he drew up a chair to her side and remarked in his old benevolent way:

"I feel guilty of cruelty, madam, in repeating a question you have already answered. But the conditions are such that I must, and do it now. When this young lady fell so unexpectedly at your feet, was your first look at her or at the opposite gallery?"

For an instant her eyes held his—something which did not often happen to him.

"At her," she vehemently declared. "I never thought of looking anywhere else. I saw her at my feet, and fell on my knees at her side. Who wouldn't have done so! Who would have seen anything but that arrow—*that arrow*! Oh, it was terrible! Do not make me recall it. I have sorrows enough—"

"Mrs. Taylor, you have my utmost sympathy. But you must realize how important it is for me to make sure that you saw nothing in the place from which that arrow was sent which would help us to locate the author of this accident. The flitting of an escaping figure up or down the opposite gallery, even a stir in the great tapestry confronting you from that far-away wall, might give us a clue."

"I saw nothing," she replied coldly but with extreme firmness, "nothing but that lifeless child and the picture of desolation which rose in my own mind. Do not, I pray, make me speak again of that. It would sound like delirium, and it is my wish to impress you with my sanity, so that you will allow me to go home."

"You shall go, after the Coroner has had an opportunity to see you. We expect him any moment. Meanwhile, you will facilitate your release and greatly help us in what we have to do, if you will carry your fortitude to the point of showing me in your own person just where you were standing when this young girl dashed by you to her death."

"Do you mean for me to go back to that—that—"

"Yes, Mrs. Taylor. Surely you can do so if you will. When you have time to think, you will be as anxious as ourselves to know through whose carelessness (to call it nothing worse) this child came to her death. Though it may prove to be quite immaterial whether you stood in one place or another at that fatal moment, it is a question which will be sure to come up at the inquest. That you may be able to answer correctly I urge you to return with me to the exact spot, before your recollection of the same has had time to fade. After that we will go below and I will see that you are taken to some quiet place where you can remain undisturbed till the Coroner comes."

Had she been a weak woman she would have succumbed again at this. But she was a strong one, and after the first moment of recoil she rose tremulously to her feet and signified her willingness to follow him to the scene of death.

"Is—is she there alone?" was her sole question as they crossed the corridor separating the room they had been in from the galleries.

"No—you will find an officer there. We could not leave the place quite unguarded."

If she shuddered he did not observe it. Having summoned up all her forces to meet this ordeal, she followed him without further word, and re-entering the spot she had so lately left in great agony of mind, stopped for one look and for one look only at the sweet face of the dead girl smiling up at her from the cold floor, then she showed Mr. Gryce as nearly as she could just where she had paused in shock and horror when the poor child smitten by the fatal arrow fell back almost into her arms.

The detective, with a glance at the opposite gallery, turned and spoke to the officer who had stepped aside into the neighboring section.

"Take the place just occupied by this lady," he said, "and hold it till you hear from me again." Then offering his arm to Mrs. Taylor, he led her out.

"I see that you were approaching the railing overlooking the court when you were stopped in this fearful manner," he remarked when well down the gallery toward its lower exit. "What did you have in mind? A nearer glimpse of the tapestry over there and the two great vases?"

"No, no." She was wrought up by now to a tension almost unendurable. "It was the court—what I might see in the court. Oh!" she impulsively cried: "the child! the child! that innocent, beautiful child!" And breaking away from his arm, she threw herself against the wall in a burst of uncontrollable weeping.

He allowed her a moment of unrestrained grief, then he took her on his arm again and led her down into the court where he gave her into the charge of Correy. He had gone as far as he dared in her present hysterical condition. Besides, he could no longer defer the great experiment by means of which he hoped to reach the heart of this mystery.

Taking the slip of paper handed him by Sweetwater, he crossed the court to where the various visitors, detained, some against their will and some quite in accordance with it, stood about in groups or sat side by side on the long benches placed along the front for their comfort. As he confronted them, his face beamed with that benevolent smile which had done so much for him in days gone by. Raising his hand he called attention to himself; then, when he was quite sure of being heard by them all, he addressed them with a quiet emphasis which could not fail to gain and hold their attention:

"I am Detective Gryce, sent here from Police Headquarters to look into this very serious matter. Till the Coroner arrives, I am in authority here, and being so, will have to ask your indulgence for any discomfort you may experience in helping me with my investigation. A young girl, full of life an hour ago, lies dead in the gallery above. We do not know her name; we do not know who killed her. But there is some one here who does. The man or woman who, wittingly or unwittingly, launched that fatal shaft, is present with us in this building. This person has not spoken. If he will do so now, he will save us and himself, too, no end of trouble. Let him speak, then. I will give him five minutes in which to make this acknowledgment. Five minutes! If that man is wise—or can it be a woman?—he will not keep us waiting."

Silence. Heads moving, eyes peering, excitement visible in every face, but not a word from anybody. Mr. Gryce turned and pointed up at the clock. All looked—but still no word from man or woman.

One minute gone!
Two minutes!
Three!

The silence had become portentous. The movement, involuntary and simultaneous, which had run through the crowd at first had stopped. They were waiting—each and all—waiting with eyes on the minute-hand creeping forward over the dial toward which the detective's glance was still turned.

The fourth minute passed—then the fifth—and no one had spoken.

With a sigh Mr. Gryce wheeled himself back and faced the crowd again.

"You see," he quietly announced, "the case is serious. Twenty-two of you, and not one to speak the half-dozen words which would release the rest from their present embarrassing position! What remains for us to do under circumstances like these? My experience suggests but one course: to narrow down this inquiry to those—you will not find them many—who from their nearness to the place of tragedy or from some other cause equally pertinent may be looked upon as possible witnesses for the Coroner's jury. That this may be done speedily and surely, I am going to ask you, every one of you, to retake the exact place in the building which you were occupying when you heard the first alarm. I will begin with the Curator himself. Mr. Jewett, will you be so good as to return to the room, and if possible to the precise spot, you were occupying when you first learned what had occurred here?"

The Curator, who stood at his elbow, made a quick bow and turned in the direction of the marble steps, which he hastily remounted. A murmur from the crowd followed this action and continued till he disappeared in the recesses of the right-hand gallery. Then, at a gesture from Mr. Gryce, it suddenly ceased, and with a breathless interest easy to comprehend, they one and all waited for his next word. It was a simple one.

"We are all obliged to Mr. Jewett for his speedy compliance with so unusual a request. He has made my task a comparatively easy one."

Then, glancing at the list of names and addresses which had been compiled for him by Sweetwater, he added:

"I will read off your names as recorded here. If each person, on hearing his own, will move quickly to his place and remain there till my young man can make a note of the same, we shall get through this matter in short order. And let me add"—as he perceived here and there a shoulder shrugged, or an eye turned askance—"that once the name is called, no excuse of non-recollection will be accepted. You must know, every one of you, just where you were standing when the cry of death rang out, and any attempt to mislead me or others in this matter will only subject the person making it to a suspicion he must wish to avoid. Remember that there are enough persons here for no one to be sure that his whereabouts at so exciting a moment escaped notice. Listen, then, and when your own name is spoken, step quickly into place, whether that place be on this floor or in the rooms or galleries above.—Mrs. Alice Lee!"

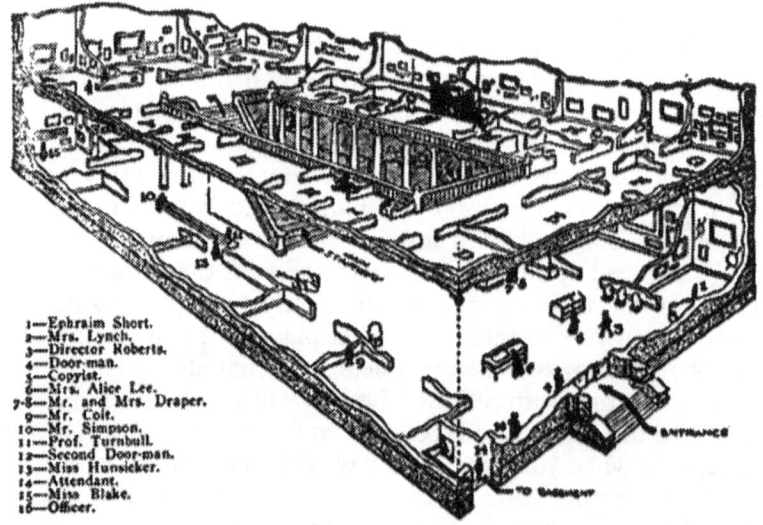

1—Ephraim Short.
2—Mrs. Lynch.
3—Director Roberts.
4—Door-man.
5—Copyist.
6—Mrs. Alice Lee.
7-8—Mr. and Mrs. Draper.
9—Mr. Colt.
10—Mr. Simpson.
11—Prof. Turnbull.
12—Second Door-man.
13—Miss Hunsicker.
14—Attendant.
15—Miss Blake.
16—Officer.

You can imagine the flurry, the excitement and the blank looks of the average men and women he addressed. But not one hesitated to obey. Mrs. Lee was on the farther side of one of the statues before her name had more than left his lips. Her example set the pace for those who followed. Like soldiers at roll-call, each one responded to the summons, going now in one direction and now in another until on reaching the proper spot he or she stopped.

Only six persons followed the Curator upstairs—an old woman who shook her head violently as she plodded slowly up the marble steps; Correy; a man with a packet of books under his arm (the same who had been studying coins in Section II); a young couple whose movements showed such a marked reluctance that more than one eye followed them as they went hesitatingly up, clinging together with interlocking hands and stopping now on one step and now on another to stare at each other in visible consternation; and a boy of fourteen who grinned from ear to ear as he bounded gayly up three steps at a time and took his position on the threshold of one of the upper doors with all the precision of a soldier called to sentry-duty—a boy scout if ever there was one.

There were twenty-two names on the list, and with the calling out of the twenty-second, Mr. Gryce perceived the space before him entirely cleared of its odd assortment of people. As he turned to take a look at the result, a gleam of satisfaction crossed his time-worn face. By this scheme, which he may be pardoned for looking upon as a stroke of genius worthy of his brilliant prime, he had set back time a full hour, restoring as by a magician's wand the conditions of that fatal moment of initial alarm. Surely, with the knowledge of that hidden bow in his mind, he should be able now to place his hand upon the person who had made use of it to launch the fatal arrow. No one, however sly of foot and quick of action, could have gone far from the gallery where that bow lay in the few minutes which were all that could have elapsed between the shooting of the arrow and the gasping cry which had brought all within hearing to the Apache section. The man or woman whom he should find nearest to that concealed door in the northern gallery would have to give a very good account of himself. Not even the Curator would escape suspicion under those circumstances.

However, it is only fair to add that Mr. Gryce had no fear of any such embarrassing end to his inquisition as that. He had noticed the young couple who had betrayed their alarm so ingenuously to every eye, and had already decided within himself that the man was just such a fool as might in a moment of vacuity pick up a bow and arrow to test his skill at a given mark. Such things had been and such results had followed. The man was a gawk and the woman a ninny; a few questions and their guiltiness would appear—that is, if they should be found near enough the tapestry to warrant his suspicion. If not—the alternative held an interest all its own, and sent him in haste toward the stairway.

To reach it Mr. Gryce had to pass several persons standing where fate had fixed them among the statuary grouped about the court, and had his attention been less engrossed by what he expected to discover above, he would have been deeply interested in noting how these persons, or most of them at least, had so thoroughly accepted the situation that they had taken the exact position and the exact attitude of the moment preceding the alarm. Those who were admiring the great torsos or carved chariots of the ancients, made a show of admiring them still. The man or woman who had been going in an easterly direction, faced east; and those who had been on the point of entering certain rooms, stood halting in the doorways with their backs to the court.

Unfortunately, he did not take note of all this, or give the poor pawns thus parading for his purpose more than a cursory glance. When he did think, which was when he was halfway up the staircase, it was to look back upon a changed scene. For with his going, interest had flagged and the tableau lost its pointedness. No one had ventured as yet to leave his place, but all had turned their faces his way, and on many of these faces could be seen signs of fatigue if not of absolute impatience. He had ordered them to stand and they had stood, but to be left there while he went above was certainly trying. The one spot which held the interest was in the southern gallery. If they could only follow him there—

All this was to be seen in their faces, and possibly the cunning old man read it there; but if he did, it was to ask himself if their conclusions were quite correct. The locale of interest had shifted in the last half hour; and while most of these people believed him to be searching for the witness who could tell him what had occurred in the death gallery, he really was hunting for one who

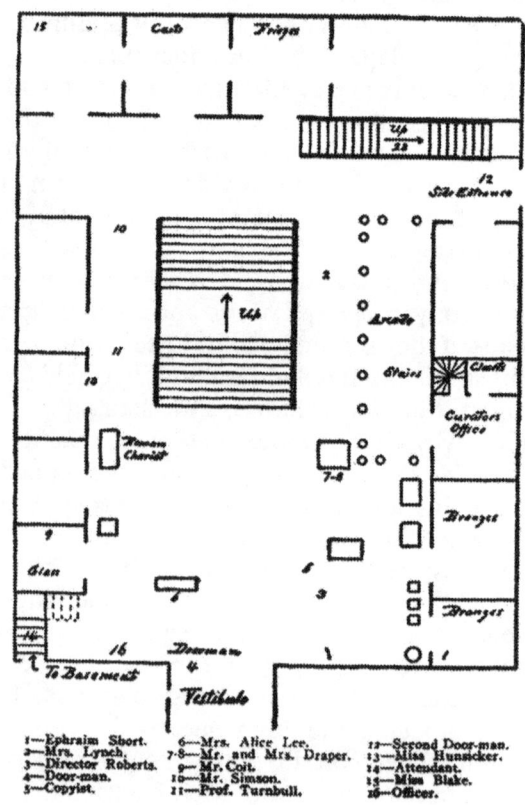

1—Ephraim Short.   6—Mrs. Alice Lee.   12—Second Door-man.
2—Mrs. Lynch.   7-8—Mr. and Mrs. Draper. 13—Miss Hunsicker.
3—Director Roberts.   9—Mr. Coit.   14—Attendant.
4—Door-man.   10—Mr. Simson.   15—Miss Blake.
5—Copyist.   11—Prof. Turnbull.   16—Officer.

could add to his knowledge of what had happened in the opposite one. And this witness might not be found in the gallery, or even on the upper floor. It was well among the probabilities that there might be among the various persons he saw posing in the court below some who by an upward look might take in a part of if not the whole broad sweep of that huge square of tapestry upon which his thoughts were centered. It was for him to make a note of these persons. A diagram of the court as it looked to him at that moment is shown for your enlightenment.

Sixteen persons! Ten in view from the steps and six not. Of the sixteen, only the following seemed to afford any excuse for future interrogation: Numbers Two, Six, Ten, Seven, Eight and Thirteen. Making a mental note of these, during which operation the poor unfortunates who had just been considering themselves as quite out of the game revived in a startling manner under his eye, he proceeded on his way.

As the action has now shifted to the upper floor, a diagram of this second story is now in order.

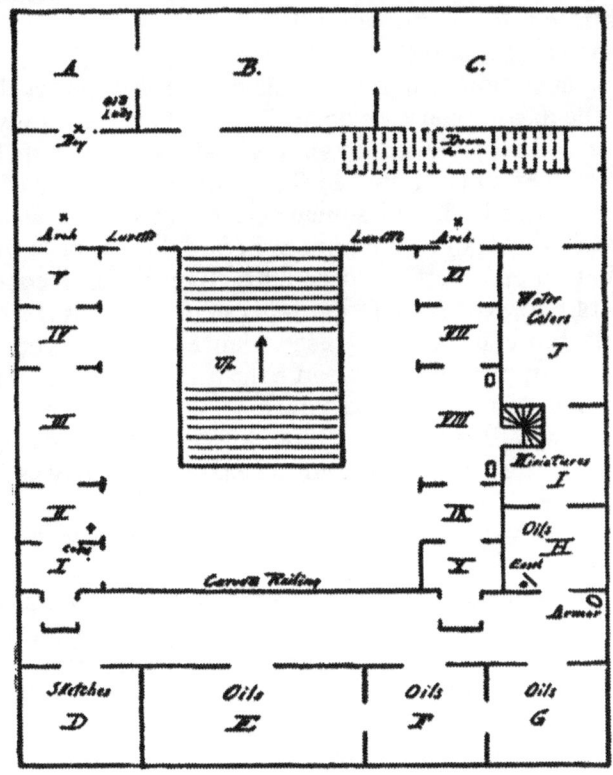

As you will see, a straight glimpse is given down either gallery from the arches opening into the broad corridor into which Mr. Gryce had stepped on leaving the central staircase. He had therefore only to choose which of the two would better repay his immediate investigation.

He decided upon the northern one, which you will remember was the one holding the tapestry; since, to find anybody there, no matter whom, would certainly settle the identity of the person responsible for that flying arrow. For, as all conceded, too little time had elapsed between its delivery and the discovery of the victim for the quickest possible attempt at escape to have carried the concealer of the bow very far from the spot where he had thrown it. It was possible—just possible—that he might have got as far as one of the four large rooms opening into the corridor stretching across the front, but that he was not in the gallery itself Mr. Gryce soon convinced himself by a rapid walk through its entire length.

That he did not follow up this move by an immediate searching of the rooms I have mentioned was owing to a wish he had to satisfy himself on another point first.

What was this point?

In passing along the rear on his way to this gallery, he had noticed the narrow staircase opening not a dozen feet away to his left. This undoubtedly led down to the side-entrance. If by any chance the user of the bow had fled to the rear instead of to the front, he would be found somewhere on this staircase, for he never could have got to the bottom before the cry of "Close the doors! Let no man out!" rendered this chance of immediate exit unavailable. So Mr. Gryce retraced his steps, and barely stopping to note the boy eying him with eager glances from the doorway of Room A, he approached the iron balustrade guarding the small staircase, and cautiously looked over.

A man was there! A man going down—no, coming up; and this man, as he soon saw from his face and uniform, was Correy the attendant.

"So that is where *you* were," he called down as he beckoned the man up.

"As near as I can remember. I was on my way in search of Mr. Jewett, for whom I had a message, and had got as far as you saw me, when I heard a cry of pain from somewhere in the gallery. This naturally quickened my steps and I was up and on this floor in a jiffy."

"Did you notice, as you stepped from the landing, whether

the boy staring at us from the doorway over there was facing just as we see him now?"

"He was. I remember his attitude perfectly."

"Coming out of the door—not going in?"

"Sure. He was on the run. He had heard the cry too."

"And followed you into the gallery?"

"Preceded me. He was on the scene almost as soon as the man who stepped in from the adjoining section."

"I see. And this man?"

"Was well within my view from the minute I entered the first arch. He seemed more bewildered than frightened till he had passed the communicating arch and nearly stumbled over the body of the girl shot down almost at his elbow."

"And yourself?"

"I knew by his look that something dreadful had happened, and when I saw what it was, I didn't think of anything better to do than to order the doors shut."

"On your own initiative? Where was the Curator?"

"Not far, it seems. But he gets awfully absorbed in whatever he is doing, and there was no time to lose. Some one had shot that arrow, some one who might escape."

Mr. Gryce never allowed himself—or very rarely—to look at anyone full and square in the face; yet he always seemed to form an instant opinion of whomever he talked with. Perhaps he had already gauged this man and not unfavorably, for he showed not the slightest distrust as he remarked quite frankly:

"You must have had some suspicion of foul play even then, to act in so expeditious a manner."

"I don't know what my suspicions were. I simply followed my first impulse. I don't think it was a bad one. Do you, sir?"

"Far from it. But enough of that. Do you think"—here he drew Correy into the gallery out of earshot of the boy, who was watching them with all the curiosity of his fourteen years—"that this lad could have stolen from where we are standing now to the door where you first saw him, during the time you were making your rush up the stairs? Boys of his age are mighty quick, and—"

"I know it, sir; and I see what you mean. But even if he had been able to do this,—which I very much doubt,—no boy of his age could have strung that bow, or had he found it strung, have shot an arrow from it with force enough to kill. Only a hand accustomed to its use could handle a bow like that with any success."

"You know the bow, then? Saw it nearer than you said—possibly handled it?"

"No, sir; but I know its kind and have handled many of them."

"In this building?"

"Yes, sir, and in other museums where I have been. I have arranged and rearranged Indian exhibits for years."

"Then you think that the bow we saw behind the tapestry is an Indian one?"

"Without question."

The detective nodded and left him. One word with the boy, and he would feel free to go elsewhere.

It proved to be an amusing one. The boy, for all his enthusiasm as a scout, proved to be so hungry that he was actually doleful. More than that, he had a ticket for that afternoon's ball game in his pocket and feared that he would not be let out in time to see it. He therefore was quick with his answers, which certainly were ingenuous enough. He had been looking at the model of a ship (which could be seen through an open door), when he heard a woman cry out as if hurt, from somewhere down the gallery. He was running to see what it meant when a man came along who seemed in as great a hurry as himself. But he got there first—and so on and on, corroborating Correy's story in every particular. He was so honest (Mr. Gryce had been at great pains to trip him up in one of his statements and had openly failed) and yet so anxious for the detective to notice the ticket to the ball game which he held in one hand, that the old man took pity on him and calling an officer, ordered him to let the boy out—a concession to youth and innocence he was almost ready to regret when a woman of uncertain years and irate mien attacked him from the doorway he had just left, with the loud remark:

"If you let him go, you can let me go too. I was in this room at the same time he was and know no more about what happened over there than the dead. I have an appointment downtown of great importance. I shall miss it if you don't let me go at once."

"Is it of greater importance than the right which this dead girl's friends have to know by whose careless hands the arrow killing her was shot?" And without waiting for a reply, which was not readily forthcoming, Mr. Gryce handed her over to Correy with an injunction to see that she was given a comfortable seat below and proceeded to finish up this portion of the building by a search through the three great rooms extending along the rear.

He found them all empty and without clue of any kind, and satisfied that his real work lay in front, he returned thither with as much expedition as old age and rheumatism would admit. Why, in doing so, he went for the third time through the gallery instead of through rooms J, H and I, he did not stop to inquire, though afterward he asked that question of himself more than once. Had he taken this latter course, he might not have missed—

But that will come later. What we have to do now is to accompany him to the front of the building, where matters of importance undoubtedly await him. He had noted, in his previous passage to and fro, that the young man who had been nearest to the tragedy was in his place before the case of coins in Section I. This time he noted something more. The young man was in the selfsame spot, but during this brief interval of waiting, the passion he evidently cherished for numismatics had reasserted itself, and he now stood with his eyes bent as eagerly upon the display of coins over which he hung, as if no shaft of death had crossed the space without and no young body lay in piteous quiet beyond the separating partition.

It was an exhibition of one of the most curious traits of human nature, and Mr. Gryce would undoubtedly have expended a few cynical thoughts upon it if, upon entering the broad front corridor which he had hitherto avoided, he had not run upon Sweetwater pointing in a meaning way toward two huge cases which, stacked with medieval arms, occupied one of the corners.

"Odd couple over there," he whispered as the older detective paused to listen. "Been watching them for the last five minutes. They pretend to be looking at some old armor, but they are mighty uneasy and keep glancing up at the window overhead as if they would like to jump out."

Mr. Gryce indulged in one of his characteristic exclamations. This was the couple whose queer actions he had noticed on the staircase. "I'll have a talk with them presently. Anyone in the rooms opposite?"

"Yes, the Curator. He's in Room A, where there are a lot of engravings waiting to be hung. I guess he was pretty well up to his neck in business when that fellow Correy set up his shout. And have you noticed that he's a bit deaf, which is the reason, perhaps, why he was not sooner on the scene?"

"No, I hadn't noticed. Anyone else at this end?"

"Only the young couple I speak of."

Mr. Gryce gave them a second look. They were by many paces farther from the pedestal from behind which the bow had been flung back of the tapestry than would quite fit in with the theory he had formed, and by means of which he hoped to single out the person who had sent the deadly arrow. But then, under the stress of fear, people can move very swiftly; and besides, what guarantee did he have that these poor, frightened creatures had located themselves with all the honesty the occasion demanded? According to Sweetwater there was nobody sufficiently near to notice where they had been at the critical instant, or where they were now. The student's back was toward them, and the Curator quite out of sight behind a close-shut door.

With this doubt in his mind, Mr. Gryce started to approach the couple. As he did so, he observed another curious fact concerning them. They were neither of them in the place natural to people interested in the contents of the great cases which they had crossed the hall to examine. Instead of standing where a full view of these cases could be had, they had withdrawn so far behind them that they presented the appearance of persons in hiding. Yet as he drew nearer and noted their youth and countrified appearance, Mr. Gryce was careful to assume his most benign deportment and so to modulate his voice as to call up the pink into the young woman's cheek and the deep red into the man's. What Mr. Gryce said was this: "You are interested I see in this show of old armor? I don't wonder. It is very curious. Is this your first visit to the museum?"

The man nodded; the woman lowered her head. Both were self-conscious to a point painful to see.

"It is a pity your first visit should be spoiled by anything so dreadful as the accidental death of this young girl. It seems to have frightened you both very much."

"Yes, yes," muttered the man. "We never saw anybody hurt before."

"Did you know the young lady?"

"Oh, no; oh, no!" they both hastened to cry out in a confused jumble, after which the man added:

"We—we're from up the river. We don't know anybody in this big town."

As he spoke, he began to edge away from the wall, the girl following.

"Wait!" smiled the detective. "You are getting out of place. You were looking at the armor when you first heard the hubbub over there?"

Both were silent.

"What were you looking at?"

"I was looking at her, and her was looking at me," stammered the man. "We were—were talking together here—we didn't notice—"

"Just married, eh?"

"Yesterday noon, sir. How—how did you know?"

"I didn't know; I only guessed. And I think I can guess something else—what your reason was for stealing into this dark corner."

It was the man who now looked down, and the woman who looked up. In a pinch of this kind, it is the woman who is the more courageous.

"He was a-kissin' of me, sir," she whispered in a frank but shamefaced way. "There was no harm in that, was there? We're so fond of one another, and how could we know that anyone was dying so near?"

"No, there was no harm," Mr. Gryce reluctantly admitted. Caught in an absurdity amusing enough in its way, he would certainly under less strenuous circumstances have rather enjoyed his own humiliation. But the occasion was too serious and his part in it too pronounced for him to take any pleasure in this misadventure. In the prosecution of so daring a scheme for locating witnesses if not of discovering the actual user of the bow, it would not do to fail. He *must* find the man he sought. If the Curator—but one glance into the room where that gentleman stood amid a litter of prints satisfied him that Sweetwater was right as to the impossibility of getting any information from this quarter. Nor could he hope, remembering what he had himself seen, that he would succeed any better with the last person now remaining on this floor—the young man busy with the coins in No. I.

That he was to be so fortunate as to lay an immediate hand on the person who had shot the fatal arrow was no longer regarded by him as among the possibilities. Whoever this person was, he had found a way of escape which rendered him for the time being safe from discovery. But there was another possible miscalculation which he felt it his duty to recognize before he proceeded further in his difficult task. The bow found back of the tapestry had every appearance of being the one used for the delivery of the arrow. But was it? Might it not, in some strange and unaccountable way, have been flung there previous to the present event and by some hand no longer in the building? Such coincidences have been known, and while as a rule this old and experienced detective put little confidence in coincidences of any kind, he had but one thought in mind in approaching this final witness, which was to get from him some acknowledgment of having seen, on or about the time of the accident, a movement in the tapestry behind which this bow lay concealed. If once this fact could be established, there could be no further question as to the direct connection between the bow there found and the present crime.

But Mr. Gryce might have spared his pains, so far as this young man was concerned. He had been so engrossed in his search for a particularly rare coin, that he had had no eyes for anything beyond. Besides, he was abnormally nearsighted, not being able, even with his glasses, to distinguish faces at any distance, much less a movement in a piece of tapestry.

All of this was discouraging, even if anticipated; but there were still the people below, some one of whom might have seen what this man had not. He would go down to them now, but by a course which would incidentally enlighten him in regard to another matter about which he had some doubts.

In his goings to and fro through the hall, he had passed the open door of Room H and noted how easily a direct flight could be made through it and Rooms I and J to the small staircase running down at the rear. Whether or not this explained the absence of anyone on this floor who by the utmost stretch of imagination could be held responsible for the accident which had occurred there, he felt it incumbent upon him to see in how short a time the escape he still believed in could be made through these rooms.

Timing his steps from the pedestal nearest this end, he found that even at his slow pace it took but three minutes for him to reach the arcade leading into the court from the foot of the staircase. A man conscious of wrong and eager to escape would do it in less; and if, as possibly happened, he had to wait in the doorway of Room J till Correy and the boy had cleared the way for him by their joint run into the farther gallery, he would still have time to be well on his way to the lower floor before the cry went up which shut off all further egress. Relieved, if not contented with the prospect this gave of a new clue to his problem, he reëntered the court and was preparing to renew his investigations when the arrival of the Coroner put a temporary end to his efforts as well as to the impatience of the so-called pawns, who were now allowed, one and all, to leave their posts.

V

THREE WHERE TWO SHOULD BE

It was a good half-hour before Mr. Gryce again found himself in a position to pursue the line of investigation thus summarily interrupted. The condition of Mrs. Taylor, which had not been improved by delay, demanded attention, and it was with a sense of great relief that Mr. Gryce finally saw her put into a taxi. Her hurried examination by Coroner Price had elicited nothing new, and of all who had noticed her distraught air on leaving the building, there was not one, if we except the detective, but felt convinced that if she had not been of unsound mind previous to this accident, she certainly had become so since. He still held to his theory that her story, fantastic and out of character as it seemed, was true in all its essentials, and that it was the warning she believed herself to have received of her husband's death, rather than what had taken place under her eyes, which had caused her such extreme suffering and temporarily laid her reason low.

With the full approbation of the Coroner, to whom he had explained his idea, Mr. Gryce began the sifting process by which he hoped to discover the one witness he wanted.

To subject to further durance such persons as from their position at the moment of tragedy could have no information to give bearing in any way upon their investigation was manifestly unfair. The old woman who had been found in Room A was of this class, and accordingly was allowed to go, together with such others as had been within twenty feet or more of the main entrance. These eliminated (it was curious to see how loath these few chosen ones were to depart, now that the opportunity was given them), Mr. Gryce settled down to business by asking Mrs. Lynch to come forward.

She, as you will see by consulting the chart, answered to the person marked "2." A little, dried-up, eager woman rose from the bench on which were collected the few people still remaining, and met his inquiring look with a nervous smile. She, of all the persons moving about on the main floor at the moment of alarm, had been in the best position for seeing the flight of the arrow and the fall of the victim in Section II. Had she seen them? The continued jigging of the small, wiry curls hanging out from either side of her old-fashioned bonnet would seem to betray an inner perturbation indicative of some hitherto suppressed information. At all events

Mr. Gryce allowed himself this hope and was most bland and encouraging in his manner as he showed her the place which had been assigned her on the chart drawn up by Sweetwater, and asked if the position given her was correct.

Perhaps a ready reply was too much to expect—women of her stamp not knowing, as a rule, very much about charts. But when he saw her hasten to the very spot assigned her by Sweetwater, he took heart and with a suggestive glance at the gallery intimated that he would be very glad to hear what she had seen there. Her surprise was evident, much too evident for his satisfaction. The little curls jigged about more than ever, and her cheeks grew quite pink as she answered hastily:

"I didn't see anything. I wasn't looking. Did you think I saw anything?"

"I hoped you had," he smiled. "If your eyes had chanced to be turned toward that end of the gallery—"

"But I was going the other way. My back was to it, not my face—like this." And wheeling herself about, she showed him that she had been walking toward the rear of the building rather than advancing toward the front.

His disappointment was great; but it would have been greater if he had not realized that under these conditions she was in the precise position to meet face to face any person emerging into the court from the foot of the small staircase. If she could tell him of having seen any such person, and closely enough to be able to give a description of this person's appearance, then she might prove to be his prime witness, after all. But she could not satisfy him on this point. She had been on her way out, and was too busy searching in her bag for her umbrella check to notice whether there were people about her or not. She had not found it when the great shout came.

"And then?"

Oh, then she was so frightened and so shocked that everything swam before her eyes and she nearly fell! Her heart was not a strong one and sometimes missed a beat or two, and she thought it must have done so then, for when her head steadied again, she found herself clinging to the balustrade of the great staircase.

"Then you have nothing whatever to add to what the others have told?"

Her "no," if a shaky one, was decisive, and seeing no reason for detaining her further, he gave her permission to depart.

Disturbed in his calculations, but not disheartened, Mr. Gryce next proceeded to interrogate the door-man at this end of the building. From his position, facing as he did the approach from the small staircase, he should be able to say, if the old lady could not, whether anyone had crossed the open strip of court toward which she had been advancing. But Mr. Gryce found him no more clear-headed on this point than she. He was the oldest man connected with the museum, and had been very much shaken up by what had occurred. Really, he could not say whether anyone had passed across his line of vision at that time or not. All he could be sure of was that no attempt had been made by anyone to reach the door after he had been bidden to close it.

So this clue ended like the rest in no thoroughfare. Would he have any better luck with the subject of his next inquiry? The young lady tabulated as No. 13 was where she could have seen the upper edge of the tapestry shake if she had been looking that way; but she was not. She also was going from instead of toward the point of interest—in other words, entering and not leaving the room on whose threshold she stood.

Only two men were left from whom he could hope to obtain the important testimony he was so anxiously seeking: Nos. 10 and 11. He had turned back toward the bench where they should be awaiting his attention and was debating whether he would gain more by attacking them singly or together, when he suddenly became aware of a fact which drove all these small considerations out of his mind.

According to every calculation and according to the chart, there should be only these two men on that bench. But he saw *three*. Who was this third man, and where had he come from?

VI

THE MAN IN THE GALLERY

Beckoning to Sweetwater, Mr. Gryce pointed out this extra man and asked him if he recognized him as one of the twenty-two he had tabulated.

The answer was a vigorous no. "It's a new face to me. He must have dropped from the roof or come up through the flooring. He certainly wasn't anywhere about when I made out my list. He looks a trifle hipped, eh?"

"Troubled—decidedly troubled."

"You might go a little further and say done up."

"Good-looking, though. Appears to be of foreign birth."

"English, I should say, and just over."

"English, without a doubt. I'll go speak to him; you wait here, but watch out for the Coroner, and send him my way as soon as he's at leisure."

Then he reapproached the bench, and observing, with the keenness with which he observed everything without a direct look, that with each step he took the stranger's confusion increased, he decided to wait till after he had finished with the others, before he entered upon an inquiry which might prove not only lengthy but of the first importance.

He was soon very glad that he had done this. He got nothing from Mr. Simpson; but the questions put to Mr. Turnbull were more productive. Almost at the first word, this gentleman acknowledged that he had seen a movement in the great square of tapestry to which Mr. Gryce drew his attention. He did not know when, or just where he stood at the time, but he certainly had noticed it shake.

"Can you describe the movement?" asked the gratified detective.

"It swayed out—"

"As if blown by some wind?"

"No, more as if pushed forward by a steady hand."

"Good! And what then?"

"It settled back almost without a quiver."

"Instantly?"

"No, not instantly. A moment or two passed before it fell back into place."

"This was before the attendant Correy called out his alarm, of course?"

Yes, of course it was before; but how long before, he couldn't say. A minute—two minutes—five minutes—how could he tell! He had no watch in hand.

Mr. Gryce thought possibly he might assist the man's memory on this point but forbore to do so at the time. It was enough for his present purpose that the necessary link to the establishment of his theory had been found. No more doubt now that the bow lying in the niche of the doorway overhead had been the one made use of in this desperate tragedy; and the way thus cleared for him, he could confidently proceed in his search for the man who had flung it there. He believed him to be within his reach at that very moment, but his countenance gave no index to his thought as reapproaching the young man now sitting all alone on the bench, he halted before him and pleasantly inquired:

"Do I see you for the first time? I thought we had listed the name of every person in the building. How is it that we did not get yours?"

The tide of color which instantly flooded the young man's countenance astonished Mr. Gryce both by its warmth and full-ness. If he were as thin-skinned as this betokened, one should experience but little difficulty in reaching the heart of his trouble.

With an air of quiet interest Mr. Gryce sat down by the young man's side. Would this display of friendliness have the effect of restoring some of his self-possession and giving him the confi-dence he evidently lacked? No, the red fled from his cheek, and a ghastly white took its place; but he showed no other change.

Meantime the detective studied his countenance. It was a good one, but just now so distorted by suffering that only such as were familiar with his every look could read his character from his present expression. Would a more direct question rouse him? Pos-sibly. At all events, Mr. Gryce decided to make the experiment.

"Will you give me your name?" he asked, "—your name and residence?"

The man he addressed gave a quick start, pulled himself together and made an attempt to reply.

"My name is Travis. I am an Englishman just off the steamer from Southampton. My home is in the county of Hertfordshire. I have no residence here."

"Your hotel, then?"

Another flush—then quickly: "I have not yet chosen one."

This was too surprising for belief. A stranger in town without rooms or hotel accommodations, making use of the morning hours to visit a museum!

"You must be very much interested in art!" observed his inquisitor a little dryly.

Again that flush and again the quick-recurring pallor.

"I—I am interested in all things beautiful," he replied at last in broken tones.

"I see. May I ask where you were when that arrow flew which killed a young lady visitor? Not in this part of the court, I take it?"

Mr. Travis gave a quick shudder and that was all. The detective waited, but no other answer came.

"I am told that as she fell she uttered one cry. Did you hear it, Mr. Travis?"

"It wasn't a cry," was his quick reply. "It was something quite different, but dreadful, dreadful!"

Mr. Gryce's manner changed.

"Then you did hear it. You were near enough to distinguish between a scream and a gasp. Where were you, and why weren't you seen by my man when he went through the building?"

"I—I was kneeling out of sight—too shocked to move. But I grew tired of that and wanted to go; but on reaching the court, I found the doors closed. So I came here."

"Kneeling! Where were you kneeling?"

He made a quick gesture in the direction of the galleries.

The detective frowned, perhaps to hide his secret satisfaction.

"Won't you be a little more definite?" he asked; then as the man continued to hesitate he added, but as yet without any appreciable loss of kindliness: "Every other person here has been good enough to show us the exact place he was occupying at that serious moment. I must ask you to do the same; it is only just."

Was the look this called up one of fear or of simple repugnance? It might be either; but the detective was disposed to consider it fear.

"Will you lead the way?" he pursued. "I shall be glad to follow."

A glance of extreme reproach; then these words, uttered with painful intensity:

"You want me to go back there—where I saw—where I can see again—*I cannot*. I'm not well. I suffer. You will excuse me. You will allow me to say what I have to say, *here*."

"I'm sorry, but I cannot do that. The others have gone without question to their places; why should not you?"

"Because—" The word came brokenly and was followed by silence. Then, seeing the hopelessness of contending with police authority, he cast another glance of strong repulsion in the direction of the gallery and started to his feet. Mr. Gryce did the same, and together they crossed the court. But they got no further at this time than the foot of the staircase. Coroner Price, by an extra effort which seemed to be called for by the circumstances, had succeeded in picking up a jury from the people collected on the street, and entering at this moment, created a diversion which effectively postponed the detective's examination of his new witness.

When the opportunity came for resuming it, so much time had elapsed that Mr. Gryce looked for some decided change in the manner or bearing of the man who, unfortunately for his purposes, had thus been given a quiet hour in which to think. Better, much better, for the cause of justice, if he could have pushed him to the point at once, harried him, as it were, in hot blood. Now he might find him more difficult.

But when, in company with the Coroner, who now found himself free to assist him in his hunt for witnesses, he reapproached the Englishman sitting as before alone on his bench, it was to find him to all appearance in the same mind in which he had left him. He wore the same look and followed with the same reluctance when he was made to understand that the time had now come for him to show just where he was standing when that arrow was sped on its death-course. And greatly impressed by this fact, which in a way contradicted all his expectations, Mr. Gryce trod slowly after, watching with the keenest interest to see whether, on reaching the top of the steps, this man upon whose testimony so much depended would turn toward the southern gallery where the girl had fallen, or toward the northern one, where Correy had found the bow.

It looked as if he were going to the left, for his head turned that way as he cleared the final step. But his body soon swayed aside in the other direction, and by the time the old detective had himself reached the landing, Travis, closely accompanied by the Coroner, had passed through the first of the three arches leading to that especial section of the gallery where the concealing tapestry hung.

"The man is honest," was Mr. Gryce's first thought. "He is going to show us the bow and confess to what was undoubtedly an accident." But Mr. Gryce felt more or less ready to modify this impromptu conclusion when, on passing through the arch himself he came upon the young man still standing in Section VI, with his eyes on the opposite gallery and his whole frame trembling with emotion.

"Is she—the young lady who was shot—still lying on those cold stones alone, forsaken and—"

Mr. Gryce knew misery when he saw it. This man had not overstated the case when he had said "I suffer." But the cause! To what could this excess of sensibility be attributed? To remorse or to an exaggerated personal repulsion? It looked like remorse, but that there might be no doubt as to this, Mr. Gryce hastened to assure the Englishman that on the departure of the jury the body had been removed to one of the inner rooms. The relief which this gave to Mr. Travis was evident. He showed no further reluctance to proceed and was indeed the first of the three to enter where the great drapery hung, flanked by the two immense vases. Would he pause before it or hurry by into the broad corridor in front? If he hurried by, what would become of their now secretly accepted theory?

But he did not hurry by; that is, he did not pass beyond the upper end, but stopped when he got there and looked back with an air of extreme deprecation at the two officials.

"Have we arrived?" asked Mr. Gryce, his suspicions all returning, for the man had stepped aside from the drapery and was standing in a spot conspicuously open to view even from the lower court.

The Englishman nodded; whereupon Mr. Gryce, approaching to his side, exclaimed in evident doubt:

"You were standing *here*? When? Not at the moment the young girl fell, or you would have been seen by some one, if not by everyone, in the building. I want you to take the exact place you occupied when you first learned that something had gone wrong in the opposite gallery."

The stranger's distress grew. With a show of indecision scarcely calculated to inspire confidence in either of the two men watching him, he moved now here and now there till he finally came to a standstill close by the pedestal—so close, indeed, to its inner corner that he was almost in a line with its rear.

"It was here," he declared with a gulp of real feeling. "I am sure I am right now. I had just stepped out—"

"From behind the tapestry?"

"No." His blank astonishment at the quickness with which he had been caught up left him staring for a moment at the speaker, before he added:

"From behind the pedestal. The—the vase, as you see, is a very curious one. I wanted to look at it from all sides."

Without a word the Coroner slipped past him and entering the narrow space behind the pedestal took a look up at the vase from his present cramped position.

As he did this, two things happened: first Sweetwater, who had stolen upon the scene, possibly at some intimation from Mr. Gryce, took a step toward them which brought him in alignment with the Englishman, of whose height in comparison with his own he seemed to take careful note; and secondly, the sensitive skin of the foreigner flushed red again as he noticed the Coroner's sarcastic smile, and heard his dry remark:

"One gets a better view here of the opposite gallery than of the vase perched so high overhead. Had you wished to look at those ladies, without being seen by them, you could hardly have found a better loophole than the one made by the curving in of this great vase toward its base." Then quickly: "You surely took one look their way; that would be only natural."

The answer Mr. Travis gave was certainly unexpected.

"It was after I came out that I saw them," he stammered. "There were two ladies, one tall and one very young and slight. The older lady was stepping toward the front, the other entering from behind. As I looked, the younger made a dash and ran by the first lady. Then—"

"Proceed, Mr. Travis. Your emotion is very natural; but it is imperative that we hear all you have to tell us. She ran by the older lady, and then?"

Still silence. The Englishman appeared to be looking at Coroner Price, who in speaking emerged from behind the pedestal; but it is doubtful if he saw him. A tear was in his eye—a tear!

Seeing it, Mr. Gryce felt a movement of compassion, and thinking to help him, said kindly enough:

"Was it so very dreadful?"

The answer came with great simplicity:

"Yes. One minute she was all life and gaiety; the next she was lying outstretched on the hard floor."

"And you?"

Again that look of ingenuous surprise.

"I don't remember about myself," he said. "I was thinking too much about her. I never saw anyone killed before."

"Killed? Why do you say killed? You say you saw her fall, but how did you know she was killed?"

"I saw the arrow in her breast. As she fell backward, I saw the arrow."

As he uttered these words, the three men watching him perceived the sweat start out on his forehead, and his eyes take on a glassy stare. It was as if he were again in gaze upon that image of youthful loveliness falling to the ground with the arrow of death in her heart. The effect was strangely moving. To see this event reflected as it were in horror from this man's consciousness made it appear more real and much more impressive than when contemplated directly. Why? Had remorse given it its poignancy? Had it been his own hand which had directed this arrow from behind the pedestal? If not, why this ghastly display of an emotion so far beyond what might be expected from the most sentimental of onlookers?

In an endeavor to clear the situation, the Coroner intervened with the following question:

"Have you ever seen a shot made by a bow and arrow before, Mr. Travis? Archery-practice, I mean. Or—well, the shooting of wild animals in India, Africa or elsewhere?"

"Oh, yes. I come from a country where the bow and arrow are used. But I never shoot. I can only speak of what I have seen others do."

"That is sufficient. You ought to be able to tell, then, from what direction this arrow came."

"It—it must have come from this side of the gallery. Not from this section, as you call it, but from some one of the other open places along here."

"Why not from this one?"

"Because there was nobody here but me," was the simple and seemingly ingenuous answer.

It gave them an unexpected surprise. Innocence would speak in this fashion. But then the bow—the bow which was lying not a dozen feet from where they stood! Nothing could eliminate that bow.

After a short consultation between themselves, which the Englishman seemed not to notice, the Coroner addressed him with the soothing remark:

"Mr. Travis, you must not misunderstand me. The accident which has occurred (we will not yet say crime) is of so serious a nature that it is imperative for us to get at the exact facts. Only yourself and one other person whom we know can supply them. I allude to the lady you saw, first in front of and then behind the girl who was shot. Her story has been told. Yours will doubtless coincide with it. May I ask you, then, to satisfy us on a point you were in a better position than herself to take note of. It is this: When the young girl gave that bound forward of which you both speak, did she make straight for the railing in front, or did she approach it in a diagonal direction?"

"I do not know. You distress me very much. I was not thinking of anything like that. Why should I think of anything so immaterial. She came—I saw her smiling, beaming with joy, a picture of lovely youth—then her arms went suddenly up and she fell—backward—the arrow showing in her breast. If I told the story a hundred times, I could not tell it differently."

"We do not wish you to, Mr. Travis. Only there must be somewhere in your mind a recollection of the angle which her body presented to the railing as she came forward."

The unhappy man shook his head, at which token of helplessness Mr. Gryce beckoned to Sweetwater and whispered a few words in his ear. The man nodded and withdrew, going the length of the gallery, where he disappeared among the arches, to reappear shortly after in the gallery opposite. When he reached Section II, Mr. Gryce again addressed the witness, who, to his surprise and to that of the Coroner as well, had become reabsorbed in his own thoughts to the entire disregard of what this movement might portend. It took a sharp word to rouse him.

"I am going to ask you to watch the young man who has just shown himself on the other side, and tell us to what extent his movements agree with those made by the young lady prior to her collapse and fall to the floor."

For an instant indignation robbed the stranger of all utterance. Then he burst forth:

"You would make a farce of what is so sad and dreadful, and she scarcely cold! It is dishonoring to the young lady. I cannot look at that young man—that hideous young man—and think of her and of how she looked and walked the instant before her death."

The two officials smiled; they could not help it. Sweetwater was certainly no beauty, and to associate him in any kind of physical comparison with the dead girl was certainly incongruous. Yet they both felt that the point just advanced by them should be settled and settled now while the requisite remembrance was fresh in the mind of this invaluable witness. But in order to get at what they wanted, some show of consideration for his feelings was evidently necessary. Police persistence often defeats its own ends. If he was to be made to do what they wished, it would have to be through the persuasion of some one outside the Force. To whom should they appeal? The question answered itself. Mr. Roberts was approaching from the front, and to him they turned. Would he use his influence with this stranger?

"He may listen to you," urged the Coroner in the whispered conference which now followed, "if you explain to him how much patience you and all the rest of the people in the building have had to exercise in this unhappy crisis. He seems a good enough fellow, but not in line with our ideas."

Mr. Roberts, who saw the man for the first time, surveyed him in astonishment.

"Where was he standing?" he asked.

"Just where you see him now—or so he says."

"He couldn't have been. Some one would have observed him—the woman who was in the compartment with the stricken girl, or the man studying coins in the one next to it."

"So it would seem," admitted the Coroner. "But if he were behind the pedestal—"

"Behind the pedestal!"

"That's where we think he was. But no matter about that now!—we can explain that to you later. At present all we want is for you to reassure him."

Not altogether pleased with his task, but seeing no good reason for declining it, the affable director approached the Englishman, who, recognizing one of his own social status, seemed to take heart and turn a willing ear to Mr. Roberts' persuasions. The result was satisfactory.

When the Coroner again called Mr. Travis' attention to Sweetwater awaiting orders in the opposite gallery he did not refuse to look, though his whole manner showed how much he was affected by this forced acquiescence in their plans.

"You will watch the movements of the young man we have placed over there," the Coroner had said; "and when he strikes a position corresponding to that taken by the young lady at the moment she was shot, lift up your hand, thus. I will not ask you to speak."

"But you forget that there is blood on that floor. That man will step in it. I cannot lend myself to such sacrilege. It is wrong. Let the lady be buried first."

The outburst was so natural, the horror so unfeigned, that not only the men he addressed but all within hearing showed the astonishment it caused.

"One would think you knew the victim of this random shot!" the Coroner intimated with a fresh and close scrutiny of this very reluctant witness. "Did you? Was she a friend of yours?"

"No, no!" came in quick disavowal. "No friend. I have never exchanged a word with her—never."

"Then we will proceed. One cannot consider sensibilities in a case like this." And he made a signal to Sweetwater, who turned his body this way and that.

The distressed Englishman watched these movements with slowly dilating eyes.

"It's the angle we want—the angle at which she presented her body to the gallery front," explained the relentless official.

A shudder, then the rigidity of fixed attention, broken in another moment, however, by an impulsive movement and the unexpected question:

"Is it to find the man who did it that you are enacting this horrible farce?"

Somewhat startled, the Coroner retorted:

"If you object on that account—"

But Mr. Travis as vehemently exclaimed:

"But I don't! I want the man caught. One should not shoot arrows about in a place where there are beautiful young women. I want him caught and punished."

As they were all digesting this unexpected avowal, they saw his hand go up. The Coroner gave a low whistle, and the detective in obedience to it stood for one instant stock-still—then bent quickly to the floor.

"What is he doing?" cried Mr. Travis.

"Yes, what is he doing?" echoed Mr. Roberts.

"Running a mark about his shoes to fix their exact location," was the grim response.

VII

"YOU THINK THAT OF ME!"

"We're certainly up against it this time," were the words with which Dr. Price led the detective down the gallery. "What sort of an opinion can a man form of a fellow like that? Is he fool or knave?"

Mr. Gryce showed no great alacrity in answering. When he did speak it was to say:

"We shall have to go into the matter a little more deeply before we can trust our judgment as to his complete sincerity. But if you want to know whether I believe him to have loosed the arrow which killed that innocent child, I am ready from present appearances to say yes. Who else was there to do it? He and he only was on the spot. But it was a chance action, without intention or wish to murder. No man, even if he were a fool, would choose such a place or such a means for murder."

"That's true; but how does it help to call it accident? Accident calls for a bow in hand, an arrow within reach, an impulse to try one's skill at a fancied target. Now the arrow—whatever may be said of the bow—was not within the reach of anyone standing in this gallery. The arrow came from the wall at the base of which this young woman died. It had to be brought from there here. That does not look like accident, but crime."

Yet as the Coroner uttered this acknowledgment, he realized as plainly as Mr. Gryce how many incongruous elements lay in the way of any such solution of the mystery. If they accepted the foreigner's account of himself,—which for some reason neither seemed ready to dispute,—into what a maze of improbabilities it at once led them! A stranger just off ship! The victim a mere schoolgirl! The weapon such an unusual one as to be *outré* beyond belief. Only a madman—But there! Travis had less the appearance of a lunatic than Mrs. Taylor. It must have been an accident as Gryce said; and yet—

If there is much virtue in an *if,* there is certainly a modicum of the same in a *yet,* and the Coroner, in full recognition of this stumbling-block, remarked with unusual dryness:

"I agree with you that some half-dozen questions are necessary before we wade deeper into this quagmire. Where shall we go to have it out?"

"The Curator will allow us to use his office. I will see that Mr.

Travis joins us there."

"See that he comes before he has a chance to fall into one of his reveries."

But quickly as Mr. Gryce worked, he was not speedy enough to prevent the result mentioned. The man upon whose testimony so much hinged did not even lift his eyes when brought again into their presence.

The Coroner, in his determination to be satisfied on this point, made short work of rousing him from his abstraction. With a few leading questions he secured his attention and then without preamble or apology asked him with what purpose he had come to America and why he had been so anxious to visit the museum that he hastened directly to it from the steamer without making an effort to locate himself in some hotel.

The ease with which this apparently ingenuous stranger had managed to meet the opening queries of this rough-and-ready official was suddenly broken. He stammered and turned red and made so many abortive attempts to reply that the latter grew impatient and finally remarked:

"If the truth will incriminate you, you are quite justified in holding it back!"

"Incriminate me!" With the repetition of this alarming word, a change of the most marked character took place in young Travis' manner. "What does that mean?" he asked. "I am not sure that I understand your use of that word *incriminate*."

Dr. Price explained himself, to the seeming horror of the startled Englishman.

"You think that of me!" he cried, "of me, who—"

But here indignation made him speechless, till some feeling stronger than the one subduing him to silence forced him again into speech, and he supplemented in broken tones: "I am only a stranger to you and consequently am willing to pardon your misconception of my character and the principles by which I regulate my life. I have a horror of crime and all violence; besides, the young lady—she awakened my deepest admiration and reverence. I,"—again he stopped; again he burst forth,—"I would sooner have died myself than seen such angel graces laid low. Let my emotion be proof of what I say. It was a man of the hardest heart who killed her."

"It would seem so."

It was the Coroner who spoke. He was nonplussed; and Mr. Gryce no less so. Never had either of them been confronted by a blinder or more bewildering case. An incomprehensible crime and a suspect it was impossible to associate with a deed of blood! There must be some other explanation of the mournful circumstance they were considering. There had been twenty or more people in the building, but—and here was the rub—if the chart which they had drawn up was correct and the calculations which they had drawn from it were to be depended upon, this man was the only person who had been in this gallery when the arrow was shot.

With a side glance at Mr. Gryce, who seemed content to remain silent in the background, Dr. Price turned again to Mr. Travis.

"Your admiration of the young lady must have been as sudden as it was strong. Or possibly you had seen her before you hid behind the pedestal. Had you, Mr. Travis? She was a charming child; perhaps you had been attracted by her beauty before you even entered the galleries."

Instantly the man was another being.

"You are right," he acquiesced with undue alacrity. "I had seen her crossing the court. Her beauty was heavenly. I am a gentleman, but I followed her. When she moved, I moved; and when she went upstairs, I followed her. But I would not offend. I kept behind,—far behind her,—and when she entered the gallery on one side, I took pains to enter it on the other. This is how I came to be looking in her direction when she was struck down. You see, I speak with candor; I open my whole heart."

Dr. Price, stroking his long beard, eyed the man with a thoughtful air which changed to one of renewed inquiry. Instead of being convinced by this outburst, he was conscious of a new and deepening distrust. The transition from a low state of feeling to one so feverishly eager had been too sudden. The avidity with which this man just off ship had made a grasp at the offered explanation had been too marked; it lacked sincerity and could impose on no one. Of this he seemed himself aware, for again the ready flush ran from forehead to neck, and with a deprecatory glance which included the silent detective he vehemently exclaimed:

"I am poor at a lie. I see that you will have the whole truth. It was on her account I crossed the ocean. It was by dogging her innocent steps that I came to the museum this morning. I am a man of means, and I can do as I please. When I said that I had never exchanged a word with her, I spoke the truth. I never have; yet my interest in her was profound. I have never seen any other girl or woman whom I was anxious to make my wife. I hoped to meet and woo her in this country. I had no opportunity for doing so in my own. I did not see her till a night or so before she sailed, and then it was at the theater, where she sat with some friends in an adjoining box. She talked, and I heard what she said. She was leaving England. She was going to America to live; and she mentioned the steamer on which she expected to sail. It may strike you as impetuous, unnatural in an Englishman, and all that, but next morning I secured my passage on that same ship. As I have just said, I am my own master and can do as I please, and I pleased to do that. But for all the opportunity which a voyage sometimes gives, I did not succeed in making her acquaintance on shipboard, much as I desired it. I was ill for the first three days and timorous the rest. I could only watch her moving about the decks and wait for the happy moment in which I might be able to do her some service. But that moment never came, and now it never will come."

The mournfulness with which this was uttered seemed genuine. The Coroner was silenced by it, and it was left to Mr. Gryce to take up the conversation. This he did with the same show of respect evinced by Dr. Price.

"We are obliged to you for your confidence," said he. "Of course you can tell us this young girl's name."

"Angeline—Angeline Willetts. I saw it in the list of passengers."

"What ship?"

"The *Castania*, from Southampton."

"We are greatly obliged to you for this information. It gives us the much-wanted clue to her identity. Angeline Willetts! Whom was she with?"

"A Madame Duclos, a French lady. I once spoke to *her*."

"You did? And what did you say?"

"I bade her good morning as we were passing on the main-deck stairs. But she did not answer, and I was not guilty of the impertinence again."

"I see. Such, then, was the situation up to this morning. But since? How did it happen that a young girl, six hours after landing in this country, should come to a place like this without a chaperon?"

"I don't know what brought her here; I can only tell you why I came. When she left the dock, I was standing near enough to hear the orders Madame Duclos gave on entering a cab. Naturally, mine were the same. I have been in New York before, and I knew the hotel. If you will consult the Universal's register for the day, you will find my name in it under hers. You will understand why I shrank from confessing to this fact before. I held her in such honor—I was and am so anxious that no shadow should fall upon her innocence from my poor story of secret and unrecognized devotion. She knew nothing of what led me to follow every step she took. I was a witness of her fate, but that is all the connection between us. I hope you believe me."

It would be difficult not to, in face of his direct gaze, from which all faltering had now vanished. Yet the matter not being completely thrashed out, Mr. Gryce felt himself obliged to say in answer to this last:

"We see no reason to doubt your word or your story, Mr. Travis. All that you have said is possible. But how about your following the young girl here? How did that come about?"

"That was occasioned by my anxiety for her—an anxiety which seems to have been only too well-founded."

"How? What?" Both of the officials showed a greatly increased interest. "Please explain yourself, Mr. Travis. What reason had you for any such feeling in regard to a person with whom you had held no conversation? Anything which you saw or heard at the hotel?"

"Yes. I was sitting in the foyer. I knew that the ladies were in the house, but I had not seen them. I was anxious to do so (see, I am telling all) and was watching the door of the lift from behind my journal, when they both stepped out. Miss Willetts was dressed for the street, but Madame Duclos was not, which seemed very strange to me. But I felt no concern till I caught some fragments of what Madame said in passing me. She spoke in French, a language I understand, and she was exclaiming over her misfortune at not being allowed to accompany her young charge to whatever place she was going. It was bad, bad, she cried, and she would not have a moment's peace till her dear Angeline got back. Anxiety of this kind was natural in a Frenchwoman not accustomed to see a young lady enter the streets alone; but the force with which she expressed it betrayed a real alarm—an alarm which communicated itself to me. Where could this unprotected girl be going, alone and in a hotel cab?

"I could not imagine, and when I saw Madame stop in the middle of her talk to buy some fresh flowers and pin them to Miss Willetts' corsage, I got a queer feeling, and flinging my newspaper aside, I strolled to the door and so out in time to hear Madame's orders to the chauffeur. The young lady was to be taken to a museum. To a museum, at this early hour! and alone, alone! Such a proceeding is not at all in accord with French ideas, and I feared a plot. Though it was far from being my affair, I determined to make it so; and as soon as I dared, I followed her just as I had followed her from the dock. But fruitlessly! Not knowing the danger, how could I avert it? I was in one gallery, she in the other. It was my evil fate to see her fall, but by whose hand I am as ignorant as yourselves. *Now* I have told it all. Will you let me go?"

"Not yet," interposed the Coroner. "There are one or two questions more which you will undoubtedly answer with the same frankness. Were you standing in front of the pedestal or behind it when you saw Miss Willetts fall?"

"I was standing just where I said, somewhere near it in the open gallery."

This seemed so open to question that the Coroner paused a moment to recall the exact situation and see if it were possible for a man as conspicuous in figure as Mr. Travis to have stood thus in full view of gallery and court, without attracting the attention of anyone in either place. He found, after a moment's consideration, that it was possible. Mr. Gryce, for all his efforts and systematic inquiry into the position which each person had held at or near this time, had been able to find but one who chanced to be looking in the direction of this gallery, and he with a limited view which took in only the upper part of the tapestry.

A probe in a fresh direction might reach a more vulnerable spot.

"But you had been behind the pedestal?" Dr. Price suggested.

"Yes"—the quick flush coming again. "My old timidity led me to conceal myself where I could watch undetected her bright young figure pass from arch to arch along the opposite gallery. Not till she had got past my line of view did I step out, and then—then it was to see what I have already told you—her rush toward the front—the start she gave—the fall—that cruel arrow! I own that I shrank back into my narrow hiding-place when I realized that all was at an end—that she was dead."

"Why? You had been witness to a deed of blood—a deed which must have recalled to you the anxiety expressed by the woman whom you regarded as the young girl's guardian; and yet you shrank back—out of sight—away from those who had the right to make inquiries! How do you explain that, Mr. Travis?"

"I cannot, except that I was so dazed, so stricken, that I was hardly conscious of what I did. And, sirs, believe me or not, had it not been for the refuge afforded by that narrow space behind the pedestal, I think I should have fallen headlong to the floor. When I came again to myself, which was after some of the confusion had abated, I had only one thought in mind: to suppress myself and my story lest some shadow should fall across her sweet purity. Waiting till the attention of the man you had placed on guard over her body was attracted another way, I slid out and hastened to the front, where I managed to find a quiet room in which to sit down and brood again over my misfortune. Forewarned, as you have said, and on the spot, with every wish to protect her, I had failed to do so. I fear it will make me mad some day."

Had it made him insane already? Was his story to be trusted? It was full of incongruities; were they those of a disordered mind? Such had been the excuse made for Mrs. Taylor when she had been thought guilty of this attack; why should it not be applied to this man who certainly had given evidences of not being of the usual type of young Englishman? With a sidelong look at Mr. Gryce, which that individual perfectly understood, Dr. Price thanked Mr. Travis for his candor and asked if he could point out the room in which he had sat while their young man had gone through the building checking off the position of everybody in it.

To his surprise, the Englishman answered quite simply, "I will try," and rose when they rose.

The glances exchanged between the other two men were eloquent. Where was he about to take them? Sweetwater was no fool; how had this man of marked appearance and generous proportions managed to elude him?

As has happened before, it proved to be easily explainable when once the conditions were known. The room to which he led them was that on the upper story marked H on Chart Two. It was devoted, like one or two others near it, to a line of famous paintings at once the hope and despair of young girl copyists. The one most favored for this purpose hung just behind the door "X," which, half-open as they found it, made with the easel, the canvas upon it and an apron hanging carelessly over all, an impromptu screen behind which a man crouched in misery on the copyist's stool might easily remain unnoticed by anyone passing hurriedly by him.

And thus vanished one hindrance to a full belief in young Travis' story.

But a greater one remained. The bow! the bow found behind the tapestry at the edge of which he had stood in timorous hiding! In the hope that a shock might startle him into some admission which would give a different aspect to the case, they now led him back to this place of first concealment. He was showing strain by this time, and no delay was made to press their point. Giving the tapestry a pull, the Coroner bade him tell what he saw behind it.

The answer came with much emotion.

"The bow! The bow which sped the arrow which killed Miss Willetts. I do not want to see it. It hurts me—hurts me physically. Let me go, I entreat."

"Mr. Travis," urged the Coroner as they again emerged upon the open gallery, "you have said that there was no one with you in the section where you stood. If that was so, how came this bow to be where you have just seen it?"

A bewildered look, a slow shake of the head and nothing more.

"Did you know it was there? Did you see it thrown there?"

"No, I saw nothing. I am an honest man. You may believe me."

The Coroner scrutinized him closely but not unkindly.

"We shall know before night who handled that bow, Mr. Travis. It carries its own clue with it."

A gleam of unmistakable joy lighted up the Englishman's features.

"I am glad," he cried. "I am glad."

Coroner Price was a man of experience. He recognized the ring of truth in the Englishman's tones, and saying no more, led the way from the gallery.

A few minutes later he was on the lower floor. He had a short conversation with the two doormen; then he proceeded to the telephone and called up the Universal.

The result was startling.

Asked if the name of Rupert Henry Travis, Hertfordshire, England, was on their register, the answer was yes.

"The date of his arrival?"

"Early this morning."

"Any other arrivals today from the other side?"

"Yes, a Madame Duclos and a Miss Willetts."

The Coroner's tone altered. So much of the stranger's story was true, then.

"Will you connect me with Madame Duclos. I have important news to give her. Some woman had better be with her when she receives it."

"I am sorry, but I cannot do this. Madame Duclos has left."

"Left? Gone out, you mean?"

"No, left the hotel. She's been gone about half an hour. The young lady who came with her has gone out too, but we expect her back."

"You do. And what took the older woman away? What excuse

did she give, and where has she gone?"

"I cannot tell you where she has gone. She left after receiving a telephone message from some one in town. Came down to the desk looking extremely distressed, said that she had had bad news and must go at once. I made out her bill and, at her request, that of the young lady, whom she said would be called for by a friend on her return to the hotel. These bills she paid; after that she left the hotel on foot, carrying her own bag. The young lady has not returned—"

"Enough. The young lady is dead, killed by chance here at the museum. A plain-clothes man will be with you shortly from Headquarters. Meanwhile keep your eyes and ears open. If a message comes for either Madame Duclos or Miss Willetts, notify me here; and if anyone calls, detain the party at all hazards. That's all; no time to talk."

And now Gryce entered the room. He was accompanied by an inspector. This was a welcome addition to their force. Coroner Price greeted him with cordiality:

"You've come in good time, Inspector. The death of this young girl struck down by an arrow shot by an unknown hand from the opposite side of the building bids fair to make a greater call on your resources than on mine. The woman who appears to have acted as companion to Miss Willetts has fled the hotel where they both took rooms immediately upon leaving the steamer. Either she has heard of the accident which has occurred here— and if so, how?—or she's but carrying out some deep-laid plan which it is highly important for us to know. It looks now like a premeditated crime."

"With this Englishman involved?"

"I doubt that; I seriously doubt that—don't you, Gryce? A more subtle head than his planned this strange crime."

"Yes; there can be little doubt about that. Shall I set the boys to work, Inspector? This Frenchwoman must be found."

"At once—a general alarm. You can get a description of her from the clerk at the Universal. She must not be allowed to leave town."

Mr. Gryce sat down before the telephone. Coroner Price proceeded to acquaint the Inspector with such details of the affair as were now known. The Curator moved restlessly about. Gloom had settled upon the museum. On only one face was there a smile to be seen, but that was a heavenly one, irradiating the countenance of her who had passed from the lesser to the larger world with the joy of earth still warm in her innocent heart.

BOOK II
MR. X

VIII

ON THE SEARCH

It was late in the afternoon. The Inspector's office had hummed for hours with messages and reports, and the lull which had finally come seemed grateful to him. With relaxed brow and a fresh cigar, he sat in quiet contemplation of the facts brought out by the afternoon's inquiries. He was on the point of dismissing even these from his mind, when the door opened and Gryce came in.

Instantly his responsibilities returned upon him in full force. He did not wait for the expected report, but questioned the detective at once.

"You have been to the hotel," he said, pointing out a chair into which the old man dropped with a sigh as eloquent of anxiety as of fatigue. "What more did you learn there?"

"Very little. No message has come; no persons called. For them and for us these two women, Madame Duclos and Miss Willetts, are still an unknown quantity. Their baggage, which arrived while I was there, supplied the only information I was able to obtain."

"Their baggage! But that should tell us everything."

"It may if you think best to go through it. It is not heavy—a trunk for each, besides the one they brought with them from the steamer. From the pasters to be seen on them, they have come from the Continental Hotel, Paris, by way of the Ritz, London. At this latter place their stay was short. This is proved by the fact that only the steamer-trunk is pasted with the Ritz label. And this trunk was the one I found in their room at the Universal. From it Miss Willetts had taken the dress she wore to the museum. Her other clothes—I mean those she wore on arriving—lay in disorder on the bed and chairs. I should say that they had been tossed about by a careless if not hasty hand, while the trunk—"

"Well?"

"Stood open on the floor."

"Stood open?"

"Yes, I went through it, of course."

"And found nothing?"

"Nothing to help us today. No letters—no cards. Some clothing—some little trifles (bought in Paris, by the way) and one little book."

"A name in it?"

"Yes—*Angeline*; and one line of writing from some poem, I judge. I put it back where I found it. When we know more, it may help us to find her friends."

"And is that all?"

"Almost, but not quite. The young girl had a bag too. It stood on a table—"

"Well?"

"Empty. Everything had been tumbled out—turned upside down and the contents scattered. I looked them carefully over. Nothing, positively nothing, but what you would be likely to find in any young girl's traveling-bag. There's but one conclusion to be drawn."

"And what is that?"

"That all these things, such as they were, had been pushed hastily about after being emptied out on the table. That was not the young girl's work."

"Madame Duclos'!"

"You've hit it. She was in search of some one thing she wanted, and she took the quickest way of finding it. And—"

"Yes, Gryce?"

"She was in a desperate hurry, or she wouldn't have left the trunk open or all those dainty things lying about. Frenchwomen are methodical and very careful of their belongings. One other thing I noted. There was a loose nail in the lock of the trunk. Sticking to this nail was a raveling of brown wool. Here it is, sir. The woman—Madame Duclos—wore a dress of brown serge. If my calculations are not wrong and we succeed in getting a glimpse of that dress, we shall find a tear in the skirt—and what is more, one very near the hem."

"Made today?"

"Yes—another token of haste. She probably jerked at the skirt when she found herself caught. She could not have been herself to have done this—for which we may be glad."

"You mean that by this thoughtless action she has left a clue in our hands?"

"That and something more. That tear in her decent skirt will bother her. She will either make an immediate attempt to mend it, or else do the other obvious thing—buy a new one. In either case it gives us something by which to trace her. I have put Sweetwater on that job. He never tires, never wearies, never lets go. No report in yet from the terminals?"

"Not a word. But she will not get far. Sooner or later we shall find her if she does not come forward herself after reading the evening papers."

"She will never come forward."

"I am not so sure. Something not a little peculiar happened at the museum after you left. We had Reynolds up, and he made a most careful examination of that bow for finger-prints. He did not find any. But fortune favored us in another way almost as good."

"Now you interest *me*."

"We had brought the bow into the Curator's office, and it lay on the long table in the middle of the room. I had been looking it over (this was after Reynolds had gone, of course) and had already noted a certain defect in it, when on chancing to look up, my eyes fell on a mirror hanging in a closet the door of which stood wide open. A face was visible in it—a very white face which altered under my scrutiny into a semblance more natural. It was that of Correy—you remember Correy, one of the assistants, and an honest fellow enough, but more troubled at this moment than I had ever seen him. What could have happened?

"Wheeling quickly about, I caught him just as he started to go. He had openly declared that he did not know this bow; but it was evident that he did, and I did not hesitate to say so. Taken unawares, he could not hide his distress, which he proceeded to explain thus: He did remember the bow, now that he had the opportunity of seeing it closer. He pointed to the nick I had myself noticed and said that owing to this defect the bow had been cast aside, and the last time he had handled it—Here he caught his breath and stopped. Another memory had evidently returned to embarrass him."

"Did you succeed in getting him to acknowledge what it was?"

"Yes, after I had worked with him for some time. He didn't want to talk. In a moment you will see why. Going back to the time he had seen it before, he said that he had found it in the cellar in an old box, the contents of which he had been pulling over in a search for something very different. Amazed to find it there, he had taken it out, examined it carefully, noted the nick I mentioned and tossed it back again into the box. This he told, but reluctantly.

"Why reluctantly, I was soon to find out. He was not alone in the cellar. The shadow of some person at his back had fallen across the lid of the box as he was closing it. He did not recognize the shadow and had not given it at the time a second thought, but the remembrance of it came back vividly when he saw the bow lying before him and realized the part it had played in the morning's tragedy. Was it because he knew that only a person actively connected with the museum would have access to that part of the cellar? I asked. I did not expect an answer, and I did not get it. We looked at each other for a moment, then I let him go."

A momentary silence, which the Inspector broke by saying:

"Later I called the Curator in, and he also recognized the bow as belonging to the museum. But he volunteered no explanations and in fact had little to say on the subject. He was evidently too much startled by the direct connection which had thus been made between the crime (or accident, if you will) and the personnel of the museum."

"That was natural. He should be the first to see that the bow which shot the arrow must of necessity have been brought into the building by some other door than those at which the doormen stood guard. I had a talk with those men, and they both declared that no sticks or umbrellas or anything of that nature ever went by them or would be allowed to go by them, no matter how concealed or wrapped up. But to revert to the matter in hand. So Correy made absolutely no attempt to explain how this weapon had been carried from cellar to gallery without his knowledge?"

"No. He for one will have a sleepless night."

"Not he alone. I must and will see a way through this maze. Tomorrow may bring luck. Ah, I forgot to say that I spent an hour of the three you allowed me with the captain of the steamer which brought over these two women. As might be expected, he had no information of any significance to give me; nor could I obtain much from such members of the crew as I could get hold of. One steward remembered the Englishman, chiefly because he never showed himself unless the young lady was on deck. But he never saw them speak."

"Which bears out Travis' story to the last detail."

"Exactly. I think we can depend upon *him*; otherwise we *should* be at sea."

"Yet his story is a very strange one."

"The whole affair is strange—the strangest I ever knew. But that isn't against it. It's the commonplace case which baffles. We shall get the key to the whole mystery yet."

"I've no doubt. Is Mr. Travis to be detained?"

"Yes, as witness."

"Does he object?"

"Not at all. Having spoken—told his whole story, as he says— he is rather glad than otherwise to be relieved from the common curiosity of strangers. He's a rare bird, Gryce. If he stops to think, he must see that he stands in a more or less ticklish position. But he does not betray by look or action any doubt of our entire belief in the truth of all his statements. His only trouble seems to be that he has lost, by these inhuman means, the girl upon whom he had set his heart. Tomorrow we will confront him with Mrs. Taylor. She should be able to say whether he did or did not stand out in the open gallery at the moment Miss Willetts fell."

But Mr. Gryce had no encouragement to give him on this head.

"Mrs. Taylor is ill—very ill, as I take it. I stopped at her hotel to inquire. I was anxious about her for more than one reason and the report I got of her condition was far from favorable. She is suffering cruelly from shock. How occasioned, whether by the peculiar and startling death to which she was a witness or by the strangely coincident fancy to which she herself attributes her deep emotion, will have to be decided by further developments. Nothing which I was able to learn from doctor or nurse settled this interesting question. Meanwhile, no one is allowed to see her—or will be till she is on the direct road to recovery. Let us hope that this may be soon, or the inquest may be delayed indefinitely."

"I don't know as that is to be deplored. I imagine we shall find enough to fill in our time.... Any communications made by her before she collapsed? Did she send out or receive messages of any kind since her return from the museum?"

"She received none; but it is impossible to say whether or not she sent any out. There is a letter-chute very near her door. She may have dropped a letter in that any time before a watch was put upon her. You are thinking, of course, of the anxiety she expressed about her husband, and whether she took any measures for ascertaining if her fears for him had any foundation in fact?"

"I was, yes; but I presume this fancy had passed, or else she is too ill to remember her own aberrations. Were you able to effect an understanding with her nurse?"

"Yes; that's fixed. I had a short talk, too, with the proprietor of the hotel. He thinks very highly of Mrs. Taylor. She has lived in the one apartment for years, and he cannot say enough of her discreet and uniform life. Though she made no secret of the fact that she does not live with her husband, her conduct has always been such as to insure universal respect. He did not even make mention of eccentricities. If she is crazy, it is a late development. She seemed to have been all right up to this morning. Whichever way you turn, you encounter mystery and a closed door."

"The papers may spring the lock of that door at any moment.

Publication does much in a case of this kind. Tomorrow we may be in a much more favorable position. Meantime, let us recount the facts it is our business to clear up."

"On what hypothesis?"

"On all hypotheses. We are not sure enough of our premises, as yet, to confine ourselves to one."

"Very good, these are the ones which seem to me to be of the greatest importance:

"Whose hand carried the bow from cellar to gallery?

"Was it the same which carried the arrow from one gallery to the other?

"Is it possible for an arrow, shot through the loophole made by the curving-in of the vase, to reach the mark set for it by Mr. Travis' testimony?

"Which one of the men or women known to be in the museum when this arrow was released has enough knowledge of archery to string a bow? A mark can be reached by chance; but only an accustomed hand can string a bow as unyielding as this one.

"Who telephoned to Madame Duclos; and of what nature was the message which sent her from the hotel so precipitately that she not only left the most important part of her baggage behind but went away without making adequate provision for the young girl confided to her charge?

"Does this mean that she had been made acquainted with the fate of the young girl; and if so, by whom?"

"Business enough for us all," was the Inspector's comment as Gryce paused in this enumeration. "As you put it, I am more and more convinced that the key you spoke of a short time ago will be found in this missing woman's tightly shut hand."

"Which brings us round full-circle to our first conclusion: that Miss Willetts' death is not only a crime, but a premeditated one."

"Carried out, not by the one benefited, but by an agent selected for the purpose."

"An agent, moreover, who knew the ways and possibilities of the place."

"A logical conclusion; but still too incredible for belief. I find it hard to trust to appearances in this case."

"And I also. But as we have both said, time may clear away some of its incongruities. Meanwhile I have an experiment to propose." And leaning close to the Inspector, notwithstanding the fact that there was nobody within hearing and he knew it, he whispered a few words in his ear.

The Inspector stared.

"Tonight?" he asked.

The detective nodded.

IX

WHILE THE CITY SLEPT

Night—the night of a great city with its myriad of garish lights and its many curious and incongruous activities.

Who has not felt his imagination stirred by the contrasts thus offered—contrasts never more apparent than at these hours of supposed rest? Grim walls, with dimpled children sleeping behind them! Places of merrymaking athrob with music and dazzling with jets of incandescent light, with grief in the heart of the dancer and despair making raucous the enforced laugh!

But nowhere in the great city of which we write on this night of May 23, 1913, was there to be found a scene of greater contradictions than in the court and galleries of its famous museum.

Lighted as for a reception, the architectural beauties of its Moorish arcades and carven balustrades flashed in full splendor. Gems of antique art, casts in which genius had stored its soul and caused to live before us the story of the ancients, pillars from desert sands, friezes from the Parthenon and bas-reliefs from Nineveh and Heliopolis, filled every corner, commanding the eye to satisfy itself in forms of deathless grace or superhuman power. And no one to heed! Not an eye to note that the Venus in one corner seemed to smile in the soft light with more than its accustomed allurement, or that the armor in which kings had fought wore a menacing sparkle exceeding that of other times and quieter days. Ghosts of vanished ages might parade at will among the chattels of their time or drain the iridescent beaker to their unknown gods—no one would have noticed or turned aside to see. For there was something else within these walls tonight for the men assembled there to look upon, and a story to be read which shut the imagination upon the past by amply filling it with the present.

What is this something? Let us follow the gaze of the half-dozen persons grouped in front of the tapestry hanging in the northern gallery, and see.

But first, of whom is this small and mystic group composed? Who are these men who in the middle of the night, in the security of a completely shuttered building, busy themselves, not with the inestimable treasures surrounding them, but with an odd and seemingly mountebank adventure totally out of keeping with the place and their absorbed demeanor? We will name them:

Mr. Roberts and a second director seen here for the first time, Inspector Jackson, Mr. Gryce, two lesser detectives, and a strange young man of undoubted Indian extraction who kept much in the background and yet stood always at attention like one awaiting orders.

Are these all? Yes, in the one gallery; but in the other, shadowy figures are visible among the arches at one end, with whose identity we shall probably soon be made acquainted.

At what are these various persons, in the one gallery as in the other, looking so intently that all are turned one way—the way of greatest interest—the way the fatal arrow had flown some fourteen hours before, carrying death to the innocent girl smiling upon life in youthful exuberance? Is it at some image of herself they see restored to hope and joy? An image is there, but alas! it is but a dummy taken from one of the exhibits and so set up as to present the same angle to the gallery-front as her young body had done, according to Mr. Travis' reluctant declaration.

Why so placed, and why regarded with such concentrated interest by the men confronting it from the opposite gallery, will become apparent when, upon the Indian's being summoned from his place of modest retirement, it can be seen that the bow he carries in one hand is offset by the arrow he holds in the other. A test is to be made which will settle, or so they hope, the truth of Mr. Travis' story. If an arrow launched from before the pedestal or even from behind it through the loophole made by the curving-in of the vase toward its base can be made to reach its mark in the breast of this dummy, then they would feel some justification in doubting his statement that the arrow, whatever the appearances, was not shot from this gallery. If it could not, belief in his statements would be confirmed and their minds be cleared of a doubt which must hamper all their future movements.

The second director, whose name was Clayton, stood at the left of the Inspector and close against the tapestry. To him that official now turned with this explanation:

"The bow you see in Mr. La Flèche's hand is similar in length and weight to the one found lying strung for use in the doorway back of where you are now standing. The arrow is from the same quiver as the one which entered Miss Willetts' breast.... Did you speak?"

No, Mr. Clayton had not spoken; yet for some reason a thrill had passed through the small group surrounding him, which had heightened the consciousness of them all. Eyes and ears became alert; only the Indian showed stolidity.

"Mr. La Flèche, you will first stand here," continued the Inspector, pointing to the spot which Mr. Travis had finally settled upon as the one where he had been standing at the moment he saw Miss Willetts fall.

The Indian took the place, sighted the figure diagonally opposite and laid his finger on the string.

"An inch to the left of the bunch of flowers pinned on the dummy's breast," murmured Mr. Gryce almost in his ear.

It was a breathless moment; even the two detectives showed excitement.

But the Indian failed to shoot. Instead, he looked around at the Inspector and quietly remarked:

"I will shoot standing, since you so request, but I think you will find that the arrow which caused death was delivered by a man kneeling."

A flash of the eye between the two detectives, which only one man saw! All the others were watching the lightning flight of the arrow. It struck the dummy full and square. Everyone shuddered, even the Inspector; it brought the real tragedy so vividly to mind.

Meanwhile a movement had taken place in the small group of men watching from the other side. One of them stepped fully into view and approaching the figure thus attacked, drew out the arrow and made close examination of the hole it had made and shook his head. It was Coroner Price.

"Try again, and from behind the pedestal this time," he called out across the intervening space as he stepped back into his former place of observation.

The Inspector motioned his wishes to the Indian, who with a subtle twist of his body slipped behind the pedestal.

"That's better," was the Inspector's quick comment. "Can you handle the bow easily from where you now stand?"

"There is plenty of room."

"Very well. But wait! Before we proceed further, there is a matter to which I wish to call the attention of these gentlemen. It must have been apparent to you all that a person standing where Mr. La Flèche did a moment ago would be easily visible to anyone looking up from the court or across from the opposite gallery, or even from the broad corridors at either end of the building. But would the same hold true if instead of being in front he had been behind the pedestal, as Mr. La Flèche is now? Run below, Barney; and, gentlemen, disperse yourselves in different directions and give me your opinion. Now!" he demanded after a few minutes' wait, during which there had been a scattering to right and left along the galleries, "what do you say?"

"If anyone chanced to be looking directly there, yes," was shouted up from below.

"What do you say, Coroner Price?"

"Ask the man to kneel."

The Inspector gave the word.

"Ah, that's different! The bulge of the vase hides the upper part of his head, and the pedestal itself the lower. He might shoot from his present position with impunity."

"Do you all agree?"

"Yes, yes!" came from different parts of the building.

"Then, Mr. La Flèche, here's another arrow from the same quiver. Take fresh aim and shoot."

Another breathless moment—more breathless than the other; then a second arrow flew across the court and hung quivering in the breast of the dummy.

From both ends of the gallery men came running, and leaning eagerly over the gallery-rail they watched the Coroner as he stepped again into view to make a second examination.

This time he kept them several minutes in suspense, and when he had drawn out the arrow, he looked long at the hole it had made. Then, instead of shouting his decision across the court, he could be seen leaving the gallery and coming around their way.

What had he to say? As they waited, a clock struck from some neighboring steeple—three sonorous peals! The two directors glanced at each other. Doubtless they felt the weirdness of the hour as well as of the occasion. It was a new experience for these amateurs in police procedure.

Arrived on their side, the Coroner advanced quickly. When close upon the reassembled group, he remarked quickly but with great decision:

"Mr. Travis seems to have been correct in denying that the arrow flew either from before or behind this pedestal. The first arrow sent by Mr. La Flèche entered the dummy almost at a right angle; the last departed but a little from this same line. But the real wound which I probed and located to a hair was a decidedly slanting one. It must have been sent from a place further off."

"From behind the other pedestal!" spoke up Mr. Gryce, all fire and interest at once. "Either the Englishman deceived us, or each pedestal had its man."

"We'll see! Another shot, and from behind the further pedestal, Mr. La Flèche!"

The Indian glided into view and started for the other end of the tapestry, followed by the Inspector, his detectives and the two directors. As they passed one by one across the face of the great hanging, they had the appearance not of living men but of a parade of specters, so silent their step and so somber their air. The dread of some development hitherto unacknowledged made their movements slow instead of hasty. The upper pedestal instead of the lower! Why should this possible fact make any difference in their feelings. Yet it did—perhaps because it meant deception on the part of one they had instinctively believed trustworthy, or—

But why pursue conjecture when actuality only is of moment? Let us proceed with our relation and await the result.

Arrived at the upper pedestal, Mr. La Flèche took his place, received the third arrow and presently delivered it. The Coroner, who had already started for the other side, hastily approached the dummy, made his examination and threw up his hand with the loud shout:

"The shot was made from there; the matter is settled!"

Question: Had Mr. Travis wilfully misled them, or had the presumption in his favor been strengthened by this proof that it had been shown possible for another hand than his to have shot the arrow from this same section of the gallery, without disturbing his belief that he was the only person in it at the time?

X

"AND HE STOOD *HERE*?"

The Inspector, finding himself very much disturbed by the doubt just mentioned, felt inclined to question whether any perceptible advancement had been made by this freak business of his canny subordinate. He was hardly ready to say yes, and was not a little surprised when on his way toward the head of the staircase he heard the exultant voice of Mr. Gryce whisper in his ear:

"That's all right. We've gained a point. We know now the exact place from which the arrow was shot."

"But not who shot it."

"No—except that it was not the man Travis."

"How can you be sure of that?"

"For two reasons. This is the first one: If it is difficult to understand how a man could slip from behind the eastern pedestal and make his way along the open gallery to Room H, without attracting the attention of the officer posted opposite, how next to impossible we should find it, if thirty feet were added to his course—which is the distance between the two pedestals!"

"What was that fellow doing, that he shouldn't have seen this effort at escape, whether it involved a short flight or a long one?"

"He says he was not given detective-duty—that he was placed there to keep watch over the body of the young girl;—that at a certain moment he imagined himself to hear a stealthy footstep approaching from the farther end of the gallery, and anxious to spot the man yielding to so doubtful a curiosity, he approached the arch separating his section from the adjoining one, and stopping just inside, stood for a moment or so, listening. As this involved the turning of his back upon the court and consequently upon the opposite gallery, it gave Travis just the opportunity he needed for an unobserved escape. But I see you are not very much impressed by the reason I have advanced for believing his story and placing him where he says he was placed, behind the eastern pedestal. You doubtless think that if the officer opposite had stood long enough with his back to the court, Travis might have taken those extra thirty steps as easily as the twenty he had confessed to. Listen, then, to my second reason, or rather, step this way."

Leading his superior toward Room B, the door of which stood wide open, he paused just outside the threshold to note the effect produced upon the Inspector by what he saw inside. Evidently it was as marked with surprise as the detective had calculated upon, for with an air of great astonishment the Inspector turned upon him with the whispered exclamation:

"Travis here! where he could listen—see—"

"Yes. Take a good look at him, Inspector. It won't trouble him any. I doubt if he would notice us if we stepped into the room."

And such was the opinion of the Inspector himself, as he remarked the extreme excitement under which the Englishman was laboring. Absorbed in thoughts of his own, he was pacing the room with long strides, turning mechanically as he met some impediment, but otherwise oblivious to his surroundings, even to the point of not noting the presence of Sweetwater, who stood quietly watching him from one of the corners.

This display of feeling was certainly eloquent enough to attract anyone's attention, but what gave it impressiveness to the official mind was this: his excitement was that of triumph, not fear, of hope without any trace of confusion.

"It is not of himself he is thinking," muttered Gryce.

"And he stood *here*?"

"No—we left him free to move about at will, and his will carried him into full view of the whole performance."

"And Sweetwater?"

"Was near enough to note his every move, but of course kept himself well out of sight."

Then as they both stepped back from the doorway: "Mr. Travis didn't know he was being watched. He thought himself alone; and having an expressive countenance,—very expressive for an Englishman,—it was easy enough for Sweetwater to read his thoughts."

"And those thoughts?"

"Relief to find an explanation of the phenomenon he had doubtless been puzzling over for hours. The moments he had spent in hiding behind one pedestal had evidently failed to suggest that another man might have been in hiding behind the other."

"I am not surprised. Coincidences of this astonishing kind are not often met with even by us," was the Inspector's dry retort.

During the interchange of these hurried sentences, they had withdrawn still farther out of sight and hearing of the man discussed. But at this point Inspector Jackson reapproached the doorway, and entering in a manner to intercept Mr. Travis in his nervous goings to and fro, remarked in an off-hand way:

"I see that you have met with a surprise, Mr. Travis. Like ourselves, you gave little thought to what that upper pedestal might conceal."

"You are right. I never even glanced that way. But if I had, I should have seen nothing. He was well hid, exceedingly well hid, whoever he was. But he cannot escape now; you'll get him, won't you, Inspector? He could not have left the building—all say that this was impossible. He was one, then, of the people I saw moving about when I went down into the court. Find him! Find this murderer of innocence! of the sweetest, purest child—"

He turned away; grief was taking the place of indignation and revenge. At this sight the two men left him. The Inspector was at last convinced, both of the man's probity and of one stern, disconcerting fact: that the real culprit—the man whose guilty fingers had launched the fatal arrow—had been, as Travis said, one of the twenty-two persons who had been moving about for hours not only under his eyes but under those of the famous detective posted there.

XI

FOOTSTEPS

WANTED—A WOMAN CALLING HERSELF ANTOIN-
ETTE Duclos, just arrived from Europe on the steamer *Castania*, who after taking rooms at the Universal for herself and
her steamer companion, Angeline Willetts, left the hotel in
great haste late in the afternoon of May twenty-third and has
not been heard of since.

In person she is of medium height, but stocky for a
Frenchwoman. Dark hair, black eyes, with an affection of the
lid which causes the left one to droop. Her dress consisted of
skirt and jacket of a soft shade of brown. Hat indistinguish-
able. She carried, on leaving the hotel, a dark brown leather
bag of medium size, long and narrow in shape. Her only pe-
culiarity, saving the one drooping eyelid, is a hesitating walk.
This is particularly obvious when she attempts to hasten.

It is to be hoped that this person on hearing of Miss
Willetts' death, will communicate at once with the clerk of the
hotel.

If in two days this does not occur, a reward of five hundred dollars will be given to the man or woman who can give
definite news of this Frenchwoman's whereabouts.

Police Headquarters, Mulberry St.

This notice, appended to such particulars of the tragedy as
appeared in all the morning papers, roused the city—I may even
say the country—to even greater wonder and excitement than had
followed the first details given in the journals of the evening
before.

Would anything come of it?

Morning passed; no news of Antoinette Duclos.

Afternoon: messages of all kinds leading to much work, but
bringing no result.

Five o'clock: a missive from the directors of the museum to
the effect that under the peculiar circumstances and the seeming
absence of any friends of the deceased, they would be glad to furnish the means necessary to the proper care and burial of the
young woman killed in such an unhappy manner within their
walls.

A half-hour later, Gryce, for whose appearance the Inspector
had been anxiously waiting, came in with his report. A chair was

pushed up for him, for he was an old man and had had a sleepless night, as we know, besides two days of continued work. But he did not drop into it, as the Inspector expected, or give any other signs of exceptional fatigue; yet when he had seated himself and they were left alone, he did not hasten to speak, though he evidently had much to say, but remained quiet, holding counsel, as it were, in his old way, with some small object he had picked up from the desk before him.

At last the Inspector spoke:

"You have been on the hunt; what did you find?"

"Not much, Inspector—and yet enough to disturb me in a way I was not looking for. Of course, in studying the situation carefully, you have asked yourself how the man who shot the arrow from behind the upper pedestal got away. He did not wait as Travis did till the first excitement had abated and the way was, in a manner, cleared for an escape into the court. For X, as we will call him, was certainly among those I saw lined up before me at the moment I bade them one and all to return and stand until released, in the exact spot occupied by them when the first alarm rang out. After the surprise Travis gave us we had the building searched from roof to cellar. Not another soul was found in it whose name was not registered on the chart. As I have already said, the guilty one had managed to escape immediately upon the flight of the arrow, though how, even then, he could have got below in the time he did is a mystery which trips me up every time I think of it. But letting that go for the present, he did get there and get there unnoticed. How? Now, there are three ways of escape from behind either of those pedestals. The way Travis took, that is, toward the front, and round through the suite of rooms headed by the one marked H, to the rear staircase; the more direct one of an immediate exit from the gallery through Sections VI and VII to this same staircase; and (the only one worth considering) a straight plunge for the door behind the tapestry and so down by the winding staircase beyond, into the Curator's office. The unknown never went Travis' way, and he couldn't have gone the other without running into the arms of Correy; so he must have made use of the hidden door. So convinced was I of this, after last night's discovery eliminated Travis as a suspect, that I made it my first duty this morning to examine this door and the mysterious little passageway back of it. When first notified of this door, we had been assured that it had not been opened in years, that the only key remaining to it was the one the Curator showed us hanging from the ring he drew from his own pocket; and acting upon these statements, which I would not allow myself to doubt for a moment, we decided to open the door in our own way, which we immediately did. The result was the instant discovery that some one had passed through this door and down these stairs very much later than years ago. We could see, without taking a step beyond the doorway, traces of a well-shod foot in the dust lying thickly on every tread. These traces were so many and so confused that I left them for Stevens' experienced eye and deft manipulation to separate and make plain to us. He is making an examination of them now, and will be able to report to you before night."

The Inspector was a man of little pretense. He felt startled and showed it.

"But this is a serious matter, Gryce."

"Very serious."

"No mere visitor to the museum would have presumed upon this venture."

"No."

"Which means—"

"That some one actively connected with it had a guilty hand in this deplorable affair."

"I am afraid so."

"Some one well acquainted with the existence of this door and who had means of opening it. The question is—who?"

In saying this, Mr. Gryce studiously avoided the Inspector's eye; while the Inspector in his turn looked up, then down—anywhere but in the detective's direction. It was a moment of mutual embarrassment, broken, when it was broken, by a remark which manifestly avoided the issue.

"Possibly those traces you speak of were not made at the time you specify. They may have been made since, or they may have been made before. Perhaps the Curator was curious and tried his hand at a little detective work on his own account."

"He hadn't the chance. Every portion of the building has been very thoroughly guarded since first we entered it. He may have gone up prior to the shooting. That is open to dispute; but if he had done so, why did he not inform us of the fact when he showed us the key? The Curator is the soul of honor. He would hardly deceive us in so important a matter."

The quick glance which this elicited from the Inspector awoke no corresponding flash in the eye of the imperturbable detective. He continued to shake his head over the small object he was twirling thoughtfully about between his thumb and finger, and only from his general seriousness could the Inspector gather that his mind was no more at rest than his fingers. Was this why his remark took the form of a question?

"Where was the Curator when you forced open that door behind the tapestry? Was he anywhere in the building?"

"No, sir; he has not been there today. He was ill last night, and he is ill today. He sent us his excuses. If he had been in the building, I doubt whether I would have given the order to burst open the door. I would simply have requested him to use his key. And he would have done so and kept his own counsel. I do not know as I can say as much for any of his subordinates. Happily, no spying eye was about at that time; and Stevens will be sure to see that he is not watched at his work if he has to lock the door upon the whole bunch of directors."

"This is to be a secret investigation, then?"

"I would so advise."

"With every reporter headed off, and anyone likely to report to a reporter headed off also?"

"Do not *you* advise this?"

"I do. Anything more?"

"Not till we hear from Stevens."

They had not long to wait. Sooner than they expected the expert mentioned came in. He held a batch of papers in his hand, which at a gesture from the Inspector he spread out before them. Then he spoke:

"One man and one man only has passed down those stairs. But that man has passed down them twice—once with rubbers on and once without. There are signs equally plain of his having gone up them, but only once, and at the time he wore the rubbers. I took every pains possible to preserve and photograph the prints, but as you see, great confusion was caused by the second line of steps falling half on and half off the other. All I dare read there is this: A quick run up and a quick run down by a man in rubbers, and then a second run down by the same man in shoes. That's the whole story. These other scraps of paper," he went on as he saw the Inspector's eye travel to some small bits lying on the side, "are what I have to show as the result of my search on and about the western pedestal for finger-prints. A gloved hand drew that bow. See here: this is an impression I obtained from the inner edge of the pedestal in question."

He pulled forward a small square of paper; the sewing of a kid glove was plainly indicated there.

When Stevens had gone, the Inspector exclaimed meaningly:

"Gryce! Name your man; we shall get on faster."

The aged detective rose.

"I dare not," he said. "Give me one—two days. I must have time to think—to collect my evidence. A name once mentioned leaves an echo. When my echo rings, it must carry no false sound. Remember, I did not sleep last night. When I present this case to you as I see it, I must be at my best. I am not at my best today."

This was doubtless true, but the Inspector had not discovered it.

XII

"SPARE NOBODY! I SAY, SPARE NOBODY!"

On his way home Mr. Gryce stopped at the Calderon to inquire how Mrs. Taylor was doing, and what his prospects were for a limited interview with her.

He was told that no such interview could be considered for days—that she still lay in a stupor, with brief flashes of acute consciousness, during which she would scream "No! no!"—that brain fever was feared and that increased excitement might be fatal.

Another bar to progress! He had hoped to help her memory into supplying him with a fact which would greatly simplify a task whose anomalies secretly alarmed him. She had been in a fair state of mind before her nerve was attacked by the event which robbed the little Angeline of life and herself of reason, and if carefully approached, might possibly recall some of the impressions made upon her previous to that moment. If, for instance, she could describe even in a general way the appearance of any person she may have seen advancing in the direction of the northern gallery at the moment she herself turned to enter the southern one, what a stability it would give to his theory, and what certainty to his future procedure!

But he must wait for this, as he must wait for Angeline's story from Madame Duclos. Meantime, a word with Sweetwater—after which, rest.

It was Mr. Gryce's custom, especially when engaged upon a case of marked importance, to receive this, his recognized factotum, in his own home. No prying ears, no watchful eyes, were to be feared there. He was the absolute master of everything, even of Sweetwater, he sometimes thought. For this young fellow loved him—had reason to; and when Sweetwater played the violin, as he sometimes did after one of their long talks, the aged detective came as near happiness as he ever did, now that his little grandchild was married and had gone with her husband to the other side of the world.

Tonight he was not anticipating any such relaxation as this, yet to Sweetwater, arriving later than he wished, he had never looked more in need of it, as, sitting in his old and somewhat dingy library, he mused over some little object he held in his half-closed palm, with an intent, care-worn gaze which it distressed his young subordinate to see. Uncertainty incites the young and fires them to action; but it wearies the old and saps what little strength they have; and Sweetwater detected uncertainty in his patron's troubled brow and prolonged stare at the insignificant article absorbing his attention.

However, Gryce roused quickly at the young detective's cheery greeting, and looking up with an answering welcome, plunged at once into business.

"So you have seen Turnbull! What did the man say?"

"That it was the left-hand upper corner of the tapestry he saw shaking, and not the right-hand one as we had blindly supposed."

"Good! Then we can take it for granted that our new theory is well founded. Certain things have come to light in your absence. That tapestry was pulled aside not merely for the purpose of flinging in the bow, but to let the flinger pass through the door at its back down to the Curator's office and so out into the court."

"Whew! And who...."

"If this fact had been made known to me sooner, you would have had a different day's work; not getting it until late this afternoon, we have perhaps wasted some valuable hours. But we won't fret about that. Mrs. Taylor being no better, we are likely to have all the time we want for substantiating my idea. It cannot take long if we succeed either in tracing the Duclos woman or in drawing the net I am quietly manufacturing, so closely about—well, I've decided to call him X—that it will hold against all opposition. I have hopes of finding the woman, but great doubts as to the efficacy of the net I have mentioned; it will have to be so wide and deep, and so absolutely without a single weak strand."

Sweetwater sat astonished, and what was more, silent—he who had a word for everything. Accustomed as he was to the varying moods of his remarkable friend, he had never before been met with a reticence so absolute. It made him think; but for once in his life did not make him loquacious.

Mr. Gryce seemed to be gratified by this, though he made no remark to that effect and continued to preserve his abstracted look and quiet demeanor. So Sweetwater waited, and while waiting managed to steal a glimpse at the small object to which his professional friend still paid his undivided attention.

It looked like a narrow bit of dingy black cloth—just that and nothing more—a thing as trivial as the band which clips a closed umbrella. Was it such a band, and would he presently be asked to find the umbrella from which it had fallen or been twisted away? No. Umbrellas are not carried about museum buildings. Besides, this strip of cloth had no ring on the end of it. Consequently it could not have served the purpose he had just ascribed to it. It must have had some other use.

But when, after an impatient flinging aside of this nondescript article, Mr. Gryce spoke, it was to say:

"I had a long talk with Correy today. It seems that he goes through both galleries every morning before the museum opens. Though he will not swear to it, he is of the opinion that the quiver holding the Apache arrows had its full complement when he passed it that morning. He has a way of running things over with his eye which has never yet failed to draw his attention to anything defective or in the least out of order."

"I see, sir," acquiesced Sweetwater in an odd tone, Mr. Gryce's attitude showing that he awaited some expression of interest on his part.

The elder detective either did not notice the curious note in the younger one's voice, or noticing it, chose to ignore it, for with no change of manner he proceeded to say:

"I wish you would exercise your wits, Sweetwater, on the following troublesome question: if the arrow which slew this young girl was in one gallery at ten o'clock, how did it get into the other at twelve? The bow"—here he purposely hesitated—"might have been brought up the iron staircase. But the arrow—"

His eyes were on Sweetwater (a direct glance was a rare thing with Mr. Gryce), and he waited—waited patiently for the word which did not come; then he remarked dryly:

"We are both dull; you are tired with your day's work and I with mine: we will let difficult questions rest until our brains are clearer. But"—here he reached for the strip of dingy cloth he had cast aside, and tossing it over to Sweetwater, added with some suggestion of humor,—"if you want a subject to dream upon tonight, there it is. If you have no desire to dream, and want work for tomorrow, make an effort to discover from whose clothing that fell and what was its use. It was picked up in Room B on the second floor, the one where Mrs. Taylor was detained before going downstairs."

"Ah, something tangible at last!"

"I don't know about that; I honestly don't know. But we cannot afford to let anything go by us. Little things like that have not infrequently opened up a fresh trail which otherwise might have been missed."

Sweetwater nodded, and laying the little strip along his palm, examined it closely. It was made of silk, doubled, and stitched together except at the ends. These were loose, but rough with bits of severed thread, as if the thing had been hastily cut from some article of clothing to which it had been attached by some half-dozen very clumsy stitches.

"I think I understand you, Mr. Gryce," observed Sweetwater, rising slowly to his feet. "But a dream may help me out; we will see."

"I shall not leave here till ten tomorrow morning."

"Very good, sir. If you don't mind, I'll take this with me."

"Take it, by all means."

As Sweetwater turned to go, he was induced by the silence of his patron to cast a backward glance. Mr. Gryce had risen to his feet and was leaning toward him with an evident desire to speak.

"My boy," said he, "if your dreams lead you to undertake the search I have mentioned, spare nobody; I say, spare *nobody*."

Then he sat down; and the memory which Sweetwater carried away with him of the old detective at the moment he uttered this final injunction was far from being a cheerful one.

XIII

"WRITE ME HIS NAME"

Refreshed by a good night's rest and quite ready to take up his task again, Mr. Gryce sat at the same table in the early morning, awaiting the expected message from Sweetwater. Meanwhile he studied, with a fuller attention than he had been able to give it the evening before, the memorandum which this young fellow had handed him of his day's work. A portion of this may be interesting to the reader. Against the list of people registered on his chart as present in the museum at the moment of tragedy, he had inscribed such details concerning them as he could gather in the short time allotted him.

I—Ephraim Short. A sturdy New Englander visiting New York for the first time. Has a big story to take back. Don't care much for broken marbles and pictures so dingy you cannot tell what you are looking at; but the sight of a lot of folks standing up like scarecrows in a field, here and there all over a great building, because something had happened to somebody, will make a story the children will listen to for years.

Address taken, and account of himself verified by telegraph.

II—Mrs. Lynch. Widow, with a small house in Jersey and money to support it. No children. Interested in church work. Honest and of reliable character. Only fault a physical one— extreme nervousness.

III—Mr. Carleton Roberts, director; active in his work, member of the Union League and an aspirant for the high office of U. S. Senator. Lives in bachelor apartment, 67 W. — Street. A universally respected man of unquestioned integrity and decided importance. Close friend of Curator Jewett.

IV—Eben Clarke, door-man. Been long in the employ of museum. Considered entirely trustworthy. Home in decent quarter of West 80th Street. Wife and nine children, mostly grown. Never been abroad. Has no foreign correspondence.

V—Emma Sutton, an art enthusiast, gaining her living by copying old masters. Is at museum six days in the week. It was behind her easel Travis found a hiding-place in Room H.

VI—Mrs. Alice Lee, widowed sister of Edward Cronk Tailor, — Sixth Ave. Lives with brother. Kindly in disposition, much liked and truthful to a fault. No acquaintance abroad.

VII-VIII—John and Mary Draper, husband and wife, living in East Orange, N. J. Decent, respectable folk with no foreign connections.

IX—Hetty Armstrong, young girl, none too bright but honest to the core. Impossible to connect her with this affair.

X—Charles Simpson, resident of Minneapolis. In town on business, stopping at Hotel St. Denis. Eager to return home, but willing to remain if requested to do so. Hates foreigners; thinks the United States the greatest country on earth.

XI—John Turnbull, college professor; one of the new type, alert, observant and extremely precise. Not apt to make a mis-statement.

XII—James Hunter, door-man, a little old for his work, but straight as a string and methodical to a fault. No wife, no child. Bank account more than sufficient for his small wants.

XIII—Miss Charlotte Hunsicker, one of last season's débutantes. Given to tennis and all outdoor sports generally. Offhand but stanch. It was she who gave a woman's care to Mrs. Taylor when the latter fainted in Room B.

XIV—Museum attendant coming up from basement.

XV—Eliza Blake a school-teacher, convalescing after a long illness.

XVI—Officer Rudd.

XVII—Tommy Evans, boy scout. Did not lose his game. Went to the field after lunching on pie at a bakery.

XVIII—Mrs. Nathaniel Lord, wealthy widow, living at the St. Regis.

XIX—Mrs. Ermentrude Taylor. (Nothing to add to what is already known.)

XX—Henry Abbott, Columbia student, good-hearted and reliable, but living in a world of his own to such an extent as to make him the butt of his fellow students.

XXI-XXII—Young couple from Haverstraw. Just married. He a drug-clerk, she a farmer's daughter. Both regarded in their home town as harmless.

XXIII—James Correy, attendant. Bachelor, living with widowed mother. Fair record on the whole. Reprimanded once, not for negligence, but for some foolish act unbecoming his position. Thorough acquaintance with the museum and its exhibits. A valuable man, well liked, notwithstanding the one lapse alluded to. At home and among his friends regarded as the best fellow going. A little free, perhaps, when unduly excited, but not given to drink and very fond of games. A member once of a club devoted to contests with foils and target-shooting. Always champion. Visits a certain young lady three times a week.

XXIV—Curator Jewett. A widower with two grandchildren—a daughter married to an Englishman and living in Ringold, Hants, and a son, owner of a large ranch in California. Lives, when in city, at Hotel Gorham. Known too well for any description of himself or character to be necessary here. If he has a fault, or rather a weakness, it is his extreme pride in the museum and his own conduct of its many affairs.

As on the evening before, Mr. Gryce lingered longest over one name. He was still brooding anxiously over it when the telephone rang at his elbow and he was called up from Headquarters. Cablegrams had been received from London and Paris in acknowledgment of those sent, and in both these cablegrams promises were made of a full examination into the antecedents of Madame Duclos and her companion, Miss Willetts.

That was all. No further news regarding them from any quarter. Mr. Gryce hung up the receiver with a sigh.

"It is likely to be a long road full of unexpected turns and perilously near the precipice's edge," he muttered in weary comment to himself. "Nothing to start from but—"

Here Sweetwater walked in.

Mr. Gryce showed surprise. He had not expected to see the young man himself. Perhaps he was not quite ready to, for he seemed to shrink, for one brief instant, as from an unwelcome presence.

But the cheer which always entered with Sweetwater was contagious, and the old detective smiled as the newcomer approached, saying significantly:

"I had those dreams you spoke of last night, Mr. Gryce, and found them too weighty for the telephone."

"I see, I see! Sit down, Sweetwater, and tell me how they ran. I haven't as much confidence in my own dreams as I hope to have in yours. Speak up! Mention names, if you want to. No echo follows confidences uttered in this room."

"I know that; but for the present perhaps it will be best for me to follow your lead, and when I have to speak of a certain person, say X as you do. X, Mr. Gryce, is the man who for reasons we do not yet understand brought up the discarded bow from the cellar and stored it somewhere within reach on the floor above. X is also the man who for the same unknown reason robbed the quiver hanging in the southern gallery of one of its arrows and kept the same on hand or in hiding, till he could mate it with the bow. My dreams showed me this picture:

"A man with a predominating interest in sport, but otherwise active in business, correct in his dealings and respectable in private life, sees and frequently handles weapons of ancient and modern make which rouse his interest and awaken the longing, common to such men, to test his skill in their use. Sometimes it is a sword, which he twirls vigorously in sly corners. Again, it is a bow calling for a yeoman's strength to pull. He is a man of sense and for a long time goes no further than the play I have just indicated. Perhaps he has no temptation to go further until one unfortunate day he comes upon an idle bow, rotting away in the cellar."

Here Mr. Gryce looked sharply up—a proof of awakened interest which Sweetwater did not heed. Possibly he was not expected to. At all events he continued rapidly:

"It was a fine, strong bow, a typical one from the plains. He took it up—examined it closely—noted a slight defect in it somewhere—and put it back. But he did not forget it. Before many days had passed, he goes down cellar again and brings it up and stands it on end in—where do you think, sir?—in the closet of the Curator's office!"

"How did you learn that?"

"From the woman who comes every day to wipe up the floors. I happened to think she might have something worth while to tell us, so I hunted her up—"

"Go on, boy. Another long mark in your favor."

"Thank you, sir. I'm relating a dream, you know. He stands it on end then in this closet into which nobody is supposed to go but the Curator *and* the scrubwoman, and there he leaves it, possibly as yet with no definite intention. How long it stood there I cannot say. It was well hidden, it seems, by something or other hanging over it. Nor am I altogether sure that it might not be standing there yet if the impulse swaying X had not been strengthened by seeing daily over his head a quiver full of arrows admirably fitted for this bow. Time has no place in dreams, or I might be able to state the day and the hour when he stood looking at the ring of keys lying on the Curator's desk, and struck with what it might do for him, singled out one of the keys which he placed in the keyhole of a door opening upon a certain little iron staircase. He was alone, but he stopped to listen before turning that key. I can see him, can't you? His air is a guilty one; but it is the guilt of folly, not of premeditated crime. He wants a try at that bow and recognizes his weakness and laughs.

"But his longing holds, and running up the little staircase to a second door, he unlocks this also and after another moment of hesitation pulls it open. He has brought the bow with him, but he does not take it past the drapery hanging straight down before his eyes. He simply drops it in the doorway and leaves it there within easy reach from the gallery if ever his impulse should be strong enough to lead him to make an attempt at striking a feather from the Indian headdress on the other side of the court. You think him mad. So do I, but dreams are filled with that kind of madness; and when I see him shut the door upon this bow, and steal back without relocking it or the one below, I have no other excuse than this to give in answer to your criticisms."

"I do not criticise; I listen, Sweetwater."

"You will criticise now. As Bunyan says in his *Pilgrim's Progress*: 'I dreamed again!' This time I saw the museum proper. It was filled with visitors. The morning of May twenty-second was a busy one, I am told, and a whole lot of people, singly and in groups, were continually passing up and down the marble steps and along the two galleries. Partaking of the feelings of the one whose odd impulses I am endeavoring to describe, I was very uneasy and very restless until these crowds had thinned and most of the guests vanished from the building. The hands of the clock were stealing toward twelve—the hour of greatest quiet and fewest visitors. As it reached the quarter mark, I saw what I was looking for, the man X reaching for one of those arrows hanging in the southern gallery, and slipping it inside his coat.—Did you speak, sir?"

No, Mr. Gryce had not spoken; and Sweetwater, after an interval of uncertainty, went quietly on:

"As I saw both of his hands quite free the next minute, I judge that something had been attached to the lining of that coat to hold the arrow by its feathered head. But this is a deduction rather than a fact."

He stopped abruptly. An exclamation—one of Mr. Gryce's very own—had left that gentleman's lips, and Sweetwater felt that he must pause if only for an instant, to enjoy his small triumph. But the delay was short.

"Go on," said Mr. Gryce; and Sweetwater obeyed, but in lowered tones as though the vision he was describing was actually before his eyes.

"Next, I see a sweep of tapestry, and an eager, peering figure passing slowly across it. It is that of the love-lorn Travis watching his inamorata tripping up the marble staircase and turning at its top in the direction of the opposite gallery. His is a timid soul, and anxious as he is to watch her, he is not at all anxious to be detected in the act of doing so. So he slips behind the huge pedestal towering near him, thus causing the whole gallery to appear empty to the eyes of X, now entering it at the other end. This latter has come there with but one idea in his head—to shoot an arrow across the court at the mark I have mentioned. It may have been on a dare—sometimes I think it was; but shoot it he means to, before a fresh crowd collects.

"He already has, as you will remember, the arrow hidden somewhere about his person, and it is only a few steps to the edge of the tapestry behind which he has secreted the bow. If he takes a look opposite, it is at the moment when both Mrs. Taylor and Miss Willetts are screened from his view by one of the partitions separating the various sections. For unless he felt the way to be free for his arrow, he would never have proceeded to slip behind his chosen pedestal, secure the bow, pause to string it, then crouch for his aim in such apparent confidence. For after he has left the open gallery and limited his outlook to what is visible beyond the loophole through which he intends to shoot, he can see—as we know from Mr. La Flèche—little more than the spot where the cap hangs and the one narrow line between. Unhappily, it was across this line the young girl leaped just as the arrow left the bow. Don't you see it, sir? I do; and I see what follows, too."

"The escape of X?"

"Yes. Inadvertently, as you see, he has committed a horrible crime; he can never recall it. Whatever his remorse or shame, nothing will ever restore the victim of his folly to life, while he himself has many days before him—days which would be ruined if his part in this tragedy were known. Shall he confess to it, then, or shall he fly (the way is so easy), and leave it to fate to play his game—fate, whose well-known kindness to fools would surely favor him? It does not take long for such thoughts to pass through a man's head, and before the dying cry of his innocent victim had ceased to echo through those galleries, he is behind the tapestry and on his way toward the court. Beyond that, my dream does not go. How about yours, sir?"

"My dream was of a crime, not of an accident. No man could be such a fool as you have made out this X of yours to be. Only an extraordinary purpose or some imperious necessity could drive a man to shoot an arrow across an open court where people were passing hither and yon, even if he didn't see anyone in the gallery."

"By which you mean—"

"That he had already marked the approach of his victim and was ready with his weapon."

"You are undoubtedly right, and I only wish to say this: that the purpose in my relation was merely to show the method and manner of this shooting, leaving *you* to put on the emphasis of crime if you saw fit."

The gravity with which Mr. Gryce received this suggestion had the effect of slightly embarrassing Sweetwater. Yet he presently ventured to add after a moment of respectful waiting:

"Did you know that after I woke from my dream I had a moment's doubt as to its accuracy on one point? The bow was undoubtedly flung behind the curtain, but the man—"

He paused abruptly. A morsel of clean white paper had just been pushed across the table under his eyes, and a peremptory voice was saying:

"Write me his name. I will do the same for you."

XIV

A LOOP OF SILK

Sweetwater hesitated.

"I am very fond of the one of your own choosing," he smiled, "but if you insist—"

Mr. Gryce was already writing.

In another moment the two slips were passed in exchange across the table.

Instantly, a simultaneous exclamation left the lips of both.

Each read a name he was in no wise prepared to see. They had been following diverging lines instead of parallel ones; and it took some few minutes for them to adjust themselves to this new condition.

Then Mr. Gryce spoke:

"What led you into loading up Correy with an act which to accept as true would oblige us to deny every premise we have been at such pains to establish?"

"Because—and I hope you will pardon me, Mr. Gryce, since our conclusions are so different—I found it easier to attribute this deed of folly—or crime, if we can prove it such—to a man young in years than to one old enough to know better."

"Very good; that is undoubtedly an excellent reason."

As this was said with an accent we will for want of a better word call *dry*, Sweetwater, hardy as he was, flushed to his ears. But then any prick from Mr. Gryce went very deep with him.

"Perhaps," he ventured, "you will give even less indulgence to what I have to add in way of further excuse."

"I shall have to hear it first."

"Correy is a sport, an incorrigible one; it is his only weakness. He bets like an Englishman—not for the money, for the sums he risks are small, but for the love of it—the fun—the transient excitement It might be"—here Sweetwater's words came slowly and with shamefaced pauses—"that the shooting of that arrow—I believe I said something like this before—was the result of a dare."

A halt took place in the quick tattoo which Mr. Gryce's fingers were drumming out on the table-top. It was infinitesimal in length, but it gave Sweetwater courage to add:

"Then, I hear that he wishes to marry a rich girl and shrinks from proposing to her on account of his small salary."

"What has that got to do with it?"

"Nothing so far as I can see. I am only elaborating the meager report lying there under your hand. But I recognize my folly. You ordered me to dream, and I did so. Cannot we forget my unworthy vaporings and enter upon the consideration of what may prove more profitable?"

Here he glanced down at the slip of paper he himself held— the slip which Mr. Gryce had handed him with a single word written on it, and that word a name.

"In a moment," was Mr. Gryce's answer. "First explain to me how, with the facts all in mind, and your chart before your eyes, you reconciled Correy's position on the side staircase two minutes after the shooting with your theory of a quick escape to the court by means of the door back of the tapestry? Haven't you hurried matters to get him so far in such a short space of time?"

"Mr. Gryce, I have heard you say yourself that this question of time has been, from the first, our greatest difficulty. Even with these three means of escape in our minds, it is difficult to see how it was possible for anyone to get from the gallery to the court in the minute or so elapsing between the cry of the dying girl and the appearance at her side of the man studying coins in the adjoining section."

"You are right. There was a delay somewhere, as we shall find later on. But granting this delay, a man would have to move fast to go the full length of the court from the Curator's room even in the time which this small delay might afford him. But perhaps you cut this inextricable knot by locating Correy somewhere else than where he placed himself at the making of the chart."

"No, I cut it in another way. You remember my starting to tell you just now how, in my dissatisfaction with a certain portion of my dream, I refused to believe in the escape of my Mr. X by the way of the Curator's office. The tapestry was lifted, the bow flung behind, but the man stepped back instead of forward. An open flight along the gallery commended itself more to him than the doubtful one previously arranged for. If you will accept that for fact, which of course you will not, it is easy to see how Correy might have been somewhere on that staircase when the inspiration came to turn the appearance of flight into a show of his own innocence, by a quick rush back into the further gallery and a consequent loud-mouthed alarm. But I see that I am but getting deeper and deeper in the quagmire of a bad theory badly stated. I am forgetting—"

"Many things, Sweetwater. I will only mention a very simple one. The man who shot the arrow wore gloves. You wouldn't attribute any such extraordinary precaution as that to a fellow shooting an arrow across the court on a dare?"

"You wouldn't expect it, sir. But in going about the museum that afternoon, I came upon Correy's coat hanging on its peg. In one of its pockets was a pair of kid gloves."

"You say the fellow is courting a rich girl," suggested Mr. Gryce. "Under those circumstances some show of vanity is excusable. Certainly he would not carry his folly so far as to put on gloves for the shooting match with which you credit him, unless there was criminal intent back of his folly—which, of course, would be as hard for you as for me to believe."

Sweetwater winced, but noting the kindly twinkle with which Mr. Gryce softened the bitterness of this lesson, he brightened again and listened with becoming patience as the old man went on to say:

"To discuss probabilities in connection with this other name seems futile this morning. The ease with which one can twist the appearances of things to fit a preconceived theory as exemplified by the effort you have just made warns us to be chary of pushing one's idea too far without the firmest of bases to support it. If you find a man's coat showing somewhere on its lining evidences that there had once been sewed to it a loop of the exact dimensions of the one I passed over to you last night, I should consider it a much more telling clue to the personality of X than a pair of gloves in the pocket of a man who in all probability intends to finish up the day with a call on the girl he admires."

"I understand." Sweetwater was quite himself again. "But do you know that this is no easy task you are giving me, Mr. Gryce. Where a man has but two coats, or three at best, it might not be so hard, perhaps, to get at them. But some men have a dozen, and if I don't mistake—"

"Sweetwater, I meant to give you a task of no little difficulty. It will keep you out of mischief."

XV

NEWS FROM FRANCE

For the next three days the impatience of the public met with nothing but disappointment. The police were reticent,—more reticent far than usual,—and the papers, powerless to add to the facts already published, had little but conjectures to offer.

The hunt for Madame Duclos continued, joined in now by the general public. But for all the efforts made, aided by a careful search through her entire baggage, there was as little known concerning her as on the morning of her disappearance.

Nor did any better success follow the exhibition at the morgue of the poor little victim's innocent body. The mystery covering the whole affair seemed to be impenetrable, and the rush made on the museum upon its first reopening to the public was such as to lead to its being closed again till some limit could be put upon the attendance.

And thus matters stood when one morning the country was startled, and the keenest interest again aroused in this remarkable case, by an announcement received from France to the effect that the young lady so unfortunately killed in one of the public buildings in New York City was, from the description sent, not the ward of the woman Antoinette Duclos, but her own child, Angeline Duclos. That the two were well known in St. Pierre sur Loire, where they had lived for many years in the relationship mentioned. At the convent where she was educated, she had been registered under the name of Duclos—also at the hotel where she and her mother had spent a few days before leaving for England. Though of pure French descent, the father being a Breton, they could not furnish her birth-certificate, as she had not been born in France. According to the records to be seen at the convent, the father, Achille Duclos, was a professor of languages, whom her mother had met in England and married in France before going to the States. So far as known, their story was a simple one, affording no reason, so far as could be learned, for any change of name on the part of the young woman, in her visit to America.

This was supplemented by a word from Scotland Yard, England, received a few hours after the other, to the effect that Madame Duclos and Miss Willetts arrived at the Ritz from Dover, on the morning of May 16th, and left the next morning for Southampton. They spent the evening at the theater with friends who called for them in a public automobile. These people had not been found, but they had been advertised for and might yet show up. Nothing more could be learned of either of them.

Now here was an astonishing discovery! That two women known and recognized as mother and daughter in France should pass for unrelated companions on leaving that country to enter ours. What were we Americans to think of this, especially in the light of the tragic event which so soon terminated this companionship.

That the French records, imperfect as they were, were to be relied upon as stating the truth as to the exact nature of the connection between these two, there could be no doubt. But granting this, what fresh complexities were thus brought into an affair already teeming with incongruities—nay, absolute contradictions.

Madame Duclos' conduct, as shown toward her young charge, had seemed sufficiently strange and inconsistent when looked upon as that of governess or guardian. But for a mother, and a French mother at that, to allow a young and inexperienced girl to go alone to a strange museum on the very day of their arrival, and then, with or without knowledge of what had happened to her there, to efface herself by flight without promise of return, was inconceivable to anyone acquainted with the most ordinary of French conventions.

Some sinister secret, despite the seeming harmlessness of their lives, must hide behind such unnatural conduct! Was it one connected with or entirely dissociated from the tragedy which had terminated the poor child's existence? This was the great question. This was what gave new zest to the search for the dark-skinned Frenchwoman, with her drooping eyelid and hesitating walk, and led Sweetwater to whisper into Gryce's ear, as they stepped out that same day from Headquarters:

"No more nonsense now. We must find that woman or her dead body before the next twenty-four hours have elapsed. With our fingers on that end of the string—"

"We will get hold of some family secret, but not of the immediate one which especially concerns us. Madame Duclos sent her daughter unattended to the museum, but she did not direct the shaft which killed her. That was the work of our friend X. Let us then make sure that we fit the right man to this algebraic symbol, and trust to her testimony to convict him."

By this time they had reached the taxi which was to convey Mr. Gryce home. But though Sweetwater lent his arm to help the old man in, he did it with such an air of hesitation that it caused the other to remark:

"You have not ended your argument. There is something more you want to say. What is it? Speak up."

"No, no. I am quite satisfied, so far as the Duclos matter is concerned. It is only—would you mind stepping aside for a moment till I tell you a bit of gossip which has just come to my ears? Thank you, sir. Forbes is all right" (Forbes was the chauffeur), "but confidences are sacred and this thing was told me in confidence."

The humorous twist of his features as he said this quite transformed his very plain countenance. Mr. Gryce, noting it, began to stare at the first isolated object handy, which in this case happened to be the crooked end of his umbrella—a sign, to those who knew him well, of awakened interest.

"Well? Let's hear," he said.

"It doesn't sound like much; but it will probably be news to you, as it certainly was to me. It's this, Mr. Gryce: A certain gentleman we know has been contemplating matrimony; but since this accident happened at the museum,—that is, within the last two days,—the engagement has been broken off."

"So! But I thought he had not got so far as an engagement. You mean young Correy—"

"No, Mr. Gryce, I do not. I mean—*the other.*"

"The other! Well, that's worth listening to. Engaged, eh, and now all of a sudden free again? At whose instance, Sweetwater, his or hers? Did you hear?"

"Not exactly, but—it's quite a story, sir. I had it from his chauffeur and will tell it to you later if you are in a hurry to go home."

"Home! Come back with me into Headquarters. I've got to sleep tonight."

Sweetwater laughed, and together they retraced their steps.

"You see, sir," the young detective began as they drew their chairs together in an unoccupied corner, "you gave me a task the other day which called for the help of a friend—one at court, I mean, a fellow who not only knows the gentleman but has access to his person *and* his wardrobe. X does not keep a man-servant—men of his intellectual type seldom do—but does own a limousine and consequently employs a chauffeur. To meet and make this chauffeur mine took me just two days. I don't know how I did it. I never know how I do it," he added with a sheepish smile as Mr. Gryce gave utterance to his old-fashioned "Umph!"

"I don't flatter and I don't bring out my pocketbook or offer drinks or even cigars, but I get 'em, as you know, and get 'em strong, perhaps because I don't make any great effort.

"After an evening spent in the garage with this man, he was ready to talk, and this is what slipped out, among a lot of nonsensical gossip. Mr. X, the real Mr. X this time, has, besides his apartment in New York, a place on Long Island. The latter has been recently bought and, though fine enough, is being added to and refitted as no man at his age would take the trouble of doing, if he hadn't a woman in mind. The chauffeur—Holmes is his name—is no fool, and has seen for some time that Mr. X, for all his goings to and fro and the many calls he is in the habit of making on a certain young lady, did not expect him—that is, Holmes—to notice anything beyond the limits of his work, or to recognize in any way his employer's secret intentions. But fortunately for us, this man Holmes is just one of those singularly meddlesome people whose curiosity grows with every attempt at repression; and when, coincident with that disastrous happening at the museum, all these loverlike attentions ceased and no calls were made and no presents sent, and gloom instead of cheer marked his employer's manner, he made up his mind to sacrifice a portion of his dignity rather than endure the fret of a mystery he did not understand. This meant not only keeping his eyes open,—this he had always done,—but his ears as well.

"The young lady, whose name he never mentioned, lives not in the city but in that same Long Island village where Mr. X's country-house is in the process of renovation. If he, Holmes, should ever be so fortunate as to be ordered to drive there again, he knew of a gravel walk running under the balcony where the two often sat. He would make the acquaintance of that gravel walk instead of sitting out the hour somewhere in the rear, as he had hitherto been accustomed to do. What's the use of having ears if you don't use them? Nobody would be any the worse, and his mind would be at rest.

"And do you know, sir, that he did actually carry this cowardly resolution through. There came a night—I think it was Tuesday—when the order came, and they took the road to Belport. Not a word did his employer utter the whole way. Solemn and still he sat, and when they arrived he descended without a word, rang the bell and entered the house. It was very warm, that night, Holmes said, and before long he heard the glass doors open onto the balcony, and knew that his wished-for chance had come. Leaving the limousine, he crept around to secure a place among the bushes, and what he heard while there seemed to compensate him for what he called his loss of dignity. The young girl was crying, and the man was talking to her kindly enough but in a way to end whatever hopes she may have had.

"Holmes heard him say: 'It cannot be, now. Circumstances have changed for me lately, and much as I regret it I must ask you to be so good as to forgive me for giving up our plans.' Then he offered her money,—an annuity, I believe they call it,—but she cried out at that, saying it was love she wanted, to be petted and cared for—money she could do without. When he showed himself again in front, he was stiffer and more solemn than ever, and said 'Home,' in a dreary way which made the chauffeur feel decidedly uncomfortable.

"Of course Holmes is quite blind to what this all means, but you may possibly see some connection between this sudden act of sacrifice on X's part and the work of the arrow. At all events, I thought you ought to know that Mr. X's closet holds a skeleton which he will doubtless take every pains to keep securely locked from general view. Holmes says that his last word to the disappointed girl was in the way of warning. No mention of this break in their plans was to be made without his sanction."

"Good work, Sweetwater! You have strengthened my hands wonderfully. Does this fellow Holmes know you for a police-detective?"

"Indeed not, sir. That would be fatal to our friendship, I am sure. I haven't even let him discover that what he was burning to tell had any especial interest for me. I let him ramble on with just a word here and there to show I wasn't bored. He hasn't an idea—"

"Very good. Now, what do you propose to do next?"

"To take up my residence in Belport."

"Why Belport?"

"Because X proposes to move there, bag and baggage, this very week."

"Before his house is done?"

"Yes. He hates the city. Wants to have an eye to the changes being made. Perhaps he thinks a little work of this kind may distract him."

"And you?"

"Was a master carpenter once, you know."

"I see."

"And have a friend on the spot who promises to recommend me."

"Are workmen wanted there?"

"A good one, very much."

"I'm sure you'll fill the bill."

"I shall try to, sir."

"But for the risk you run of being recognized, I should bet on you, Sweetwater."

"I know; people will not forget the unfortunate shape of my nose."

"You were up and down the museum for hours. He must know your face like a book."

"It can't be helped, I shall keep out of sight as much as possible whenever he is around. I am an expert workman in the line wanted. I understand my trade, and he will see that I do and doubt his eyes rather than stretch probabilities to the point of connecting me with the Force. Besides, I get quite another expression when my hands get in touch with the wood; and I can look a man in the eye, if I have to, without a quiver of self-consciousness. His will drop before mine will."

"Your name as carpenter?"

"Jacob Shott. It's the name by which Holmes already knows me."

"Well, well, the game may be worth the candle. You can soon tell. I will keep you posted."

The rest was business with which we need not concern ourselves.

BOOK III
STORM IN THE MOUNTAINS

XVI

FRIENDS

A shaded walk, with a glimpse of sea beyond, embowering trees, a stretch of lawn on one side, and on the other the dormer windows of a fine old house half hidden by scaffolding, from which there came now and then the quick strokes of a workman's hammer.

It was half-past four, if the sharp little note of a cuckoo-clock, snapping out one, told the time correctly.

Two men are pacing this leafy retreat, both of whom we have seen before, but under circumstances so distracting that we took little note of their appearance, fine as it undoubtedly was in either case. However, we are more at leisure now, and will pause for an instant to give you some idea of these two prominent men, with one of whom our story will henceforth have very much to do.

One of them—the Curator of our famous museum—lacks comeliness of figure, though at moments he can be very impressive. We can therefore recognize him at a distance by means of a certain ungainliness of stride sometimes seen in a man wholly given over to intellectual pursuits. But when he turns and you get a glimpse of his face, you experience at once the scope of mind and charm of spirit which make his countenance a marked one in the metropolis. A little gray about the temples, a tendency—growing upon him, alas!—to raise his hand to his ear when called upon to listen, show that he has already passed the meridian of life; but in his quick glance, and clear and rapid speech, youth still lingers, making of him a companion delightful to many and admirable to all.

The other—Carleton Roberts, his bosom friend, and the museum's chief director—is of a different type, but no less striking to the eye. For him, personality has done much toward raising him to his present status among the leading men of New York. While not tall, he is tall enough never to look short, owing to the trim elegance of his figure and the quiet dignity of his carriage. He does not need to turn his face to impress you with the idea that he is handsome; but when he does so, you find that your expectations are more than met by the reality. For though he may not have the strictly regular features we naturally associate with one of his poise and matchless outline, there is enough of that quality, and more than enough of that additional elusive something which is an attraction in itself, to make for handsomeness in a marked degree. He, like his friend, has passed his fortieth year, but no-where save in his abundant locks can one see any sign of approaching age. They are quite white—cut close, but quite white, so white they attracted the notice of his companion, who stole more than one look at them as he chatted on in what had become almost a monologue, so little did Roberts join in the conversation.

Finally the Curator paused, and stealing another look at that white head, remarked anxiously:

"Have you not grown gray very suddenly? I don't remember your being whiter than myself the day I dined with you just preceding the horrible occurrence at the museum."

"I have been growing gray for a year," rejoined the other. "My father was white at forty; I am just forty-three."

"It becomes you, and yet—Roberts, you have taken this matter too much to heart. We were not to blame in any way, unless it was in having such deadly weapons within reach. How could one suppose—"

"Yes, how could one suppose!" echoed the director. "And the mystery of it! The police seem no nearer solving the problem now than on the night they practised archery in the galleries. It does wear on me, possibly because I live so much alone. I see—"

Here he stopped abruptly. They had been strolling in the direction of the house, and at this moment were not many paces from it.

"See what?" urged the Curator with an accent one might almost call tender—would have been called tender, if used in addressing a woman.

"See *her*, that dead girl!—constantly—at night when my eyes are shut—in the daytime while I go about my affairs, here, there and everywhere. The young, young face! so white, so still, so strangely and so unaccountably familiar! Do you feel the same? Did she remind you of anyone we know? I grow old trying to place her. I can say this to you; but not to another soul could I speak of what has become to me a sort of blind obsession. She was a stranger. I know of no Madame Duclos and am sure that I never saw her young daughter before; and yet I have started up in my bed more than once during these past few nights, confident that in another moment memory would supply the clue which will rid my mind of the eternal question as to where I have seen a face like hers before? But memory fails to answer; and the struggle, momentarily interrupted, begins again, to the destruction of my peace and comfort."

"Odd! but you must rid yourself of what unnerves you so

completely. It does no good and only adds to regrets which are poignant enough in themselves."

"That is true; but—stop a minute. I see it now—her face, I mean. It comes between me and the house there. Even your presence does not dispel it. It is—no, it's gone again. Let us go back once more and take another look at the sea. It is the one thing which draws me away from this pursuing vision."

They resumed their stroll, this time away from the house and toward the oval cut in the trees for a straight view out to the sea. Across this oval a ship was now sailing which attracted the eyes of both; not till it had passed, did the Curator say:

"You live too lonely a life. You should seek change—recreation—possibly something more absorbing than either."

"You mean marriage?"

"Yes, Roberts, I do. Pardon me; I want to see your eye beam again with contentment. The loss of your late companion has left you desolate, more desolate than you have been willing to acknowledge. You cannot replace her—"

"I am wedded to politics."

"An untrustworthy jade. When did politics ever make a man happy?"

"Happy!" They were turned toward the house again. When near, Roberts capped his exclamation with the remark:

"You ask a great deal for me, more than you ask for yourself. You have not married again."

"But my mistress is not a jade. I find joy in my work. I have not had time to woo a woman as she should be wooed if she's to be a happy second wife. I should have so much to explain to her. When I get looking over prints, the dinner-bell might ring a dozen times without my hearing it. A letter from an agent telling of some wonderful find in Mesopotamia would make me forget whether my wife's hair were brown or black. I don't need diversion, Roberts."

"Yet you enjoy a couple of hours in the country, a whiff of fresh air—"

"And a chat with a friend. Yes, I do; but if the museum were open—"

Mr. Roberts smiled.

"I see that you are incorrigible." Then, with a gesture toward the house: "Come and see my new veranda. Its outlook will surprise you."

As you have already surmised, he was the owner of this place; and the man for whose better understanding Sweetwater had again taken up the plane and the hammer.

XVII

THE CUCKOO-CLOCK

As they made their way through scattered timber and the litter of fresh carpentry-work, the man who was busy there and who certainly had outstayed his time took up his kit and disappeared around the corner of the house. Neither noted him. The cuckoo-clock was chirping out its five small notes from the cheerful interior, and the Curator was remarking upon it.

"That's a merry sound both sweet and stimulating; and what is still better, I can hear it without effort. I believe I should like to have a clock of that kind."

"It goes where I go," muttered its strange owner with what seemed an involuntary emphasis. Then as the Curator turned upon him in some surprise, he added with studied indifference: "I brought it from Switzerland when I was younger than I am now—a silly memento, but I fancy it."

A commonplace explanation surely; why, then, did that same workman, who had stopped short after rounding the corner to pick up something which he as quickly threw down, turn a quick head and listen eagerly for what might be said next. Nothing came of it, for the veranda door was near and the two gentlemen had stepped in; but to one who knew Sweetwater, the smile with which he resumed his work had an element in it which, if seen, would have darkened still further the gloom in the troubled eye of the speaker.

Switzerland! He had said Switzerland.

It was not long after this that the Curator and his host left for New York.

The house was not quite ready for occupancy, but was in the process of being made so by the woman who had done duty as housekeeper for Mr. Roberts both before his marriage and since his wife's death. During the fifteen years which had intervened, she had been simply the cook.

This woman, Huldah Weston by name, did not accompany them. She was in Belport to stay, and as it behooves us to remain there for a while longer ourselves, we will join her in the quiet rest she is taking on the kitchen steps before shutting up the house for the night.

She is not alone. A young man is with her—one to whom she is giving temporary board and lodging in exchange for the protection of his presence and such slight help as he can afford her in the heavy task of distributing and arranging the furniture.

We know this man. It is the one we have just seen halting at the corner of the house, on quitting his work on the new veranda—Sweetwater.

He is a genial soul; she, though very old for the responsibilities she still insists upon carrying, enjoys a good laugh. Nor is she averse to the numberless little kindly attentions with which he shows his respect for her age if not a personal liking for herself. In short, they are almost friends, and she trusts him as she has never trusted any young man yet, save the boy she lost when she was still a comely widow.

Perhaps this is why, on this night when we find the two together, he ventures to turn the talk upon the man she had so devotedly served during the better part of her life.

He began with the cuckoo-clock. Where did it come from? How long had they had it? What a jolly little customer the wee bird was, darting out and darting in with his hurry-call to anyone who would listen! It made a fellow feel ashamed to dawdle at his work. It wouldn't do to let any mere bird get ahead of him—a wooden bird at that!

He got her talking. She had known Mr. Roberts' mother, and she had been in the house (a young girl then) when he went away to Europe. He had not wanted to go. He was in love, or thought he was, with a woman older than himself. But the mother did not approve of the match, though the lady had a mint of money and everything in her favor but those seven years. She afterward became his wife and for all his mother's fears they lived together very happily. Since her death which occurred about a year ago he's been a different man; very sad and much given to sitting alone. Anyone can see the effect it has had upon him if they look at him closely.

"She was a good woman, then?"

"Very good."

"Well, life must be lonesome for a widower, especially if he has no children. But perhaps he has some married or at school?"

"No, he has no children, and no relations, to speak of."

"And he brought that clock from Switzerland? Did he ever say from what part of Switzerland?"

"If he did, I don't remember; I've no memory for foreign names."

This sent Sweetwater off on another tack. He knew such a good story, which, having told, he seemed to have forgotten all about the clock, for he said nothing more about it, and not much more about Mr. Roberts.

But when, a little later, he followed her into that gentleman's room for the purpose of unlocking a trunk which had been delivered that day, he took advantage of her momentary absence in search of the key to pull out that cuckoo-clock from the wall where it hung and read the small slip of paper pasted across its back. As he hoped, it gave both the name and address of the merchant from whom it had been bought. But that was not all. Running in diagonal lines across this label, he saw some faded lines in fine handwriting, which proved to be a couplet signed with five initials. The latter were not quite legible, but the couplet he could read without the least difficulty. It was highly sentimental, and might mean much and might mean nothing. If the handwriting should prove to be Mr. Roberts', the probabilities were in favor of the former supposition—or so he said to himself, as he swung the clock back into place.

When Mrs. Weston returned, he was standing as patiently as possible in the middle of the room, saying over and over to himself to insure remembrance till he could jot the lines down in his notebook: *Bossberg, Lucerne.... I love but thee—and thee will I love to eternity.*

His interest in this slight and doubtful clue, however, sank into insignificance when, having unlocked and unstrapped the trunk which Mrs. Weston pointed out, he saw to his infinite satisfaction that it held Mr. Roberts' clothing—the one thing in the world toward which at this exact moment his curiosity mainly pointed. If only he might help her handle the heavy coats which lay so temptingly on top! Should he propose to do so? Looking at her firm chin and steady eye, he felt that he did not dare. To rouse the faintest suspicion in this woman's intelligent mind would be fatal to all further procedure, and so he stood indifferent, while she lifted garment after garment and laid them carefully on the bed. He counted five coats and as many vests—and was racking his brains for some plausible excuse for a nearer inspection, when she stopped in the midst of her work, with the cheery remark:

"That will do for tonight. Tomorrow I will look them all over for moths before hanging them away in the closet."

And he had to go, leaving them lying there within reach of his hand, when one glance at the lining of a certain coat which had especially attracted his eye might have given him the one clue he most needed.

The room which had been allotted to him in this house was in the rear and at the top of a steep flight of stairs. As he sought it that night, he cast a quick glance through the narrow passageway opening just beyond his own door. Would it be possible for him to thread those devious ways and reach Mr. Roberts' room without rousing Mrs. Weston, who in spite of her years had the alertness of a watchdog with eye and ear ever open? To be found strolling through quarters where he had no business would be worse than being suspected of taking a personal interest in the owner's garments. He was of an adventurous turn, and ever ready to risk something on the turn of a die, but not too much. A false move might hazard all; besides, he remembered the airing these clothes were to get and the nearness of the clothes-yard to the pump he so frequently patronized, and all the chances which this gave for an inspection which would carry little danger to one of his ready wit.

So he gave up the midnight search he might have attempted under other circumstances, and shut his room from the moon and his eyes to sleep, and dreamed. Was it of the great museum, with its hidden mystery enshrouding its many wonders of high art, or of a far-off time and a far-off scene, where in the stress of some great emotion the trembling hand of Carleton Roberts had written on the back of this foolish clock for which he still retained so great a fancy the couplet which he himself had so faithfully memorized:

> *I love but thee,*
> *And thee will I love to eternity.*

At eight o'clock on the following morning the quick strokes of the workman's hammer reawakened the echoes at the end of the building where the big enclosed veranda was going up.

As the clock struck nine Mrs. Weston could be seen hanging up her master's coats and trousers on a long line stretched across the clothes-yard. They remained there two hours, viewed from afar by Sweetwater, but not approached till he saw the old woman disappear from one of the gates with a basket on her arm. Then he developed thirst and went rearward to the pump. While there, he took a look at the sea. A brisk wind was springing up. It gave him an idea.

Making sure that his fellow workmen were all busy, he loosened one end of the line holding the fluttering garments and then went back to his work. As the wind increased, the strain on the line became too great, and soon he had the satisfaction of seeing the whole thing fall in one wild flap to the ground. With an exclamation calculated to draw the attention of the men about him to what had happened, he rushed to the rescue, lifted the line and rearranged the clothes. Then refastening—this time securely—the end of the line which had slipped loose, he returned to his post, with just one quick and disappointed look thrown back at the now safe if wildly fluttering garments.

He had improved his opportunity to examine the inside of every coat and had found nothing to reward his scrutiny. But it was not this which had given him his chief annoyance. It was the fact that the one coat from which he had expected the anticipated clue—the coat which Mr. Roberts had certainly worn on that tragic day at the museum—was not there. A summer overcoat had filled out the number, and his investigation was incomplete.

Why was that one coat lacking? He was sure he had seen it the night before lying on the bed with the others. Was it still there, or had it been stowed away in drawer or closet, irrespective of its danger from moths, for a reason he would give his eyeteeth to know but dared not inquire into till he had clinched his friendship with this old woman so thoroughly that he could ask her any-thing—which certainly was not the case as yet.

The absence of the one coat he wanted most to see afflicted him sorely. He told Mrs. Weston, on her return, how the line had fallen and how he had replaced it, but for all his wits, he could not get any further. With the close of the day's work and the reappear-ance of Mr. Roberts, he slipped away to the village, to avoid an encounter of the results of which he felt very doubtful. His dinner would not be ready till after Mr. Roberts had been served, and the three hours which must necessarily elapse before that happy mo-ment looked very long and very unproductive to him, especially as he had found no answer as yet to the question which so grievously perplexed him.

He had paced the main street twice and had turned into a narrow lane ending in the smallest of gardens and the most infini-tesimal of houses, when the door of this same house opened and a man came out whose appearance held him speechless for a mo-ment—then sent him forward with a quickly beating heart. It was not the man himself that produced this somewhat startling effect; it was his clothes. So far as his hat and nether garments went, they were, if not tattered, not very far from it; but the coat he wore was not only trim but made of the finest cloth and without the smallest sign of wear. It was so conspicuously fine, and looked so gro-tesquely out of place on the man wearing it, that he could pass no one without rousing curiosity, and he probably had all he wanted to do for the next few days in explaining how a fine gentleman's coat had fallen to his lot.

But to Sweetwater its interest lay in something more important than the amusing incongruity it offered to the eye. It looked exactly like the one belonging to Mr. Roberts which had escaped his scrutiny in so remarkable a way. Should it prove to be that same, how fortunate he was to have it brought thus easily within his reach and under circumstances so natural it was not necessary for him to think twice how best to take advantage of them.

Father Dobbins—for that is the name by which this old codger was known to the boys—was, as might be expected, very proud of his new acquisition and quite blind to the contrast it offered to his fringed-out trouser-legs. He had a smile on his face which broadened as he caught Sweetwater's sympathetic glance.

"Fine day," he mumbled. "Are ye wantin' somethin' of me that ye're comin' this way?"

"Perhaps and perhaps," answered Sweetwater, "—if that fine coat I see you wearing is the one given you by Mrs. Weston up the road."

"'Deed, sir, and what's amiss? She gave it to me, yes. Came all the way into the village to find me and give it to me. Too small for her master, she said; and would I take it to oblige him. Does she want it back?"

"Oh, no—not she. She's not that kind. It's only that she has since remembered that one of the pockets has a hole in it—an inside one, I believe. She's afraid it might lose you a dime some day. Will you let me see if she is right? If so, I was to take you to the tailor's and have it fixed immediately. I am to pay for it."

The old man stared in slow comprehension; then with the deliberation which evidently marked all his movements, he slowly put down his basket.

"I warrant ye it's all right," he said. "But look, an ye will. I don't want to lose no dimes."

Sweetwater threw back one side of the coat, then the other, felt in the pockets and smiled. But Gryce, and not ignorant Father Dobbins, should have seen that smile. There was comedy in it, and there was the deepest tragedy also; for the marks of stitches forcibly cut were to be seen under one of the pockets—stitches which must have held something as narrow as an umbrella-band and no longer than the little strip at which Mr. Gryce had been looking one night in a melancholy little short of prophetic.

XVIII

MRS. DAVIS' STRANGE LODGER

"If you will look carefully at this chart, and note where the various persons then in the museum were standing at the moment Correy shouted his alarm, you will see that of all upon whom suspicion can with any probability be attached there is but one who could have fulfilled the conditions of escape as just explained to you."

Stretching forth an impressive finger, Mr. Gryce pointed to a certain number on the chart outspread between him and the Chief Inspector.

He looked—saw the number "3" and glanced anxiously down at the name it prefigured.

"Roberts—the director! Impossible! Not to be considered for a moment. I'm afraid you're getting old, Gryce." And he looked about to be sure that the door was quite shut.

Mr. Gryce smiled, a little drearily perhaps, as he acknowledged this self-evident fact.

"You are right, Chief: I am getting old—but not so old as to venture upon so shocking an insinuation against a man of Mr. Roberts' repute and seeming honor, if I had not some very substantial proofs to offer in its support."

"No doubt, no doubt; but it won't do. I tell you, Gryce, it won't do. There cannot be any such far-fetched and ridiculous explanation to the crime you talk about. Why, he's next to being the Republican nominee for Senator. An attack upon him, especially of this monstrous character, would be looked upon as a clear case of political persecution. And such it would be, and nothing less; and it would be all to no purpose, I am sure. I hope you are alone in these conclusions—that you have not seen fit to share your ideas on this subject with any of the boys?"

"Only with Sweetwater, who did some of the work for me."

"And Joyce? How about him?"

"He had the same opportunities as myself, but we have not reached the point of mentioning names. I thought it best to consult with you first."

"Good! Then we'll drop it."

It was decisively said, but Gryce gave no signs of yielding.

"I'm afraid that's impossible," said he. Then with the dignity of long experience, he added with quiet impressiveness:

"I have, as you know, faced crime these many years in all its aspects. I have tracked the ignorant, almost imbecile, murderer of the slums, and laid my hand in arrest on the shoulder of so-called gentlemen hiding their criminal instincts under a show of culture and sometimes of wide education. Human nature is not so very different in high and low; and what may lead an irresponsible dago into unsheathing his knife against his fellow may work a like effect upon his high-bred brother if circumstances lend their aid to make discovery appear impossible.

"Mr. Roberts is the friend of many a good man who would swear to his integrity with a clear conscience. I would have sworn to it myself, a month ago, had I heard it questioned in the slightest manner; and I may live to swear to it again, notwithstanding the doubts which have been raised in my mind by certain strange discoveries which link him to this unhappy affair by what we are pleased to call circumstantial evidence. For, as I am obliged to acknowledge, the one great thing we rely upon, in accusations of this kind, is so far lacking in his case: I mean, the motive.

"I know of none—can, in fact, conceive of none—which would cause a gentleman of even life and ambitious projects to turn a deadly weapon upon an innocent child with whom he is not, so far as we can discover, even acquainted. Dementia only can account for such a freak, and to dementia we must ascribe this crime, if it is necessary for us to find cause before proceeding to lay our evidence before the District Attorney. All I propose to do at present is to show you my reasons for thinking that the arrow which slew Angeline Willetts—or, as we have been assured by unimpeachable authority, Angeline Duclos masquerading under the name of Angeline Willetts—was set to bow and loosed across the court by the gentleman we have just mentioned."

Here Mr. Gryce stopped for a look of encouragement from the severely silent man he was endeavoring to impress. But he did not get it. With a full sense of his years weighing upon him as never before, he sighed, but continued with little change of tone:

"In the first day or two of keen surprise following an event of so many complicated mysteries, I drew up in my own mind a list of questions which I felt should be properly answered before I would consider it my duty to submit to you a report to the disadvantage of any one suspect. This was Question One:

"'Whose was the hand to bring up into the museum gallery the bow recognized by Correy as the one which had been lying by for an indefinite length of time in the cellar?'

"Not till yesterday did I get any really definite answer to this.

Correy would not talk; nor would the Curator; and I dared not press either of them beyond a certain point, for equally with yourself, I felt it most undesirable to allow anyone to suspect the nature of my theory or whom it especially involved.

"The Curator had nothing to hide on this or any other point connected with the tragedy. But it was different with Correy. He had some very strong ideas about that visit to the cellar—only he would not acknowledge them. So yesterday, after the satisfactory settlement of another puzzling question, I made up my mind to trap him—which I did after this manner. He has, as most men have, in fact, a great love for the Curator. In discussing with him the mysterious fetching up of the bow and its subsequent concealment in the Curator's office, I remarked, with a smile I did not mean to have him take as real, that only the Curator himself would do such a thing and then forget it; that it must have been his shadow he saw; and I begged him, in a way half jocose, half earnest, to say so and have done with it.

"It worked, sir. He flushed like a man who had been struck; then he grew white with indignation and blurted forth that it was no more his shadow than it was Mr. Roberts'—that indeed it was much more like Mr. Roberts' than the Curator's. At which I simply remarked: 'You think so, Correy?' To which he replied: 'I do not think anything. But I know that Curator Jewett never brought up that bow from the cellar, or he would have said so the minute he saw it. There's no better man in the world than he.' 'Nor than Mr. Roberts either,' I put in, and left him comforted if not quite reassured.

"So much for Question One—

"Number Two is of a similar nature. 'Was the transference of the arrow from one gallery to the other due to the same person who brought up the bow?' Now, in answer to that, I have a curious thing to show you." And lifting into view a bundle of goodly size, wrapped in heavy brown paper, he opened it up and disclosed a gentleman's coat. Spreading this out between them lining side out, and pointing out two marks an inch or so apart showing the remains of stitches for which there seemed to have been no practical use, he took from his own vest-pocket what looked like a bit of narrow black tape. This he laid down on the upturned lining in the space bounded by the two lines of marks I have mentioned, and drawing the Chief's attention to it, observed in quiet explanation:

"The one fits the other—stitch for stitch. Look closely at them both, I beg, and tell me if in your judgment it is not evident that this strap or loop, or whatever we may call it, has been cut away from this coat to which it had been previously sewed—and by no woman either."

Anyone could see that this had been so. There could be but one reply:

"This coat I bought from an old man to whom it had been given by Mr. Roberts' housekeeper on their arrival at his new home on Long Island. The strip was picked up at the museum in the room where Mrs. Taylor spent an hour or so immediately upon leaving the scene of crime. With her at the time was the young lady who had kindly offered to look after her and two or three men directly associated with the museum, of whom Mr. Roberts was one. These and these only. Now, this strap or let us say loop, since we are beginning to see for what purpose it was used, was not on the floor previous to the entrance of these few persons into this room—or, indeed, for some little time afterward. Otherwise this young lady, who was the one to open my eyes to this clue, surely would have seen it in the half-hour she stood at Mrs. Taylor's side with no one to talk to and quite free to look about her. But it *was* there after that lady had revived from her fainting-fit—dropped, as you see—cut from its owner's coat and dropped! Chief, let me ask why this should have been done in a time of such suspense if it had had nothing to do with the crime then occupying everybody's attention—a good coat too, almost new, as you will observe?"

The Chief, possibly with a shade less of irony in his manner, answered this direct question with one equally direct:

"And what connection have you succeeded in establishing between this abominable crime and the coat with or without a loop worn by the museum's leading director? One as straight and indisputable, no doubt, as that you have just attempted to make between this same gentleman and the museum bow," he added with biting incredulity.

"Yes," returned the other in calm disregard of the sarcasm, "straighter and more indisputable, if anything. We are asking, as you will remember, how an arrow could have been carried from the southern to the northern gallery without attracting anyone's attention. I will show you how."

With a rap on the table which brought Sweetwater into the room, he proceeded to pin again into its old place on the lining of Mr. Roberts' coat the so-called tag. Then, taking the arrow which Sweetwater proceeded to hand him, he slipped it into the loop thus made and showed how securely it could be held there by its feather end.

"A man of Mr. Roberts' upright carriage might, with his coat well buttoned up, walk the length of Broadway without disclosing the presence of this stick," remarked Mr. Gryce as, at his look, Sweetwater doffed his own coat and put on the one thus discreetly weighted.

The Chief stared, paling slightly as he noted the result. Mr. Gryce, who never overemphasised his effects, motioned Sweetwater to leave and proceeded to the next question.

"Number Three," he now observed, "should have come first, as it has already been answered. It asks if it is possible to hit the mark in Section II of the museum's gallery, from behind the pedestal in Section VIII. From the pedestal nearest the front, *no*; but from the one further back—upon which, by the way, Stevens found the print of a gloved finger—*yes*.

"Who wore gloves that day—kid gloves, mind you, for the mark of the stitching is exact, as you can see in this print of the same made by Stevens? All the ladies, except a young copyist who was leaving in a hurry and had not stopped to put hers on. But of the men, only one—Mr. Roberts, the careful dresser, who was never known to enter the street without this last touch to his toilet. How do I know this? Look at the chart, Chief—this one which shows the court and the persons in it at the precise minute of first alarm. You see how near the exit Mr. Roberts was, and who was closest to him. I had a little talk—the most guarded one imaginable—with this lady, who was the very one of whom I have just said that she had omitted to put on her gloves; and she gave me the fact I have just passed on to you. She noted Mr. Roberts' hands, because they shamed hers, and she was just stopping to pull her gloves from her coat-pocket when Correy's voice rang out and everything else was forgotten.

"Corroborative, only corroborative, sir? I am quite aware of that. But what I have now to add may give it weight. The stringing of a bow is no easy task for an amateur; nor is the discharge of an arrow, under such dangerous circumstances as marked the delivery of the one we are discussing, one which would be lightly attempted by a person altogether ignorant of archery. However strong the evidence might be against a man who was not an utter fool, I would never have presumed to lay it out before you if I had not verified the fact that the director, whatever his life now, was once greatly addicted to sports, and thoroughly acquainted with the management of a bow and arrow. It has taken time. Many cablegrams were necessary, but I have at last received this copy of a report made sixteen years ago by a club in Lucerne, Switzerland, in which mention is made of a prize given to one Carleton Roberts, an American, for twelve piercings of the bull's-eye in as many shots, in an archery-contest which included all nationalities.

"Nor is that all. In a study of himself,—his home, his life, his secret interests,—we come upon things which call for closer inspection. For instance, not a day has passed since that poor child has been in the morgue that he has not been one on the line to see her. He dreams of her, he says; he cannot get her face out of his mind—you notice that he has been growing gray.

"But I will stop here. I do not wonder that you look upon all this as the ravings of a man on the verge of senility. If I were in your place, I should undoubtedly do the same. But ungracious as the task has proved, I owed it to myself to rid my mind of its secret burden. It is for you to say whether, all things considered, I am to drop the matter here or proceed blindly in search of the motive lying back of every premeditated crime. I can imagine none in this case, as I have frankly stated, save the very weak and improbable one already advanced by young Sweetwater in connection with another party upon whom he had fixed his eye—that of the irresistible desire of an expert to test his skill with a bow which comes unexpectedly into his hands."

"That wouldn't apply to Roberts—not in the least," affirmed the Chief with the emphasis of strong conviction. "Even if we should allow ourselves to regard these stray bits of circumstantial evidence as in any way conclusive of the extraordinary theory you have advanced, he's much too able and cautious a man to yield to any such fool temptation as that. But to let that matter pass for the present: why have you paid such close attention to one end of your string, and quite ignored the other? Madame Duclos' hasty flight and continued absence, in face of circumstances which would lead a natural mother to break through every obstacle put in the way of her return, offers a field of inquiry more promising, it appears to me, than the one upon which you have expended your best energies. You say nothing of her."

"I have nothing to say. I am glad to leave that particular line of investigation to you, and more than glad if it has proved or is likely to prove fruitful. Have you heard—"

"Read that."

He tossed a letter within the detective's grasp and leaned back while Gryce laboriously perused it.

It was illy written, but well worth the pains he gave to it—as witness:

To the Chief of Police:

Dear Sir:—I am told that there is a reward out for a certain woman by the name of Duclos. I do not know any such person, but there is a woman who has been lodging in my house for the last two weeks who has acted so strangely at odd times that I have become very suspicious of her, and think it right for you to know what she did here one night.

It's about a fortnight since she came to my house in search of lodgings. Had she been young, I would not have opened my doors to her, decent as she was in her dress and ways; for she was a foreign woman and I don't like foreigners. But being middle-aged and ready with her money in advance, I not only allowed her to come in but gave her my very best room. This is not saying much, because the elevated road runs by my door, darkening my whole front, besides making an awful clatter. But she did not seem to mind this, and I took little notice of her, till one of the other lodgers—a woman with a busy tongue—began to ask why this strange woman, who was so very dark and plain, went out only at night? Did she sew or write for a living? If not, what did she do with herself all day?

As the last was a question I could easily answer, I said that she spent most of her time in reading the newspapers; and this was true, because she always came in with her arms full of them. But there I stopped, as I never discuss my lodgers. Yet I must acknowledge that my curiosity had been roused by all this talk, and I began to watch the woman, who I soon saw was in what I would call a flustered state of mind, and as unhappy as anyone could be who hadn't suffered some great bereavement. But still I wasn't really alarmed, being misled by the name she gave, which was Clery.

Night before last I went to bed early. I am a heavy sleeper, as I need to be with those cars pounding by the house every few minutes. But there are certain noises which wake me, and I found myself all of a sudden sitting up in bed and listening with all my ears. Everything was quiet, even on the elevated road; but when the next train came thundering along, I heard, piercing shrilly through the rumble and roar, that same sharp *ping* which had wakened me. What was it? It seemed to come from somewhere in the house. But how could that be! I was startled enough, however, to get up and slip on some of my clothes and stand with ears astretch for the next train.

It came and passed, and right in the middle of the noise it made I heard again that quick, sharp sound. This time I was sure it came from somewhere near, and opening my door, I slid out into the hall. All my lodgers were in but one, a young gentleman who has a night-key. And most of the rooms were dark, as I can very well tell from the fact that none of the doors fit as they ought to and there is sure to be a streak of light showing somewhere about them if the gas is burning inside. Everything looked so natural, and the house was so still, that I was going back again when another train swept by and that sound was repeated. This time I was sure it came from somewhere on the lower floor, and mindful of Mrs. Clery's queer ways, I stole downstairs to her door. She was up—that was plainly enough to be seen. But what was she doing? I was just a little frightened, or I would have knocked on the door and asked.

As I was waiting for the passing by of the next train, my last lodger came in and caught me standing there before Mrs. Clery's door. I know him pretty well; so I put my finger to my lips and then beckoned him to join me. As the train approached, I seized him by the arm and pointed toward Mrs. Clery's door. He didn't know what I meant, of course, but he looked and listened, and when the train had gone by, I drew him down the hall and said, "You heard it!" and then asked him what it was. He answered that it was a pistol-shot, and he wanted to go back to see if any dreadful thing had happened. But I shook my head and told him it was one of five, each one taking place when the roar of the trains going by was at the loudest. Then he said that this woman was practising at a mark, and bade me look out or we should have a house full of anarchists. At that, I loudly declared she should go the first thing in the morning and so got rid of him. But I did not keep my word, and for this reason: When I went to do her room-work as I always do immediately after breakfast, I was all smiles and full of talk till I had taken a good look at the walls for the bullet-holes I expected to see there. But I didn't find any, and was puzzled enough you may be sure, for those bullets must have gone somewhere and I was quite certain that they had not been fired out of the window. I hardly dared to look at the ceiling, for she was watching me and kept me chatting and wondering till all of a sudden I noticed that one of the sofa-pillows was missing from its place. This set me thinking, and I was about to ask her what she had done with it when my attention was drawn away by seeing among the scraps in the wastebasket I had lifted to carry out the end and corner of what looked like a partly destroyed photograph.

This was something too strange not to rouse any woman's curiosity, but I was careful not to give it another glance till I was well out of the room. Then, as you may believe, I drew it quickly out, to find that all the middle part was gone—shot to pieces by those tearing bullets. Not a particle of the face was to be seen, and only enough of the neck and shoulders to show that it had been the portrait of a man. I enclose it for you to see; and if you want to talk to the woman, she is still here, though I only keep her in the hope of her being that Madame Duclos for whom money is offered. I will tell you why I think this: Not because of a torn skirt,—you see I have been looking over the advertisement printed in the papers,—but because she is foreign and dark and has a decidedly drooping eyelid. Then too, she halts a little on one foot, as I noticed when I called her hurriedly to the window to see something. If you want to have a look at her, come after five and before seven; we are both in then.

Yours respectfully,
Caroline Davis.

"No doubt that's the woman," commented Gryce. "We are fortunate in hitting her trail at this critical moment."

He had already glanced at the mutilated photograph lying before him, but now he took it up.

"Very little here," he remarked as he examined first the face of it and then the back. "But if you will let me take it, I may find that its place is in our incompleted chain."

"Take it, and if you would like to have a talk with the woman herself—"

"Yes, Chief; I would like that above all things."

"Very good. I'm expecting her here any minute, but—Well, what now? What's up?"

An officer had entered hurriedly after one quick knock.

"Mrs. Davis' lodger is gone," said he. "Left without a word to anybody. When they went to her room they found it empty, with a five-dollar bill pinned to the riddled cushion. As nobody saw her go, we are as much at sea as ever."

A smile, both curious and fine, crossed Mr. Gryce's lips as he listened to this, and turning earnestly to the Chief, he begged for the job of looking her up.

"I think with the little start we now have that I can find her," said he. "At all events, I should like to try."

"And let the other matter rest quiescent meanwhile?"

"If it will."

"What do you mean by that?"

"I hardly know myself, Chief. All is hazy yet, but skies clear, and so do most of our problems. If the two ends of my string should chance to come together—"

But here a look from his Chief stopped him.

"Let us pray that they won't. But if they do, we shall not shirk our duty, Gryce."

XIX

MR. GRYCE AND THE TIMID CHILD

"Assurance does it, sir—a great deal of assurance. Not that I have much—"

Here Mr. Gryce laughed, with the result that Sweetwater laughed also. A moment of fun was a welcome relief, and they both made the most of it.

"Not that I lack it entirely," Sweetwater hastened to say. Then they laughed again—after which their talk proceeded on serious lines.

"Sweetwater, what is that you once told me about a family named Duclos?"

"Why, this, sir: There is one such family in town, as Peters discovered in looking up the name in the directory a day or two after Madame's disappearance. But there's nothing to be learned from them. Mr. and Mrs. Edward Duclos are a most respectable couple and have but one answer to every question. They know no one of their name outside their own family. Though the man of the house is Breton born, he has lived many years in this country, and in all that time has never met another Duclos."

"And Peters let it go at that?"

"Had to. What else could he do? However, he did make this admission—that there was a child in the room who betrayed a nervousness under his questions which was not observable in her elders, a girl of twelve or so who put her hands behind her when she found she could not control their twitching. And I've an idea that if he could have got this child by herself, he might have heard something quite different from the plain denial he got from the mother. I've always thought so; but I've had too many other things to do to make an effort in this direction.

"Now, if you approve, I'll see what I can do with this girl, for it stands to reason there must be some place in town where this woman, just off ship, found an immediate refuge and a change of clothing and effects. Nor should I be much surprised if we should discover that she is an inmate of this very house. What do you think, Mr. Gryce? Is it worth looking into?"

"It is worth my looking into. I have other work for you. Where does this Duclos family live?"

Sweetwater told him. It was in one of the Eighties, not a quarter of a mile from the Hotel Universal.

This settled, Mr. Gryce took from his pocket the mutilated photograph which had served as a target to the woman in Fifty-third Street.

"You see this," said he. "The face is all gone; only a sweep of the hair on one side, and a bit of collar and the tip of a shoulder on the other, remain to act as a clue. Yet I expect you to find the negative from which this photograph was printed. It should not be so difficult,—that is, if in the course of time it has not been destroyed,—for look here." And turning over what remained of the mutilated photograph he displayed the following:

Cor. 9th Street
w York)

"New York! The portrait was made here and—at Fredericks'. His studio was on the corner of Ninth Street up to a few years ago. It's a trail after my own mind. If that negative is in existence, I'll find it, if I have to ransack half the photograph-studios in town. About how old do you think this picture is?"

"Old enough to give you trouble. But that you're used to. What we want to know—what we must know—is this: The name of the man who has incurred Madame's enmity to such a degree that she spends the small hours of the night in knocking out his features from a fifteen-year-old photograph. If it should prove to be that of a public man, rich or otherwise, we might consistently lay it to social hatred; but if, on the contrary, it turns out to be that of a private individual—well, in that case, I shall have a task for you which may call for a little of that assurance of which we have just acknowledged you possess a limited share."

That evening, just at dusk, a taxicab which had been wandering up and down a well-kept block in Eighty-seventh Street stopped suddenly in front of a certain drug-store to let an old man out. He seemed very feeble and leaned heavily on his cane while crossing the sidewalk toward the store. But his face was kindly, and his whole aspect that of one who takes the ills of life without bitterness or complaint. When halfway to his goal,—for twenty steps are a journey to one who has to balance himself carefully with every one,—he slipped or stumbled, and his cane flew out of his hand. Happily—because he seemed unable to reach it himself—a young girl just emerging from the drug-store saw his plight and stooping for the stick, handed it to him. He received it with a smile, and while it was yet in both of their hands, said in the most matter-of-fact way in the world:

"Thank you, little Miss Duclos." Then suddenly: "Where's your aunt?"

She did not stop to think. She did not stop to ask herself what this question meant or whether this old gentleman who seemed to know so much about her and the family's secrets had a right to ask it, but blurted out in nervous haste as if she knew of nothing else to do, "She's gone," and then started to run away.

"Come back, little one." His tone was very imperative, but for all that of a nature to win upon a frightened child. "I know she's gone," he added soothingly as she looked back, hesitating. "And I'm sorry, for I have something for her. I recognized you the moment you stepped out of the store; but I see that you don't remember me. But why should you? Little girls don't remember old men."

Again that benevolent smile as he poked about in one of his pockets and finally drew out a little parcel which he held out toward her.

"This belongs to your aunt. See, it has her name on it, Madame Antoinette Duclos. It came to the lodging-house in Fifty-third Street just after she left, and I was asked to bring it to her. I was going to your house as soon as I had done my little errand at this store, but now that I have met you, I will ask you to see that she gets it."

The girl looked down at the parcel, then up at him, and reaching out her hand, took it.

His old heart, which had almost stopped, beat again naturally and with renewed strength. He was on the correct trail. When Mrs. Duclos and the rest of them had said that they knew of no one of their name in this country but themselves, it was because the Madame of the Hotel Universal was of their family—the widow of their brother, as this child's acknowledgment showed.

He was turning back to his taxi when the child, still trembling very much, took a step toward him and said:

"I don't know where to find my aunt. She didn't tell us where she was going; and—and I had rather not take this parcel back with me. Mother don't like us to speak of Aunt Nettie; and—and I don't believe Aunt Nettie would care to have this now. Won't—won't you forget about it, sir, if I promise to tell her some day that it was brought back and I wouldn't take it?"

Mr. Gryce felt a qualm of conscience. The child really was too simple to be made game of. Besides, he felt sure that she had spoken the truth, so far as she herself was concerned. She didn't know where her erratic aunt had gone; and any further questioning would only frighten her without winning him the knowledge he sought. He therefore took the parcel back, said some soothing words and made his way across the walk to his taxi. But the number he gave the chauffeur was that of the house where this little girl lived.

He arrived there first. To him, waiting in the parlor and very near the window, her shrinking little figure looked pathetic enough, as glancing in at the taxi, and finding it empty, she realized who might be awaiting her under her mother's eye. He remembered his grandchild, and made up his mind, as she slid nervously in, that no matter what happened he would keep this innocent child out of trouble.

The lady who presently came in to receive him was one who called him instinctively to his feet in respect and admiration. She was an American and of the best type, a woman who, if she told a lie, would not tell it for her own comfort or gain, but to help some one else to whom she owed fealty or love. But would she lie for anyone? As he studied her longer, taking in, in his own way, the candid expression of her eye and the sweet but firm set of her lips, he began to think she would not, and the interest with which he proceeded to address her was as much due to herself as to the knowledge he hoped to gain from her.

"Mrs. Duclos?" he asked.

"Yes, sir. And you?"

"I am a member of the New York police. My errand is one which you can probably guess. You have a sister-in-law, the widow of your husband's brother. As her testimony is of the utmost importance in the inquiry which is to be made into the cause and manner of her daughter's death, I should be very glad to have a few minutes' talk with her if, as we have every reason to believe, she is in this house at the present moment."

Mrs. Edward Duclos was a strong and upright woman, but this direct address, this open attack, was too much for her. However, before replying, she had a question of her own to put, and she proceeded to ask it firmly, quietly and apparently with every expectation of its being answered:

"How did you learn that Mr. Duclos had a brother and that this brother had left a widow?"

"Not from you, madam," he smiled. "Nor from your husband. I very much wish we had. We have been waiting for some such word ever since our advertisement appeared. It has not come."

She gave him a quick interrogating glance, folded her hands and answered without further hesitation:

"We had our reasons for silence, reasons which we thought quite justifiable. But they don't hold good if we are to be brought into conflict with the police. Mr. Duclos told me this morning that if we were driven to speak we must do so with complete honesty and without quibble. What do you want to know?"

"Everything. First, your sister-in-law's story, then her reasons for sending her child alone to the museum, as well as the cause of her flight before she could have heard of that poor child's fate. More hangs upon an understanding of these facts than I am at liberty to tell you. She herself would agree with me in this if I could have a few minutes' conversation with her."

"She is not in the house. She left us late last night without giving us the least hint as to where she was going. She is, as you can very well see, as little anxious to talk of her great trouble as you are to have her, and recognizing that attempts were being made to find her and make her speak, she fled before it was too late. I am sorry she did so, sorry for her and sorry for ourselves. We do not approve her course, whatever reasons she may have for it. At the same time, I feel bound to assure you that to her they are all-sufficient. She is a conscientious woman, with many fine qualities, and when she says as she did to us, 'It is my duty to flee,' and again as she bade us a final adieu, 'I will die rather than speak a word of what is on my mind,' I know that it is no small matter which sends her wandering about like this."

"I should think not. A mother to leave her daughter to be exposed at the morgue, and never intervene to protect her from this ignominy or to see that she has proper burial after that dread display is over!"

"I know—it was dreadful—and we! Do you not think we felt the horror of this also?"

"Your own flesh and blood—that is, your husband's. I wonder you could stand it."

"We had promised. She made us promise the first day she came that we would keep still and make no move, whatever happened."

"It was here she came then, directly from the hotel?"

"I am obliged to admit it."

"With her torn dress and her little bag?"

"Yes."

"And you procured her different clothes and the suit-case in which she now lugs about her effects?"

"You seem to know it all."

"Mrs. Duclos, I hope you will answer my next question as

honestly as you have the previous ones. Had Madame Duclos heard of her daughter's death when she first presented herself to you?"

"Since you ask me this, I must answer. She was in great distress, but did not tell me why, till I asked her where Angeline was. Then she broke down utterly and flinging herself face down on the sofa, sobbed and wailed and finally confided to us that a terrible accident had happened to the child and that she was lying dead in one of the city's great museums."

"Did she say what accident?"

"No; she was almost delirious with grief, and we couldn't question her. After the papers came and we had read the dreadful news, we tried to get from her some explanation of what it all meant, but now she wouldn't answer; before, she couldn't."

"Did you ask her how she came to know that Angeline was dead, before the news was circulated outside the museum?"

"Yes; but she did not answer, only looked at us. It was the most despairing look I ever saw in my life. It made it easier for us to promise her all she wanted, though we regretted having done this when we came to think the matter over."

"So you positively do not know any more than this of what she has so religiously held secret?"

"No; and I have got to the point where I do not wish to."

"Did you know she was coming to this country?"

"Yes—but not her reasons for doing so. She has been a little mysterious of late."

"Did she say she was going to bring her daughter with her?"

"Yes, she mentioned Angeline. Also the name of the ship on which they expected to sail."

"Was this letter mailed from Paris or London?"

"It came from Paris."

"Did you understand that she was leaving France for good?"

"I got that idea, certainly."

"But not her reasons for it?"

"No. The letter was very short and not very explicit. I really have given you all the information I have on this subject."

"Mrs. Duclos, it is my duty to inform you that your sister-in-law had a deep and intense hatred for a man to us at present unknown. Can you name him? Is there anything in her early history or in what you know of her later life, here and abroad, to enlighten you as to his identity?"

With a steady look and a slow shake of her head, Mrs. Duclos denied any such knowledge, even showing a marked surprise at what was evidently a new development to her.

"Antoinette has had little to do with the men since our brother's death," she said. "I can hardly conceive of her being greatly interested either in favor of or against any of the opposite sex."

"Yet she is—even to the point of wishing him dead."

Mrs. Duclos rose quickly to her feet, but instantly sat again.

"How do you know?" she asked.

Should he tell her? At first he thought not; then he reconsidered his decision and spoke out plainly.

"Madam," said he, "some day you will hear what I had rather you heard now and from me. Madame Duclos left the lodging-house where she was so safe because she was detected, or was suspicious of having been detected, shooting the face from a photograph she had set up before her as a target in the small hours of the night."

"Impossible!" The woman thus exclaiming was quite sincere. "I cannot imagine Antoinette doing that."

"Yet she did. We have the remains of the photograph."

"And who was the man?"

"When we know that, we shall know all, or be in the way of knowing all."

"You alarm me!" She certainly looked alarmed.

"Why, madam? Do you not think it better for the truth to be known in such a case?"

"You forget what I told you. Antoinette will not survive the betrayal of her secret. She said she would not, and she is a woman who weighs her words. There is a firm edge to her resolves. It has always worked for good till now. I cannot bear to think of its working in any way for evil."

"Has she socialistic ideas? Can her hatred be for some of our plutocrats or supposed oppressors of the people?"

"Oh, no; she is of aristocratic descent and proud of her order. The Duclos are bourgeois, but Antoinette is a De Montfort."

Mr. Gryce suppressed all token of his instinctive amazement. This fine American woman was not without a sense of reflected glory given by this fact. Her sister-in-law was a De Montfort! Expressing his thanks for her candor, he rose to depart.

"For all that," said he, "she may be at heart a *révolutionnaire*." Then, as he noticed the negation in her look, he added softly: "The least clue as to her present refuge would make me greatly your debtor."

"I cannot give it; I do not know it."

And somehow he believed her as absolutely as even she could

desire. If he should yet be fortunate enough to find this elusive Madame, it would have to be through some other agency than these relatives of hers by marriage.

As he passed out, he heard a frightened gasp from somewhere back in the hall. Turning, he asked in the most natural manner whether there were children in the house.

Mrs. Duclos answered with some dignity that she had three daughters.

"You are fortunate, madame," he remarked with his old-fashioned bow. "I live alone. My last grandchild left me a year ago for a man many years my junior."

This brought the little one into his view. She was smiling, and he went away in a state of relief marred by but one regret:

He was as ignorant as ever where to look for the mother of Angeline.

XX

MR. GRYCE AND THE UNWARY WOMAN

Nevertheless Mr. Gryce was proud of the gain he had made in his talk with Mrs. Duclos, and he smiled as he thought of his next interview with Sweetwater. Assurance will often accomplish much, it is true, but it sometimes needs age to make it effective. He could not imagine either Mrs. Duclos or her daughter yielding to the blandishments of one even as gifted in this special direction as Sweetwater. Authority was needed as well—the authority of long experience and an ineradicable sympathy with human nature.

Thus he gratified himself with a few complacent thoughts. But when he stopped to think what a great haystack New York was, and how elusive was the needle which had escaped them now these three times, his spirits sank a trifle, and by the time he had ridden a half-block on his way back to Headquarters, he was at that low ebb of disheartenment from which only some happy inspiration can effectually lift one. He was glad to be able to report that he had learned a few important facts in regard to Madame Duclos, but he equally hated to admit that for all his haste in following up the clue given him, he knew as little as ever of her present whereabouts; and hated even worse to have to give the cue which would lead to a surveillance, however secret, over a house which held a child of so sensitive and tremulous a nature as that of the little friend who had picked up his stick in front of the drugstore.

He was recalling to mind the pathetic spectacle presented by her agitated little figure, when his eyes chanced to fall upon a small shop he was then passing. It was devoted to ladies' furnishings, and as he took in the contents of the window and such articles as could be seen on the shelves beyond, a happy thought came to him.

Madame Duclos had left her hotel in a hurry, carrying but few of her belongings with her. A lady of cultivated taste, she must have missed many articles necessary to her comfort; and having money would naturally buy them. Prevented by her fears from going downtown, or even from going anywhere in the daytime, what was left for her to do but to patronize some such small shop as this. Its nearness to her late refuge, as well as its neat and attractive appearance, made this seem all the more likely. A question or two would suffice to settle his mind on this point and perhaps lead to results which might prove invaluable in his present emergency.

Signaling to the chauffeur to stop, he got out in front of this little shop, toward which he immediately proceeded, with an uncertainty of step not altogether assumed. He did have some rheumatic twinges that day.

Entering, Mr. Gryce first cast a comprehensive glance at the shelves and counters, to make sure that he would find here the line of dress-goods in which he had decided to invest; then, approaching the middle-aged woman who seemed to be in charge, he engaged her in a tedious display of the goods, which led on to talk and finally to a casual remark from him, quite in keeping with the anxiety he had been careful to show.

"I am buying this for a woman to whom you have probably sold many odd little things within the past few days. Perhaps you knew her taste, and can help me choose what will please her. She lives down the street and buys always in the evening—a dark, genteel appearing Frenchwoman, with a strange way of looking down even when other people would be likely to look up. Do you remember her?"

Yes, she remembered her and recognized her perfectly from this description. He saw this at once, but he kept right on talking as he handled first one piece of goods and then another, seeming to hesitate between the gray and the brown.

"She went out of town yesterday, and wanted this material sent after her. Do you think you could do that for me, or shall I have to see to expressing it myself? I'll do it if I must—only I've forgotten her exact address." This he muttered self-reproachfully, "I've a shocking bad memory, and it's growing worse every day. You don't happen to know where she's gone to, do you?"

The innocence of this appeal from one of his years and benevolent aspect did not appear to raise the woman's suspicion; yet she limited her reply to this short statement:

"I'll send the goods, if you will make your choice." And it was not till long after that he learned that Madame Duclos, being very anxious for her mail and such newspapers as she wanted, had made arrangements with this woman to forward them.

Disappointed, but still hoping for some acknowledgment that would give him what he wanted, he continued to putter with the goods, when she broke in with harsh decision:

"I think she would prefer the gray."

"Oh, do you?" said he, with just a hint of disapproval at the suggestion. "I like brown best, myself; but let it be the gray. Ten yards," he ordered. "She was particular to say that she wanted ten yards, and that I was to be sure and purchase the dress at the shop adjoining the drug-store. You see I have obeyed her," he added with a touch of senility in his quiet chuckle which threw the busy woman off her guard.

"I fear," said she, "that the dress I sold her before will not prove very becoming. But gray is always good. That's why I advised it."

"I see, I see," chattered away the old man, not without some slight compunction. "But in my opinion she's too dark for such somber dresses. I've told her so a score of times." Then as he watched the woman before him rolling up the goods he proceeded to ask with fussy importunity what she thought the express charges were likely to be, for he wanted to pay the whole bill and be done with it.

She was caught—caught fairly this time, though I doubt if she ever knew it.

"We don't often send up the river," said she. "But I should say that for a package of this size and weight the charges would be about forty cents. But that you can leave her to pay. She will be quite willing to do so, I am sure."

"Of course, of course—I didn't think of that. She'll pay for it, of course she'll pay for it." And he continued to fuss and chat, with that curious mixture of native shrewdness and senile interest in little things which he thought most likely to impress the woman attending him, and trap her into giving him the complete address.

But she was too wary, or too much preoccupied with her own affairs, to let the cat any farther out of the bag, and he had to be content with her promise, that the package should be given to the expressman as early as possible the next morning.

The feebleness he showed while leaving the shop was in marked contrast, however, to the vigor with which he took down the telephone-receiver in the booth of the neighboring drug-store. But she was not there to see; nor anyone else who had the least interest in his movements. He could, therefore, give all the emphasis he desired to the demand he made upon Headquarters for a close watch to be set on the adjoining dry-goods shop, for the purpose of intercepting and obtaining the address of a certain package, on the point of being expressed from there to some place up the river.

Then he went home; for by now he was fully as tired as his years demanded.

XXI

PERPLEXED

"Elvira Brown."

"Elvira Brown? That the name on the package?"

"Yes."

"And the address?"

The name of a small town in the Catskills was given him.

"Thank you. Very good work." And Mr. Gryce hung up the receiver. Then he stood thinking.

"Elvira Brown! A very fair alias—that is, the *Brown* end. But what am I to think of *Elvira*? And what am I to think of the *Brown*, now that I remember that the woman who has chosen to hide her identity under another name is a Frenchwoman. Something queer! Let me see if I can call up the station-master at the place she's gone."

A long-distance connection proving practicable, he found himself after a little while in communication with the man he wanted.

"I'm Gryce, of the New York police. A woman in whom we're greatly interested has just entered your town under the name of Elvira Brown."

"Elvira Brown!"

Mr. Gryce was startled at the tone in which this was repeated, even making due allowance for the medium through which it came.

"Yes. What's there strange about that?"

"Only this: That's the name of a woman who has lived in these mountains for forty years, and who died here three days ago. Today we're going to bury her."

This *was* a blow to the detective's expectations. What awful mistake had he made? Or had it been made by the man detailed to steal the name from the package—or by the woman in the shop, or by all these combined? He could not stop to ask; but he caught at the first loose end which presented itself.

"Well, it isn't she we're after, that's certain. The one we want is middle-aged, and plain in looks and dress. If she came into your town, it was yesterday or possibly the night before. You wouldn't be apt to notice her, unless your attention was caught by her lameness. Do you remember any such person?"

"No, and I don't think anyone like that passed through my

station. We're off the main road, and our travelers are few. I would have noticed the arrival of a woman like that."

Mr. Gryce, with an exclamation of chagrin, hung up the receiver. He felt completely balked.

But old as he was, he still had some of the tenacity of youth. He was not willing to accept defeat without one more effort. Going downtown as usual, he wandered again into the little dry-goods shop to see if the package had been sent.

Yes, it had gone, but the expressman had had some trouble with a drunken man who actually took the package out of his hands and didn't give it back without a squabble. Strange how men can drink till they can't see, and so early in the morning, at that!

Mr. Gryce's vigorous hunch dismissed summarily this expression of opinion as altogether feminine. But he had something to say about the package itself, which kept the good woman waiting, though a customer or two demanded her attention.

"You'll think me a fussy old man," said he, "but I've worried about that package all night. She needs a new dress so much, and I'm afraid you didn't have the right address. I remember it now—it was—was—"

"Barford on the Hudson," she finished promptly. Evidently she begrudged the time she was wasting on his imbecilities.

"That's it; that's it. 'Way up in the Catskills, isn't it?"

"I don't know. Those people are waiting, sir. I shall really—"

"One moment! I want to buy something more for her. But I'll send it myself this time; I won't bother you again. Another dress, something bright and prettier than anything she has. She'll forgive me. She'll be glad to have it."

"I don't know, sir." The woman was really very much embarrassed. She was honest to the core, and though she enjoyed seeing her goods disappear from the shelves, it wasn't in her heart to take advantage of a man so old as this. "I'm afraid she wouldn't be pleased. You see, it isn't a fortnight since she bought and made up the one I sold her first, and she thought that a great extravagance. Now with the gray—"

"Are you speaking of the blue one?"

"No, it wasn't blue."

"What color was it? Haven't you a bit left to show me? I should know better what to do, then."

She pointed to a bolt of striped wool—a little gaudy for a woman whose taste they had both been speaking of as inclined to the plain and somber.

"That? But that's bright enough. I've never seen her in that."

"She didn't like it. But something made her take it. She wore it when she came in last."

"She did! Then I'm satisfied. Thankee all the same. Just give me a pair of gloves for her, and I'll be getting on."

She picked out a pair for him, and he trotted away, mumbling cheerily to himself as he passed between the counters. But once in his taxi again, he concentrated all his thought on that bolt of striped dress-goods. The colors were crimson and black, with a dot here and there of some lighter shade! He took pains to fix it in his mind, for this was undoubtedly the dress she fled in—an important clue to him, if this hunt should resolve itself into a chase with doubling and redoubling of the escaping quarry.

He spent the next two hours in acquainting himself with the location and some of the conditions of the town he now meant to visit. Though he could not understand Madame Duclos' reason for taking the name of a woman so well known as this Elvira Brown, there was something in this circumstance and the fact that the person so styled had been at that moment at the point of death, which called, as he felt, for personal investigation. He hardly felt fit for any such purely speculative expedition as this; especially as he must do without the companionship, to say nothing of the assistance, of Sweetwater, whom he hardly felt justified in withdrawing from the task he had given him. So he picked out a fellow named Perry; and together they took the West Shore into Greene County, where they stopped at a station from which a branch road ran to the small town whither the package addressed to Elvira Brown had preceded them.

Accidents frequently determine our course, as well as turn us from the one we had mapped out for ourselves. By accident I mean, in this case, an actual one which had occurred on the branch road I have mentioned, by which the trains were held up and further progress in that direction made impossible. When this came to the knowledge of Mr. Gryce, he found it necessary to choose between trusting himself to an automobile for the rest of the journey, or of remaining all night in the town where the train had stopped. A glance at the hills towering up between him and his goal decided him to wait for the running of the trains next day; and after an inquiry or two, he left the station on foot for the hotel to which he had been recommended.

A philosopher, in many regards, Mr. Gryce quieted himself, under the irritation of this annoyance, with the thought that in this world we do not always know just what is best for us; and that the few hours of rest thus forced upon him by the seemingly unfortunate break in his plans might prove in the end to be the best thing that could happen to him. He accordingly took a good room, enjoyed a good dinner and then sat down in the lobby to have an equally good smoke. He chose a chair which gave him a prospect of the river, and for a long time, while vaguely listening to the talk about him, he feasted his eyes on the view and allowed some of its calm to enter his perturbed spirit. But gradually, as he looked and smoked, he found his attention caught, first by what a man was saying in his rear, and secondly by something he saw intervening between himself and the flow of shining river which had hitherto filled his eye.

The sentence which had roused him was one quite foreign to his thoughts and seemingly of little importance to him or to anyone about. It was in connection with a factory on the other side of the river, which was running overtime, and had not help enough to fill its orders.

"It's women we want," he heard shouted out. "Young women, middle-aged women, any sort of women who are anxious for steady work and good wages."

The emphasis with which this announcement was made per-haps gave it point; at all events this one brief sentence sank into Mr. Gryce's ear just as he began to notice a woman who sat with her back to him on the hotel piazza.

He was not thinking of Madame Duclos at that moment; nor was there the least thing about this woman to recall his secret quarry to mind. Yet once his eyes had fallen on her, they remained there for several minutes.

Why?

Perhaps because she sat so unnaturally still. In all the time he stared at her simple bonnet and decently clothed shoulders, the silhouette she made against the silver band of the river did not change by an iota. He had been agaze upon the landscape too, but he was sure that he had not sat as still as this, and when, after an interval during which he had turned to see what kind of man it was who had spoken so vigorously, he wheeled back into place and glanced out again through his window, she was there yet, hat, shoulders and all, immovable as an image and almost as rigid.

Well, and what of it? There was surely nothing very remark-able in so commonplace a fact; yet during the ensuing half-hour, during which he gave, or tried to give, the greater part of his atten-tion to the political talk which followed the statements he had heard made in regard to the needs of a certain factory, his eye would turn riverward from time to time and always with a view to see if this woman had moved. And not once did he detect the least change in her attitude.

"She will sit there all night," he muttered to himself; and after a while his curiosity mounted to such a pitch that he got up and went out on the piazza for one of his short strolls.

XXII

HE REMEMBERS

Just an ordinary woman, lost in a dream of some kind while awaiting her departure on an out-going train!—or such was Detective Gryce's conclusion as he hobbled slowly past her.

Why should he give her a moment's thought? Yet he did. He noticed her dress and the way she held her hands, and the fact, not suspected before, that she was not looking out at the landscape outspread before her eyes, but down into her lap at her own hands clasped together in an unnaturally tight grip. Then he straightway forgot her in the thought of that other woman whose track he was following with such poor promise of success. Madame Duclos' image was in his mind as plainly as if she sat before him in place of this chance passenger. He knew the sort of hat she would wear (or thought he did). He also knew the color of her dress. Had he not been shown the piece of goods from which it had been taken? And had he not understood her choice, bizarre as it was, and for this very reason, that it was bizarre? Being a woman of subtle mind, she would reason that since the police were seeking one of plain exterior and simple dress, a gaudy frock would throw them off their guard and insure her immunity from any close inspection. Therefore this striped material rather than the plain black she so much preferred. Then her eyes! She would try to hide the defect which particularized them, by the use of glasses or, at least, by a very heavy veil. While her walk—well! she might successfully conceal her halting step if she were not hurried. But he promised himself that he would be very careful to see that any woman rousing his suspicion should be given some reason for hurrying.

While thus musing, he had reached the farther end of the piazza. In wheeling about to come back, the woman whose profile he now faced attracted his eye again, in spite of himself, and he gave her another idle thought. How absorbing was the subject upon which she was brooding, and how deeply it affected her!

It struck him as he quietly repassed her that he had never seen a sadder face. Then that impression passed from his mind, for he saw Perry coming toward him with a pencil and telegram-blank in hand. He had decided to let Sweetwater know where he could be reached that night, and Perry had come for the message.

It must have been fully two hours later that Mr. Gryce, sitting down in his former chair, looked up and found his view unobstructed to the river. The woman had gone.

Just for the sake of saying something to Perry, who had drawn up beside him, he remarked upon the fact, adding in explanation of his interest in so small a matter:

"It's the thoughts and feelings of people which take hold of my curiosity now. Human nature is a big book, a great book. I have only begun to thumb it, and I'm an old man. Some people betray their emotions in one way, some in another. Some are loudest when most troubled, and some are so quiet one would think them dead. The woman I was watching there was one of the quiet ones; her trouble was deep; that was apparent from her outline—an outline which never varied."

"Yes, she's a queer duck. I saw her: I even did an errand for her—that was before you sat down here."

"You did an errand for her?"

"Yes; she wanted a newspaper. Of course I was glad to get it for her, as she said she was lame."

"Lame?"

"Yes; I suppose she spoke the truth. I didn't think of her being in any special trouble, but I did think her an odd one. She seemed to be wearing two dresses."

Mr. Gryce started and turned sharply toward him.

"What's that you say? What do you mean by that?"

"Why, this: when she stopped to get her money out of some hidden pocket, she pulled up the skirt of her dress, and I saw another one under it. Perhaps she thought that was the easiest way of carrying it. I noticed that her suit-case was a small one."

"Describe that under-frock to me." Mr. Gryce's air and tone were unaccountably earnest. "What was its color?"

"Why, reddish, I think. No, it had stripes in it and something like spots. Do you suppose it was her petticoat?"

Mr. Gryce brought his hand down on his lame knee and did not seem to feel it. "Find out where she's gone!" he cried. "No, I will do it myself." And before the other could recover from his astonishment, he had started for the piazza where he had just seen the proprietor of the hotel take his seat.

"This comes from an old man's folly in thinking he could manage an affair of this kind without help," he mumbled to himself as he went stumping along. "Had I told Perry whom we were after and how he was to recognize her, I should have spent my time talking with this woman instead of staring at her. Two dresses! with the bright one under! Well, she's even more subtle than I thought."

And by this time, having reached the man he sought, he put his question:

"Can you tell me anything about the woman who was sitting here? Who she is and where she has gone?"

"The woman who was sitting here? Why, I should say she was a factory hand and has gone to her work on the other side of the river."

"Her name? Do you know her name? I'm a detective from New York—one of the regular police force. I'm in search of a woman not unlike the one I saw here, though not, I am bound to state, a factory worker except on compulsion."

"You are! A police detective, eh, and at your age! It must be a healthy employment. But about this woman! I'm sorry, but I can't tell you anything except that she came on the same train you did and wanted a boat right away to take her across the river. You see, we've no ferry here, and I told her so, and the only way she could get across was to wait for Phil Jenkins, who was going over at five. She said she would wait, and sat down here, refusing dinner, or even to enter the house. Perhaps she wasn't hungry, and perhaps she didn't wish to register, eh?"

"Had her speech an accent? Did you take her for a foreign woman?"

"Yes, I did and I didn't. She spoke very well. She's not young, you know?"

"I'm not looking for a young woman."

"Well, she's gone and you can't reach her tonight. There they are now, see! about a quarter of the way across. That small boat just slipping across the wake of the big one."

Mr. Gryce looked and saw that she was in the way of escape for tonight.

"When can I get over?" he asked.

"Not till Phil crosses again tomorrow noon."

"Meanwhile, she may go anywhere. I shall certainly lose her."

"Hardly. She's bound for the factory; you can just see the roof of it above the trees a little to the right. She asked me all sorts of questions about the work over there, and whether there were decent places to live in within walking distance of the factory."

"Then she isn't lame? My woman is a trifle lame."

"So may this woman be, for all I know. I didn't see her on her feet, but she carried no crutch—only a bag and an umbrella."

"A brown bag, neat like herself in appearance?"

"No. It was light in color and old. She herself was neat enough."

Mr. Gryce's brows came together. He was in a quandary. He felt convinced, with a positiveness which surprised him, that in watching the withdrawal of this small boat farther and farther toward the opposite shore, he was watching the escape of Antoinette Duclos from his immediate interference.

Yet, circumstantial as were the proofs which had led him to this conclusion, he felt that he would gladly welcome some further corroboration of those proofs before risking the time and opportunity he might lose in following the person of two skirts to her destination on the other side of the Hudson. There were more reasons than one why he could not afford to lose one unnecessary minute. An extra twinge or two of rheumatism warned him that he was approaching the point of disablement.

Moreover, of Mr. Gryce's secret fears there was one which loomed larger than the others and held an impulsive, unconsidered movement in check. He must have proof of her identity—which nevertheless he did not question—before hazarding himself and the success of his undertaking by a delay of so many additional hours. But what proof could he hope to obtain under the circumstances in which he found himself placed? Any appeal to Mrs. Edouard Duclos, by telephone or telegram, would certainly fail of its purpose. Even if the neat black dress in which her sister-in-law now traveled was one from her own wardrobe, he would find it impossible to establish the fact in time to make his own decision. The child—yes, he might worm that fact out of the child if he were where he could reach her; but he was miles away; and besides, something within him revolted from involving this child further in schemes honest enough from his standpoint, but certainly not helpful to her. No, he would have to trust his intuition, or—

He had thrown himself into a chair at the side of his host, but he rose quickly as his musings reached this point. The proof he had been looking for was his. In recalling the child to mind there had flashed upon his inner vision an instantaneous picture of her appearance as she stooped to pick up his stick in front of the drugstore. He saw again the bending figure, the flushed cheeks and the flaxen locks surmounted by a little hat. Ah! it was that little hat! The impression it had made upon him was greater than he thought. He found that he remembered not only its ribbons, but the bunches of curiously tinted flowers hanging down in front. And these bunches, or some precisely like them, had been the sole trimming of the hat he had been contemplating so long from the other side of the window. The woman was Madame Duclos.

These flowers had been taken from the child's hat and pinned upon the aunt's; and it was their familiar look which had given him, without any recognition of the reason, his surety as to the latter's identity.

Calmed immensely by this assurance, he turned back to have another word with the proprietor, now busily engaged with his newspaper.

"Will you be obliging enough to see that I'm given an opportunity for a few words with this Phil Jenkins on his return?" he asked. "And if you will be so good, respect my confidence till I am sure I have made no mistake in thinking what I have of his passenger."

The proprietor nodded, and Mr. Gryce settled himself again inside to watch for the rowboat's return.

What he learned that night from this man Jenkins calmed him still further. The woman had acknowledged, on leaving him, that she was going to seek work at the factory. "A little old for the job," the man volunteered, "but spry. How she did clamber up that bank!"

It was enough; Mr. Gryce was satisfied, and engaged a seat in his small boat for the following day.

XXIII

GIRLS, GIRLS! NOTHING BUT GIRLS!

The superintendent was puzzled and showed it. He listened to Mr. Gryce with a shrug, saying that so many women had been taken on that day, that he really couldn't remember whether any one of them answered to the given description.

"There's the time-keeper's book. Look it over. All the names are there," he said.

Mr. Gryce did as he advised, but of course without finding there the name of Antoinette Duclos or of anyone else of whom he had ever heard.

The next thing was for him to go through the factory itself and see if he could pick her out from those already at work. This he was greatly averse to doing; it would be too long and painful an effort for him, and he could not trust Perry with any such piece of nice discrimination. How he missed Sweetwater! How tempted he was to send for him! It was finally decided that when the hour came for the departure of the whole dayshift, he should take his stand where he could mark each employee as she filed out.

A sorry attempt followed by as sorry a failure! He did not see one among them who was over twenty-five years of age. But this did not mean the end of all hope. There was the nightshift. Might she not be put on that? A different man had charge at night. He would wait for this man's appearance, present his cause to him and see what could be done.

Not much, he found, when the night superintendent finally entered the office and he had the chance of introducing himself. Newer to authority than the superintendent of the dayshift, he was also of a more active temperament and much more self-assertive. He was not impressed by the detective's years or even by his errand. It was a busy night, a very busy night—new hands in every department. To take him through the building at present was quite out of the question. Perhaps later it might be done; but not now, not now.

With that the night superintendent bustled out. This was not very encouraging, but Mr. Gryce did not despair. He had seen with what ease he could look from the broad, rear window near which he stood, into the rooms where rows upon rows of girls were already at work. Only a narrow court divided him from these girls, and as the three stories of which the factory was composed were all brilliantly lighted, he should have little difficulty in picking out from among them the middle-aged woman who held in her closed and mysterious hand the key to that formidable affair threatening the honor of one of New York's most prominent men.

Before doing this, Mr. Gryce stopped to locate himself and recall if possible the entire plan of the building. He was in what was called the outer office. The inner one, used only by the president of the concern, opened on his left. There was no one in the latter room at present, the president seldom showing up at night. Another door led to the platform outside, and a third one, located in the middle of the right-hand partition, to a large vestibule or locker-room belonging exclusively to the girls, which in its turn communicated with the work-rooms of the factory running in unbroken continuity around a narrow central court.

He had been through this locker-room in the late afternoon. It was here he had stood to watch the girls file out at the close of their day's work. The exit for all employees was in one of the corners and out of this Antoinette Duclos would have to pass when it came her turn to leave the building—that is, if she were really in it, as he had every reason to believe.

However, certainty on this point would relieve him from much of his present impatience, and with this end in view he prepared to enter the room again in the hope of spying among the various hats with which the walls were hung the one with whose shape and trimming he was so well acquainted.

But promising as this attempt looked, it was destined to immediate failure. The room was not empty. He could hear girls whispering not a dozen steps away, and anxious as he always was not to attract any unnecessary attention to himself, he turned his back upon this door and returned to the window from the broad view of which he anticipated so much.

A brilliant scene awaited him. This building, built originally for other purposes, had been hastily reconstructed for its present use in a manner possibly open to criticism but which certainly gave those who worked in it an abundance of light and air. The narrow columns supporting its three stories were so inconspicuous at night when a blaze of electricity dominated the whole, that it presented the appearance of being made entirely of windows. One break and one only he observed in the double row of lights encircling the courtyard. This was in a spot diagonally opposite, where a space of several feet showed a dimness he failed to understand. But as no workers appeared to be there, he passed the matter over as one of no importance.

The task before him looked hopeless. In the first place there were the three floors, with no faces visible above the first one. Then of the long rectangle stretching out before him he could see but two sides, which fact was further complicated by there being as many of the workers' faces turned toward the outside of the building as toward the court. Yet having determined upon his course, he was bound to see it through.

His position near the corner of the huge rectangle precluded his seeing anyone working at his own end. He was obliged to pass them over. But of those opposite, especially those directly so, he could take easy count. They were all girls of fifteen or so, and could be passed over also without more than a cursory glance. Further on he saw a row of older women, and student as he was of human nature, there were faces among them at which he was tempted to look twice, though once answered his purpose. There was no Madame there.

Continuing his examination, he next encountered the space so unaccountably darkened, and having skipped this, came upon a stretch of benches displaying great activity. Only old hands seemed to be at work in this section. Their method and despatch showed a training which made it useless to look among them for one who had probably never worked before amid the hum of machinery.

In the corner beyond he saw nobody, but when he came to look along the end connecting the opposite rooms with those on his side, a different scene awaited him. There every bench seemed occupied both back and front, and mostly by newcomers, as was apparent from the anxious way the superintendent moved about among them, explaining the work and directing them with a zeal which not only attested his interest in the task but showed how completely he had forgotten the man he had left behind him in his office. Well, well, such is the way of the world! The old man saw that he would have to depend upon himself, and realizing this, bent all his energies to his present far-off inspection of these women, hoping against hope that he would be able at least to tell the young from the old.

Yes, he could do that, but the older women seemed to be in the majority; and this perplexed him. It was all too distant for him to see clearly, but he took heart of grace as he observed how the faces and figures he was studying so closely were resolving themselves into mere silhouettes under his gaze. For as I have already said, he had a quick eye for outline, and felt sure that he could sufficiently recall that of the woman whose head and shoulders had been so long under his eye that day, to recognize it even among fifty others. But not one of them—not one of them all—had the precise narrowness and rigidity of Madame Duclos'; and after many painful minutes of renewed effort followed by renewed disappointment he moved back from the window and sat down. There was one thing you could always count on in Mr. Gryce, and that was his patience.

But it was a patience not without its breaks. Once he rose to look out front to make sure he had not miscalculated the distance of this factory from the river. Then after another period of waiting, he got thinking how much he might discover if he could get one glimpse into that far corner contiguous to that end of the rectangle where he had seen so many raw workers receiving the assistance of the night superintendent. There was a way of doing this of which he had not thought before. He had but to step outside, walk the length of the platform where the loading of shipments was going on, and look in at one of the great windows at the further end. But when he came to make the attempt, he found himself plunged into such a turmoil and the way so blocked by the loading of boxes and the backing up and driving off of horses that he retreated precipitately. Rather than encounter all this, he would await events from the inside. So he took his old seat again and for another half-hour listened to the thump of machinery and the squeak of a rusty elevator-brake which almost robbed him of thought. He was even inclined to doze, when he suddenly became aware of some change either in himself or in what lay about him.

Had the machinery stopped? No, it was not that.

The place seemed darker, yet it was still very light.

With a restless move, he rose heavily and peered again into the court. Immediately it was evident what had occurred. The whole string of lights in the third story had been shut off, and now those of the middle story were following suit. Only the ground floor remained active with all its lights at the maximum, and every belt moving.

At this unexpected narrowing down of his field of operations he felt greatly relieved. He had dreaded those long walks through innumerable rooms. He could manage circling the building once, but three times would have been too much. In a mood of increased contentment, he started to return to his seat, but found himself stayed by something he saw in what had been but a dimly lighted space when he looked there last. It was now as bright as the rest and showed him the figure of the superintendent stooping over a woman, explaining to her some intricate manipulation of the work in hand which was evidently quite new to her. He could see him very plainly, but her figure was more or less hidden. Not for long though. The superintendent passed on and she came into full view. It was Antoinette Duclos. He was confident of this even before he noted her dress. When his eyes fell on that, he was sure; there was no mistaking the stripes and the dots. Antoinette Duclos! and she was where he could reach her in five minutes—in fact as soon as the superintendent returned. As he stood and watched her working quite assiduously but in something like isolation, he felt as though ten years had slipped from his age, and trifled with his pleasure as the rest of us do when we behold a despaired-of goal loom suddenly in sight. Was she the woman he had pictured in his mind's eye? Hardly. Yet there was an admirable directness in her movements. From the way she went about things, he could plainly see that she would master her duties in no time if Fate did not interpose to prevent. It certainly was hard to interrupt her in her work just when she was on the way to safety and competence. But there could be no question of his duty, or of the claims of Mr. Roberts to whatever help might accrue from an understanding of the relation of this woman to events threatening his reputation with such utter destruction. Her story might free him from all suspicion or it might actually determine his guilt. Therefore her story must be had, and at once—if possible, this very night.

But he must wait—wait for the coming of the superintendent. He felt safe to do this. Meanwhile he was determined not to let this woman out of his sight; so, drawing up a chair, he settled down within view of her active figure, from which all rigidity had vanished in the interest she was rapidly developing in her work. If he could have seen her countenance more clearly, he would have been glad. There seemed to be a veil between him and it, a hazy indistinctness which he found it difficult to understand; but remembering that he was looking through two windows and on a long diagonal, he accepted this slight drawback with equanimity and was about to indulge in the comfort of a cigar when he saw the scene he still held in view change, and change vividly, to the excitation of a fresh interest and a still more careful watch.

A girl had approached Madame Duclos from some place quite out of sight, and in passing her by, had slipped a note into her hand. The Frenchwoman had taken it, but in a way indicating shock. The ease which had given suppleness to her form and surety to all her movements was gone in an instant, and from the furtive way in which she sought to read the communication thus handed her Mr. Gryce saw that his own powers would soon be taxed to keep him even with a situation changing thus from moment to moment under his eye.

What did that note contain, and who could have taken advantage of the arrival of some late-comer to slip it into her hand? Mr. Gryce found this a very formidable question, and watched with ever-increasing anxiety to see what effect these unknown words would have upon their recipient when her opportunity came for reading them.

A startling one—of that he was presently a witness; for no sooner had she taken in their import than she cast a hurried look about her and left her place without fuss or flurry, but with an air of quiet determination which Mr. Gryce felt confident covered a resolution which nothing could balk.

She had not only left her bench but seemingly was in the act of leaving the building. This, of course, it was for him to prevent, and he rose to do so. It might be interesting to wait and watch her hurrying figure threading its way to the locker-room through the double row of girls on the opposite side of the court; but there were reasons why he wished to reach that last mentioned room before she did; reasons which seemed good enough to send him there without any further delay. If he could but discover her hat among the many he had seen hanging on pegs in one of the corners, how easy it would be for him to hold her back till he could make her listen to the few words which must be said before he could allow her to leave the building.

Quick of eye, if not of step, he had run in review the varying headgear depending from those isolated pegs, before he had half-circled the lockers. But hers he did not see. Could she have been given a locker on this her first night? He did not think so; and approaching closer, he looked again. The hat was there, but lying on the floor. Somebody had knocked it down; perhaps the late-comer who had given her the letter.

Greatly gratified by the advantage he now indisputably held over her, he picked up the hat and approached the door through which she must in another minute emerge.

She did not come.

He waited and waited, and still she did not come. At last, driven by impatience, he ventured to open the door he had previously hesitated to touch and took a quick look in. Girls, girls! nothing but girls! No Madame Duclos anywhere.

Something must have happened to interrupt her escape. Either she had been caught in the attempt by the superintendent or by some one else of equal authority. This, if bad for her, was also bad for him, as a quiet hold-up in the manner he had planned was certainly better than the public one which must now follow.

Sorry for her and sorry for himself, Mr. Gryce returned to the office just as the superintendent entered from the opposite door. He thought the latter looked a little queer, and in an instant he learned why.

"Was the woman you wanted a staid, elderly person, apparently a foreigner?"

"Yes—of French birth, I am told."

"Well, I guess you were all right in distrusting her. She's gone—took a notion that night work didn't agree with her and left without so much as a 'By your leave!' She must have smelt you out in some uncanny way. Too bad! She bade fair to be just the woman we wanted for a very nice part of the work."

"Do you mean she's really out of the building—that you didn't stop her—"

"I didn't know what she was up to, till she was gone. I—"

"But how did she get out? She didn't go by the employees' door for I stood there on the watch. I had seen her receive a note—"

"A note? How? Who gave it to her?"

"Some girl."

"And you saw this? How could you? Been through the workrooms?"

"No. I saw her from this window, as I was looking diagonally across the court. She was in one of the opposite rooms over there—"

The superintendent broke into a hearty laugh.

"Fooled!" he cried. "You police detectives are a smart crowd, but our old factory with its string of useless windows has led you astray for once. You weren't looking into any one of the rooms over there. You were looking at a reflection in that useless old window behind which the elevator runs. That happens when the elevator running on that side is down. I've seen it often and laughed in my sleeve at the chance it gives me to observe on the sly how things are going on at certain benches. Many a girl has got her discharge—But no matter about that. Come here.

"The room you think you see over there—you will notice that nobody is at work in it now—is on this side of the building, and the woman you have in chase escaped by the south delivery-door. We are loading cars tonight from this side of the building, and she took a flying advantage of it. Men give way to a woman. Though there's an order against any such use of that door, you can't get one of them to hold onto a woman when she once gets it into her head to skip the premises. But she can't have gone far. This is a place of few houses and no big buildings besides the factory. If you take pains to head her off at the station, you'll be safe for tonight, and in the morning you can easily find her. Now I must go; but first, what was her offense? Theft, eh?"

"No. This woman whom we have let slip through our fingers is Madame Duclos, the mother of the girl shot in a New York museum. There is a big reward out for her recovery and detention, and—"

The superintendent stood aghast.

"Why didn't you say so? Why didn't you say so at once? I'd have had the whole troop file out before you. I'd have had—"

The detective caught at his hat.

"I wasn't aware that I had reached an age when I couldn't tell the difference between a reflection and a reality," he growled, and hurried out.

The town was a small one; and Perry would see that she didn't escape from the station. Besides, she had fled without her hat. Surely, with all this in his favor, he would soon be able to lay his hand upon her, if not tonight, certainly before another day was at an end.

XXIV

FLIGHT

In leaving the building Mr. Gryce almost ran into the arms of Perry. In his anxiety to be within call, the young detective had seated himself on the steps outside and now stood ready for any emergency.

Mr. Gryce's spirits rose as he saw him there. The great door leading to the elevator opened not twenty feet to the left of him. Perhaps Perry had seen the woman and could tell which way she ran. Questions followed, rapid and to the purpose. Perry had seen a woman flash by. But she seemed to be in company with a man. He had not been able to see either clearly.

"Which way were they heading?" asked Mr. Gryce.

Perry told him.

It would look as though they were making for the station. Alarmed at the idea, Mr. Gryce stepped down into the road and endeavored to pierce the darkness in that direction. All he could see were the station lights. Everything else was in shadow. The night hung over all, and had it not been for the grinding of machinery in their rear, the silence would have been just as marked.

"Perry, is the way rough between here and the station—I mean, rough for me?"

"Not very, if you keep in the road."

"Run ahead, then, and learn how soon the next train is due— any train, going north or going south—I don't care which. If it is soon, look for a middle-aged woman in a striped dress, and if you can't prevent her getting on, without a fracas, follow her yourself and never quit her—telegraphing me at the first opportunity. Run."

Perry gave a leap and was soon swallowed up in the darkness which was intense as soon as he had passed beyond the glare from the factory. Mr. Gryce followed after, moving as quickly as he dared. It was not far to the station platform, but in his anxiety it seemed a mile; nor did he breathe with ease till he saw a flying shadow come between him and the station lights and knew that Perry had reached the platform.

It was just at the hour when the fewest trains pass, and Mr. Gryce was himself across the tracks and on the platform before a far-off whistle warned him that one was approaching. Looking hastily around, he saw Perry hurrying up behind him.

"No one," said he. "No such person around."

They waited. The train came in, stopped, took on two unimportant passengers and rushed away north.

"I'm afraid I shall have to ask you to stay here, Perry. It would be so easy for her to board one of these night trains and buy a ticket from the conductor."

But as he spoke he paused, and gripping Perry's arm, turned his ear to listen.

"A boat," said he. "A small boat leaving shore."

It was so. They could hear the dip of the oars distinctly in the quiet which had followed the departure of the train. No other sound but that was in the air, and it struck cold upon one old heart.

"It is she! I'm sure of it," muttered Gryce.

"The man across the river has warned her—sent a boat for her, perhaps. Run down to the point and see if there is anyone there who saw her go."

Perry slid into the night, and Mr. Gryce stood listening. The quiet dip of the oars was growing fainter every instant. The boat was rapidly withdrawing, carrying with it all hope of securing off-hand this desirable witness.

To be sure, there was nothing very serious in this. He had only to telephone across the river to have the woman detained till he could reach her himself in the early morning. Yet he felt unaccountably disturbed and anxious. For all his many experiences and a record which should have made him immune from the ordinary disappointments of life, he had never, or so it seemed to him, felt more thoroughly depressed or weary of the work which had given him occupation for more years than he liked to number, than in the few minutes of solitary waiting, with his face toward the river and the sense of some impending doom settling slowly over his aged heart.

But he was still too much the successful detective to allow his disheartenment to be seen by his admiring subordinate. As the latter approached, the old man's countenance brightened, and nothing could have been more deceptive than the calmness he displayed when the fellow reported that he had just been talking to a man who had recognized the boat and the oarsman. It was the same boat and the same oarsman that had brought them over earlier in the day. He had made an extra trip at this most unusual hour, for the express purpose of taking this woman back.

"I suppose there is no possibility of your drumming up

anyone to row us over in time to catch them?"

"None in the least. I have inquired."

"Then follow me into the station. I have a few messages to send."

Among these messages was a peremptory one to Sweetwater.

Morning! and an early crossing to the other side. Here a surprise awaited them. They found, on inquiry, that the man responsible for Madame's flitting was not, as they had supposed, the hotel proprietor, but Phil himself, the good-natured, easily-imposed-upon ferryman, on whose sympathies she had worked during their first short passage from one shore to the other. Perhaps a little money had helped to deepen this impression; one never knows.

But this was not all. The woman was gone. She had fled the town on foot before they were able to locate Phil, who had not made shore at his usual place but at some point up the river about which they knew nothing. When he finally showed up, it was almost daybreak.

"Where is he now?"

"At home, or ought to be."

"Show me the house."

In ten minutes the two were face to face.

The result was not altogether satisfactory to the detective. Though he used all his skill in his manipulation of this kind-hearted ferryman, he got very little from him but the plain fact that the woman insisted upon taking to the road when she heard that the train-service had stopped; that he could not persuade her to wait till daylight or to listen for a moment to what he had to say of the danger and terrors awaiting her in the darkness, and the awful loneliness of the hills. She didn't fear nature even at its worst, and she knew these hills better than many who had lived among them for years. She was bound to go, and she went.

This was six hours ago. Asked to explain the interest he had shown in her, it soon became evident that he was in complete ignorance of her identity. He had simply, on their first trip over, seen that she was middle-aged, suffering and much too good and kind to be followed up by enemies and wicked police officials. True, he had rowed them over in her pursuit in the early part of the day, but that was because he had not known their business. When on returning he had learned it, he made up his mind to help her out with a warning even if it kept him up all night. He had not expected to bring her back with him, but she had insisted upon his doing so, saying that she had friends in the mountains who would look after her. He saw that she was dreadfully in earnest, for she had not stopped to get her hat and would not have had so much as an extra stitch with her if she had not taken the precaution to hide a bag of things somewhere in the bushes near the factory, in anticipation of some such emergency. And he couldn't resist her. She made him think of a sister of his who had had a dreadful time of it in the world and was now well out of it, thank God!

When the ferryman heard that a reward of hundreds of dollars was waiting for the man who succeeded in bringing her before the police officials in New York, he betrayed some chagrin, but even this did not last. He was soon declaring with heartfelt earnestness that he didn't care anything about that. It was peace of mind he wanted, and not money.

When Mr. Gryce left him, it was with an even slower step than usual. Peace of mind! How about his own peace of mind? Was he trailing this poor unfortunate from pillar to post, for the reward it would bring him? No. With his advancing years money had lost much of its attraction. Nor, if he knew himself, was he particularly affected by the glory which attends success. Duty, and duty only, drove him on—to elucidate his problem and merit the confidence put in him by his superiors. If suffering followed, that was not his fault; his business was to go ahead.

It was in this frame of mind that he prepared himself for the automobile trip he saw before him.

There was no question in Mr. Gryce's mind now, as to this woman's destination or whither he should be obliged to go in order to find her. As he now saw into her mind, she had left New York with the intention of hiding herself in the remote village to which she had ordered her mail sent under the name of Elvira Brown, whom she evidently knew; but hearing, either on the car or in the hotel, where she was detained, the plea which was being made for workers in the factory on the east side of the river, she had modified her plans to the extent already known, only to return to her original intention as soon as the attempt to provide for herself in this independent way had proved a failure.

He would proceed then in her wake, conscious of the fresh disappointment which awaited her in the loss, through Miss Brown's sudden death, of the asylum she counted upon. Could he have gone on foot like herself, he might have been tempted to do so, for a trail is best followed slowly and with ear and eye very close to the ground. But as this was beyond his strength, he must wait till an automobile could be procured, and possibly till Sweetwater should arrive—for Perry was no man for this job. There were no automobiles in this small town, and it might be necessary to send up or down the river some distance before one could be found capable of carrying them over the precipitous road they would be obliged to take in order to avoid the washout which had driven them to this extremity.

But all would come right in time; and with Sweetwater at his elbow, the journey would be made and the woman caught, soon enough for him no doubt, hard as he felt it to wait. Why so hard, he might have found it difficult to say, since hitherto he had found it easy enough when the goal seemed sure and it was only with time he had to reckon!

XXV

TERROR

A woman fleeing from publicity as one flies from death—a refined woman, too, whose life had hitherto been passed in the open!

When Antoinette Duclos, after a night and morning of unprecedented fatigue and extraordinary fears, with little to upbear her in the way of food, stepped from the train which brought a few local passengers into the quiet village of Rexam, she hardly would have been recognized by her best friend, such marks may a few hours leave upon one battling with untoward Fate in one supreme effort.

She seemed to realize this, for meeting more than one eye fixed inquiringly upon her she drew down the veil wound about a sort of cap she wore till it concealed not only her features but her throat which a restless pulse had tightened almost to the exclusion of her breath. Ready to drop, she yet made use of the little energy left her, to approach with faltering steps a lumbering old vehicle waiting in the dust and smoke for such passengers as might wish to be taken up Long Hill.

There was no driver in sight, but she did not hesitate to take her seat inside. There was extra business at the station, for this was the first train to come in for two days; and if anyone noticed her in the shadowy recesses of the cumbrous old coach, nobody approached her; nor was she in any way disturbed. When the driver did show himself, she was almost asleep, but she woke up quickly enough when his good-natured face peered in at her and she heard him ask where she wanted to go and whether she had any baggage.

"I want to go up Long Hill and be set down at the first cross-road," she said. "My baggage is here." And she pointed to the space at her feet. But that space was empty; she had no baggage. She had dropped both bag and umbrella at the side of the road after one of her long climbs under a fitful moon and had not so much as thought of them since.

Now she remembered and flushed as she met the eyes of the man looking in at her with his hand on his whiskers, smoothing them thoughtfully down but saying nothing, though his countenance and expression showed him to be one of the loquacious sort. If any smiles remained to her from the old days, now was the time for one; but before she could twist her dry lips into any such attempt, he had uttered a cheerful "All right" and turned away to clamber up into his seat.

The relief was great, and she settled back, rejoicing in the fact that they would soon be moving and that she was likely to be the sole passenger. But she soon came to rue this fact, for the driver wanted to talk and even made many abortive attempts that way. But she could not fall in with his mood, and seeing this, he soon withheld all remarks and bent his full energies to the task of urging his horses up the interminable incline.

Houses, at which she scarcely looked, disappeared gradually from view, and groups of spreading trees and patches of upland took their places, deepening into the forest as they advanced. When halfway up, the farther mountains, which had hitherto been hidden by nearer hills, burst into view. Behind them the sun was setting, and the scene was glorious. If she saw it at all, she gave no sign of pleasure or even of admiration. Her head, which she had held straight up for the first quarter of a mile, sank lower and lower as they clambered on; yet she gave no signs of drowsiness—only of a mortal weariness which seemed to attack the very springs of life. The pomp and pageantry of the heavens, burning with all the pigments of the rainbow, failed to appeal to a soul shut within dungeon bars. Rocks and mighty gorges darkling to the eye and stirring to the imagination held no story for her; she looked neither to the right nor to the left while the beauty lasted, much less when the last gleam had faded from the mountain tops and a troop of leaden clouds, coming up from the east, added their shadows to those of premature night.

The driver, who had been eying these clouds for some little time, felt that he ought to speak if she did not. Pulling up his horses as though to give them a breathing spell, he remarked over his shoulder with a strain of anxiety in his voice:

"I hope your friends live near the top of the hill, missus. A storm is coming up, and it's getting very dark. Will you have to walk far?"

"No, no," she assured him with a quick glance up and around her. "A little way, a very little way!" Then she became quiet and absorbed again.

"I've got to go on," he broke in again as the top of the hill came in sight. "I've a passenger for the eight-fifty train waiting for me more than a mile along the road. I shall have to leave you after I set you down."

"That's right; I expect that. I can take care of myself—don't worry. Not but what you're very kind," she added after a moment, in her cultured voice, with just enough trace of accent to make it linger sweetly in the ear.

"Then here we are," he called back a moment later, jerking his horses to a standstill and jumping down into the road. "Goin' east or goin' west?" he asked as he took another glance at her frail and poorly protected figure.

"This way," she answered, pointing east.

He stopped and stared at her.

"Nobody lives that way," he said, "—that is, nobody near enough for you to reach shelter before the storm bursts."

"You are mistaken," she said, cringing involuntarily as the first big clap of thunder rolled in endless echoes among the mountains. And turning about, she started hurriedly into the shadows of the narrow cross-road.

He gave one glance back at his horses, the twitching of whose ears showed nervousness, uttered some familiar word and launched out after the woman. "Pardon me, missus," he cried, "but is it Miss Brown's you mean?"

The widow stopped, glanced back at him over her shoulder, made a quick, protesting gesture and dashed on.

With a shake of his head and a muttered, "Well, women do beat the devil!" he retraced his steps; and she proceeded on alone.

As the last sound of his horses' hoof-beats died out on the road, a second clap of thunder seemed to bring heaven and earth together. She scarcely looked up. She was approaching a little weather-beaten house nestled among trees on the edge of a deep gorge. As her eyes fell on it, her footsteps quickened, and lifting a hasty hand, she pulled off her veil. A change quite indescribable, but real for all that, had taken place in her worn and waxen features. Not joy, but a soft expectancy relieved them from their extreme tension. If a friend awaited her, that friend would have no difficulty in recognizing her now. But alas!

A few steps more, and she stood before the door. It had a desolate look; the whole house had a desolate look, possibly because every shade was drawn. But she did not notice this; she was too sure of her welcome. Raising her hand to the knocker, she gave two sharp raps. Then she waited. No answer from within—no sound of hurrying steps—only another rumble in the sky and a quick rustling of the trees on either side of her as if the wind which made the horizon black had sent an *avant-courieur* over the hill-tops.

"Elvira is out—gone to some church meeting or social gathering down in the village. She will be back. But I won't wait. I will try and get in in the old way. The storm may delay her indefinitely."

Leaving the door, which was raised only two steps above the road, she walked to the corner of the house and stooping down, felt behind a projecting stone for what she had certainly expected to find there—a key to the front door.

But her hand came away empty.

Surprised, for this was not her first visit to this house (she had once spent weeks there and knew the habits of its mistress well), she felt again in the place where the key should be, and where she had so often found it when her friend was out. But all to no avail. It was not there, and presently she was in the road again staring at the closed-up front.

As she did so, these words left her lips:

"And she knew I might come at any minute!"

Tottering from fatigue, she caught at the trunk of a great tree which held roof and wall in its embrace.

Why did it quiver? Why did the ground beneath her feet seem to rock and all nature darken as with the falling of a pall. The storm was upon her. It had rolled up with incredible swiftness and was about to break over her head. With a shock she realized her position. No shelter, and the storm of the season upon her! What should she do? There was no way of getting into the house at the rear, for the bushes were too thick. She must accept her fate, be drenched to the skin, perhaps smitten by the next thunderbolt. But Antoinette Duclos was no coward, so far as physical ills were concerned. She drew herself up straight against the trunk of the tree, thinking that this, bad as it was, was better than shelter with the enemy at the door. She would be calm, and she was fast growing so when she suddenly became aware of a man standing very near and hunting her out through the dusk.

She never knew why the scream which rose in her throat did not pass her lips. Her terror was unspeakable, for she had heard no advance; indeed, there was too much noise about her for that. But it was the silent terror of despair, for she thought it was the man from whom she had made this great effort at escape. But he soon proved to her he was not. It was just the driver of the stagecoach, returned to see what had become of her. He had feared to find her stricken down in the road, and when he saw her clinging alone and in a maddened way to this tree, he made no bones of speaking to her with all necessary plainness.

"I asked you if it was Missus Brown you had come to see," he called to her through the din. "And you wouldn't answer."

"Why should I?" she shouted back. "Why do you speak like that? Has anything happened to her?"

"Don't you know?"

"No, no—she was well when I heard from her last, and expecting me, or so she wrote. Is she—she—"

"Dead, missus. We buried her last Tuesday. I'm sorry, but—"

Why finish? She was lying out before him, straight and stark in the road. A bolt of lightning which at that moment tore its way through the heavens brought into startling view her face, white with distraction, framed in a mass of iron-gray locks released by her fall.

"Good heaven!" burst from the lips of the frightened man as he stooped to lift her. "What am I going to do now?"

The thunder answered him, or rather it robbed him for the moment of all thought. Peal after peal rattled over the neighboring peaks, rocking the air on the uplands and filling his soul with dismay. But when quiet had come again, hope returned with it. She was not only standing upright but was crying in his ear:

"Can I get into the house? If I could stay there tonight, I could go back tomorrow."

"I'll see that you get in, if I have to break in a window," he answered. "But you're sure that you will not be afraid to stay out this terrible storm in a house with no neighbors within half a mile?"

"I know the house. I have been here before, and if Elvira Brown could face the storms of forty years from her solitary home, I can surely face a single one, without losing my courage."

He said no more, but approaching the house, began to test such windows as he could reach. He finally broke in a pane and released the latch; after that, entrance was easy.

Yet after he had opened the way for her and she had stepped into the dim interior, he felt loth to leave her. Duty called him away. The passenger awaiting him up the road was a man he could not afford to disappoint; yet he stood there longer than the occasion warranted, with the knob of the door in hand, watching her struggle with the lamp, which she at last succeeded in lighting. As the walls of the hall and her anxiously bending figure burst into view, he uttered a quick "Good-by!"

She turned, smiled and tried to thank him, but the words failed to leave her lips. A nearer and fiercer bolt had shot to earth at that instant, striking a tree so near that the noise of its fall mingled with the crash of the heavens. When it had ceased, he had gone. He could not face the look with which she met this new catastrophe.

That look never again left her. When she saw herself in a glass, as she presently did, on entering one of the rooms lamp in hand, she was startled and muttered:

"My own mother would pass me by if she saw me now. I could go anywhere I wished without fear or dread. Why did I leave New York?" And setting the lamp down, she covered her face and wept.

The storm abated; a few minutes of fiercely pouring rain, and all was over. She was left in ghastly quiet—a quiet which was almost worse than the turmoil which had preceded it—to face her memories and accustom herself to the thought that the solitary woman with whose life everything she looked upon was so intimately connected was gone, never to pass through these doors again or touch with deft and careful fingers the infinite number of little belongings with which the house was filled.

For as yet nothing had been changed, nothing had been moved. How fitting this was, Antoinette knew better than anybody else, perhaps, for she was the only person whom Elvira Brown had ever allowed to spend any length of time with her, and she could remember—alas! how vividly, in spite of the one great fear forever gnawing at her heart—that an article, no matter how small, when once given place in this house, held that place always till broken or in some other way robbed of its usefulness. She looked at her friend's pet chair standing just in the one spot where she had seen it eight years before, and her heart swelled, and a tear rose in her eye. But there was not time for another. A sense of the straits in which she found herself placed by the death of this dependable friend returned upon her in full force; the past retired into its old place, and the present, with its maddening problems, seized upon her nerve and quelled her once indomitable spirit.

The fate which had pursued her ever since she had left her happy home in France had not spared her at this crisis. The storm, of so little consequence to her, had roused the driver's sympathy. This had not only fixed her image in his mind but given away her destination. All hope of hiding herself among the mountains was therefore gone. She would have to move on; but where? If she were but able to leave now, she might before morning find some covert from which help might be given her for further escape. But the condition of the roads, as well as her own weakness, forbade that. She needed food: she needed sleep. Of food she would find plenty, she was sure; but sleep! How could she sleep, with the promise of the morrow before her? Yet she must; everything depended upon her strength. How could she win that rest which alone would secure it.

Pausing in the midst of the hall whither her restless thought had driven her, she stared in a fruitless inquiry at the wall confronting her. Her mind, like her feet, was at a standstill. She could neither think nor act. In fact, she was at the point of a nervous collapse, when slowly from out the void there rose to her view and pierced its way into her mind the outline of the door upon which she had been steadily looking but without seeing it till now. Why did she start as it thus took on shape before her? There was nothing strange or mysterious about it. It led nowhere; it hid nothing, unless it was the yard upon which it directly opened.

But that yard! She remembered it well. It was unlike any other she had ever seen in this country or her own. It was small and semicircular; it was shut in by a high board fence except at the extreme end, where it was met by a swinging bridge topping a forty-foot chasm. That bridge led through a sparsely wooded forest to a road running in a quite different direction from the one by which the house was approached. As she strove to recall her memories of it, she became more and more assured that her one and only opportunity for a successful flight lay that way. Moved to joy at the thought, she bowed her head for one wild moment in heartfelt thankfulness and then quickly drew the bolts of the door which offered her this happy deliverance.

She did not mean to seek escape tonight, but an irresistible impulse, which quite robbed her of her judgment, drove her to take a look into the yard and make sure for herself that the bridge was still there and everything as she had last seen it.

But when with the help of the wind she pulled open the heavy door and stood, throbbing under the force of the gale, on the shallow step outside, she found herself confronted by a darkness so hollow and so absolute that she felt as though she had stumbled into a pit. But instead of retreating, if only to procure a lantern, she took the one step down to the narrow walk which led through grass and flowers to the edge of the plateau from which the bridge extended. Would she be satisfied now? No, she must see the bridge, or if she could not see it, must feel it with her foot or touch it with her hand. Once sure of its presence there, she would return, take off her clothing and seek refreshment.

But how was she to find her way in such absolute darkness? Alone with the dying tempest, now moaning in fitful gusts, now shrieking a last protest in her ear, she stood peering helplessly before her. Already her arms had gone out like those of a blind person loosed upon an unknown road. She was conscious of a great fear. All the solitude of her position had rushed upon her. She felt herself lost, forsaken; yet she had no idea of turning back. If she could but find some support—something upon which to lay her fingers. She thought of the fence, and her courage revived. If she could but reach and follow that!

There were obstacles in her way. She was sure of this, for she remembered some of them, and Elvira no more changed her garden than her house. But with care she succeeded in getting around these, and soon she knew by the lessened force of the wind that she was near, if not directly under, the high fence upon which she depended for guidance. A few bushes—another unexpected obstacle, followed by a bad stumble—separated her from the contact for which she had reached; then by a final effort her fingers found the boards and she went eagerly on, dragging herself through the wet without knowing it, and only stopping with a sense of shock, when her hand, sliding from the boards, fell groping about in midair with nothing to grasp at. She had come to the end of the fence and was within a foot of the bridge—if the bridge was still there.

But her fears on this score were few, and she felt about with hand and foot till the former struck the rail at her side, and the latter the narrow planking spanning the gorge.

She hesitated now. Who would not? But the impulse which had led her thus far continued to urge her on. She stepped upon the bridge and proceeded to cross it, clinging to the rail with a feverish clutch, and feeling every board with her foot before venturing to trust her full weight upon it. She found them seemingly firm, and when about halfway across she stopped to listen for the roar of the mountain stream which she knew to be rushing over its rocky bed some forty awesome feet below her.

She heard it, but the swish of the trees lining the gorge was in her straining ears and half drowned its sullen sound. With feelings impossible to describe, she tossed up her arms to the skies, where a single brilliant star was looking through the mass of quickly flying, quickly disintegrating clouds. Then she sought again the safety of the guiding rail, and clinging desperately to it, took one more step and stopped with a smothered shriek. The rail had snapped under her hand and had gone tumbling down into the abyss. She heard it as it struck, or thought she did, and for a moment stood breathless and fearing to move, the world and all it held vanishing in semi-unconsciousness from heart and mind. What was she but a trembling atom floating in an unknown void on the fathomless sea of eternity! Then, as her mind steadied, she began to feel once more the boards under her feet, and to hear the smiting together of the great limbs wrestling in the depths of the forest. She even caught such a homely sound as the violent slamming of the door she had left unlatched behind her; and summoning up all her courage, which was not small when she was released from her first surprise, she stepped firmly backward till she felt the rail strong again under her clutch. Then she turned resolutely and retraced her steps along the bridge and so across the plateau to the house whose light had acted as a beacon to her whenever the door blew wide enough to let the one inner beam be seen.

When she was inside again, she lingered for a long time in the darkening hall, her slight form and whitened head leaning against the wall in a desolation such as few hearts know. Then something within the woman flared up in a rekindled flame, and she passed quickly into the room where she had left her lamp burning; and blowing it out, she threw herself down on a couch and tried to sleep.

An hour later the moon shone in upon her pale features and wild, staring eyes upturned to meet it. Then it vanished, and she and the whole house were given up again to darkness.

She had forgotten to eat, though the cupboards, in this well-stored house, were quite full.

XXVI

THE FACE IN THE WINDOW

"Is this the place?"

"According to our instructions, yes. The first house after the first turn to the right. We took the first turn, and this is the first house. Romantic situation, eh? But a bit lonesome for a city chap? Shall I help you down?"

While talking, Sweetwater, who was already in the road, held up his elbow to Mr. Gryce, who slowly descended. It was early morning, and the glory of sunshine was everywhere misleading the eye from the ravages of the night before; yet neither of these two men wore an air in keeping with the freshness of renewed life and the joyous aspect of exultant nature. There seemed to be an oppression upon them both—a hesitation not common to either, and to all appearance without cause.

To end what he probably considered a weakness, Sweetwater approached the door staring somewhat blankly from the flat front of the primitive old house whose privacy they were about to invade, and rapped on its weather-beaten panels, first gently and then with quick insistence.

There was no response from within; no sound of movement; no token that he had been so much as heard. Sweetwater turned and consulted his companion before making another attempt.

"It's early. Perhaps she's not up yet," rejoined the old detective as he painfully advanced. The storm of the preceding night had got into his bones.

"I don't know. There's something uncanny about this silence. She ought to be here; but I'm afraid she isn't." Sweetwater rapped again, this time with decided vehemence.

Suddenly in one of the uncurtained windows a face appeared. They saw it, and both drew a deep breath. The eyes were looking their way, but they were like ghost's eyes. Without sight or speculation in them, they simply looked; then the face slowly withdrew, growing ghastlier every minute, and the window stared on, but the woman was gone. Yet the door did not open.

"I hate to use force," objected Sweetwater.

Before answering, Mr. Gryce stepped to one side and cast a glance around the corner of the house in the direction of the gorge opening in the rear.

"There is something like a yard at the back," he announced,

"but the fence which shut it in is so high and so protected by means of prickly underbrush that you would have difficulty in climbing it."

"Just so at this end," called out Sweetwater after a short run to the left. "If we get in at all," he remarked on coming back, "it will have to be by the window you see there with one pane knocked out."

"I don't like that; I don't like any of it. But we can't stay out here any longer. The looks of the woman herself forbid it. We sha'n't forget that hollow stare."

"They said the woman who lived here was dead."

"Yes. It's a bad business, Sweetwater. Rap once more, and then if she doesn't come, throw up the window and climb in."

Sweetwater did as he was bid, and meeting with no more response than before, thrust his hand through the hole made by the broken pane; and finding the window had been left unlocked, he pushed it up and entered. In another moment he appeared at the front door, where Mr. Gryce joined him, and together they took their first look at the small but surprisingly well-furnished interior.

The hall in which they stood was without staircase and had many of the appointments of a room. Doors opened here and there along its length, and in the rear they saw a closed one evidently leading into the yard. There was no one within sight. One would have said that with the death and carrying out of the owner of this little dwelling, all life had departed from it. Yet these two men knew that life was there; and raising his voice, Mr. Gryce called out in the least alarming way possible:

"Madame Duclos!" following this utterance of her name with an apology for the intrusion and a prayer for one minute's interview.

Silence was his answer—no stir anywhere.

Apprehensive of they knew not what, the two detectives started simultaneously, one for the door on their right, the other for that on the left. When they met again in the ill-lighted hall, Mr. Gryce was shaking his head, but Sweetwater had lifted a beckoning finger. Unconsciously moderating his step, Mr. Gryce followed him through one room to the door of another which he saw standing partly open.

Through the crack thus made between the hinges, they could get a very fair glimpse of what was going on inside. They saw a bed, and a woman kneeling beside this bed, her eyes upraised in prayer. The look which had awed them at the window was gone, and in its place was one so high and so full of religious faith that for an instant they were conscious of the reversal of all their ideas.

But only for an instant; for while they waited, hesitating to break in upon her evidently sincere devotions, she started to her feet and with a half-insane look about her, disappeared from their view in the direction of the hall.

Sweetwater was after her in a twinkling; but by the time he and Mr. Gryce, each going his separate way, had themselves reached the hall, it was to see the end door—the one giving upon the plateau—closing behind her.

"Madame!" called out Sweetwater, bounding briskly in her wake.

Mr. Gryce said nothing but approached with hastening steps the door which Sweetwater had left open behind him, and took a quick survey of the fenced-in plateau, the bridge and the towering trees beyond, toward which she seemed to be making.

"She cannot escape," was his ready conclusion; and he shouted to Sweetwater to go easy.

Sweetwater, who was in the act of setting foot upon the bridge down which she was running, slacked up at this command and presently stopped, for she had stopped herself and was looking back from a spot about halfway across, with the air of one willing, at last, to hear what they had to say.

"Who are you?" she cried. "And what do you want of me?"

"Are you not Madame Duclos?"

"Yes, I am Antoinette Duclos."

"Then you must know why you are wanted by the police authorities of New York. Your daughter—"

Her hand went up.

"I've nothing to say—nothing. Will you take that for your answer and let me go?"

"Alas, madam, we cannot!" spoke up Mr. Gryce in his calm, benevolent way. "Miss Duclos' death was of a nature demanding an inquest. Your testimony, hard as it may be for you to give it, is necessary for a righteous verdict. That is all we want—"

"It is too much!" she cried. And with a quick glance upward she took another step or two along the bridge till she had reached the broken rail; and before Sweetwater in his dismay could more than give a horrified bound in her direction, she had made the fatal leap and was gone from their sight into the gorge below.

BOOK IV
NEMESIS

XXVII

FROM LIPS LONG SILENT

"This finishes my usefulness as a detective. I have had my fill of horrors; all, in fact, that my old age can stand."

Thus, Mr. Gryce, as hours afterward he and Sweetwater turned their faces back toward New York.

"I appreciate your feelings," responded the latter, who had been strangely silent all day, speaking only when directly addressed. "I can assure you that in my way I'm as much cut up as you are. I wish now that I had made an attempt from the rear to head off this distracted woman, even if I had been obliged to scratch my hands to pieces tearing a board from the fence."

"It would have done no good. She was determined to die rather than give up her secret. I remember the look with which her sister-in-law warned me that she would never survive a capture. But I thought that mere exaggeration."

Then after a moment of conscious silence on the part of both, the weary old man added with bitter emphasis, "Her testimony might—I do not say would—have cleared away our suspicions of Director Roberts."

Sweetwater, who was acting as chauffeur, slowed down his machine till it came to a standstill at the side of the road. Then wheeling quietly about till he faced his surprised companion, he remarked very gravely:

"Mr. Gryce, I hadn't the heart to tell you this before, but the time has come for you to know that Mr. Roberts' cause is not so favorably affected, as you seem to think, by this suicidal death of one who without doubt would have proved to be a leading witness against him. I am sure you will agree with me in this when I inform you that in pursuing the task you set me, I came upon *this*."

Thrusting his hand into his pocket, he pulled out a large envelope from which he proceeded to draw forth first the tattered square of what had once been a cabinet portrait, and then a freshly printed proof of the same. Holding them both up, he waited for the word that was sure to follow.

It came with all the emphasis he expected.

"Roberts! Director Roberts!"

"The same, sir"; and the eyes of the two detectives met in what was certainly one of the most solemn moments of their lives.

They had paused for this short conference at a point where

the road running for a few yards on a level gave them a view of slope on slope of varying verdure, with glimpses of the Hudson between. Glancing up, with a gesture of manifest shrinking from the portrait which Sweetwater still held, Mr. Gryce allowed his glance to run over the wonderful landscape laid out to his view, and said with breaks and halts bespeaking his deep emotion:

"If my death here and now, following fast upon that of this unhappy Frenchwoman, would avail to wipe out the evidence I have so laboriously collected against this man, I should welcome it with gratitude. I shrink from ending my career with the shattering of so fine an image, in the public eye. What lies back of this crime—what past memories or present miseries have led to an act which would be called dastardly in the most uninstructed and basest of our sex, I lack the imagination to conceive. Would to God I had never tried to find out! But no man standing where Roberts does today among the leaders of a great party can fall into such a pit of shame without weakening the faith of the young and making a travesty of virtue and honor."

"Yet, if he is guilty—"

"It is our business to pursue him to the end. Only, I like the man, Sweetwater. I had a long talk with him yesterday on indifferent matters and I came away liking him."

This was certainly something Sweetwater had not expected to hear, and it threw him again into silence as he started up the machine and they pursued their course home.

Hard as the day had been for Mr. Gryce, its trials were not yet over. He had left it to Sweetwater to report the case to the New York authorities and had gone home to rest from the shock of the occurrence and to prepare for that interview with the Chief Inspector which he was satisfied would now lead to an even more exacting one with the District Attorney.

He was met by a messenger from downtown who handed him a letter. He opened it abstractedly and read the following:

"Mrs. Taylor is talking."

He had forgotten Mrs. Taylor. To have her thus brought forcibly back to mind was a shock heightened, rather than diminished, by a perusal of the few connected words which the careful nurse had transcribed as falling from her delirious patient's lips.

They were these:

> I love but thee,
> And thee will I love to eternity.

The exact lines, no more, no less, which Sweetwater had found written on the back of the Swiss clock cherished by Mr. Roberts.

XXVIII

"ROMANTIC! TOO ROMANTIC!"

Next morning Mr. Gryce left his home an hour earlier than usual. He wished to have a talk with Mrs. Taylor's nurse before encountering the Inspector.

It was an inconvenient time for a nurse to leave the sick-bed; but the matter being so important, she was prevailed upon to give him a few moments, in the little reception room where he had seated himself. The result was meagre—that is, from her standpoint. All she had to add to what she had written him the day before was the fact that the two lines of verse quoted in the note she had sent him were Mrs. Taylor's first coherent utterance, and that they had been spoken not only once but many times, in every kind of tone, and with ever-varying emphasis. That and a dreamy request for "The papers! the papers!" which had followed some action of her own this very morning comprised all she had to give in fulfillment of the promise she had made him at the beginning of this illness.

Mr. Gryce believed her and rose reluctantly to his feet.

"Then she is still very ill?"

"Very ill, but mending daily; or so the doctor says."

"If she talks again, as she is liable to do at any moment, do not check her, but remember every word. The importance of this I cannot impress upon you too fully. But do not by any show of curiosity endanger her recovery. She seems to be one of the very best sort; I would not have her body or mind sacrificed on any account."

"You may trust me, sir."

He nodded, giving her his hand.

But as he was turning away, he looked back with the quiet remark: "I should like to ask a final question. You have been in constant attendance on this lady for some time and must have seen many of her friends, as well as taken charge of her mail and of any messages which may have been left for her. Has there been anything in this experience to settle the doubt as to whether her talk of a vision in which she saw her absent husband stricken simultaneously with the poor child lying at that very moment dead at her feet simply delirium or a striking instance of telepathy recording an accomplished fact? In other words, do you believe her husband to be living or not living at the present time?"

"That is a subject upon which I have not been able to form any opinion. I have heard nothing, seen nothing to influence my mind either way. Some other people have asked me this same question. If her mail contains any news, it is still in the hands of the proprietor of the hotel. He has refrained from sending it up. She has lived here, as you know, for a long while."

"Has she no relative to share your watch or take such things in charge?"

"I have seen none. Friends she has in plenty, but no one who claims relationship with her, or who raises the least objection to anything I do."

He seemed about to ask another question, but refrained and allowed her to depart after some final injunction as to what she should do in case of certain emergencies. Then he had a talk with the proprietor, which added little or nothing to his present knowledge; and these duties off his mind, he went downtown.

As he expected, he found the Chief Inspector awaiting him. The death of Madame Duclos had added still another serious complication to the many with which this difficult affair was already encumbered, and he was anxious to talk over the matter with one who had been on the spot and upon whose impressions he consequently could rely.

But when he heard all that Mr. Gryce had to say on the subject, he grew as serious as the detective himself could wish, even going so far as to propose an immediate ride over to the District Attorney's office.

Fortunately, they found that gentleman in and ready to listen, though it was evident he expected little from the conference. But his temper changed as Mr. Gryce opened up his theory and began to substantiate it with facts. The looks which he exchanged with the Chief Inspector grew more and more earnest and inquiring, and when Mr. Gryce reached that portion of his report which connected Mr. Roberts so indisputably with the arrow, he called in his assistant and together they listened to what Mr. Gryce had further to say.

With this addition to his audience, the old man's manner changed and became a trifle more formal. He related the fact, not generally known, of Mr. Roberts' engagement to a young girl residing on Long Island, and how this was broken off immediately after the occurrence at the museum, seemingly from no other reason than the unhappy condition of mind in which he found himself, a condition added to if not explained by the pertinacity with which he had haunted the morgue and dwelt upon the image of the young girl who had perished under no random shot.

Here the old man paused, shrinking as much from what he had yet to say as they from the hearing of it. It was not till the Chief Inspector had made him an encouraging gesture that he found the requisite courage to proceed. He did so, in these words:

"I know that the evidence I have thus far advanced is of a purely circumstantial nature, capable, perhaps, of a more or less satisfactory explanation. But what I have to add cannot be so easily disposed of. Connections have developed between persons we thought strangers which have opened up a field of inquiry which brings the doubts and surmises of an old detective within the scope of this office. I do not know what to make of them; perhaps their full meaning can only be found out here. Of this only I am assured. The gentleman whom it seems presumptuous on my part to connect even in a casual way with crime has not gained but lost by what I have to tell of Madame Duclos' suicidal death. To those who see no association between the two, it looks like the opening of a new lead, but when I tell you that they knew each other, or at all events that she knew him and in the way of actual hatred, it looks more like a deepening of the old one. See here, gentlemen."

Opening a package he had hitherto held in hand, he showed them Fredericks' fifteen-year-old photograph of Mr. Roberts, together with its mutilated counterpart, and explained how the latter came to be in its present mutilated condition.

"But this is not all," he continued, as the remarks incident upon this proof of deadly hatred on the part of the mother of the victim for the man whom circumstances seemed to point out as her slayer subsided under the pressure of their interest in what he had further to impart. "As you will see after a moment's consideration, this token of animosity does not explain Madame Duclos' flight, and certainly not her death, which, as the unhappy witness of it, I am ready to declare was not the death of one driven to extremity from personal fear, but by some exalted feeling which we have yet to understand. All that I now wish to point out in its connection is the proof offered by this shattered photograph, that Mr. Roberts was in some manner and from some cause a party to this crime from which a superficial observation would completely dissociate him.

"Where is the connecting link? How can we hope to establish it? That is what it has now become my unfortunate duty to make plain to you. Carleton Roberts drawing a bow to shoot an innocent schoolgirl is incredible. In spite of all I have said and shown you, I do not believe him guilty of so inhuman an act. He drew the bow, he shot the arrow, but—Here allow me to pause a moment to present another aspect of the case as surprising as any you have yet heard. You are aware—we all are aware—that the inquest we await has been held back for the purpose of giving Mrs. Taylor an opportunity to recover from the illness into which she has been thrown by what she saw and suffered that day. Gentlemen, this Mrs. Taylor whom we all—I will not even exclude myself from this category—regarded not only as a casual visitor to the museum, but a stranger to all concerned, is, on the contrary, as I think you will soon see, more closely allied to the seemingly dispassionate director than even Madame Duclos. The shock which laid her low was not that usually ascribed to her, or even the one she so fantastically offered to our acceptance; but the recognition of Carleton Roberts as the author of this tragedy,—Carleton Roberts whom she not only knew well but had loved in days gone by, as sincerely as he had loved her. This I now propose to prove to you by what I cannot but regard as incontestable evidence."

Taking from a small portfolio which he carried another photograph, unmounted this time and evidently the work of an amateur, he laid it out before them. The silence with which his last statement had been received, the kind of silence which covers emotions too deep for audible expression, remained unbroken save for an involuntary murmur or so, as the District Attorney and his assistant bent over this crude presentation of something—they hardly knew what—which this old but long trusted detective was offering them in substantiation of the well-nigh unbelievable statement he had just made.

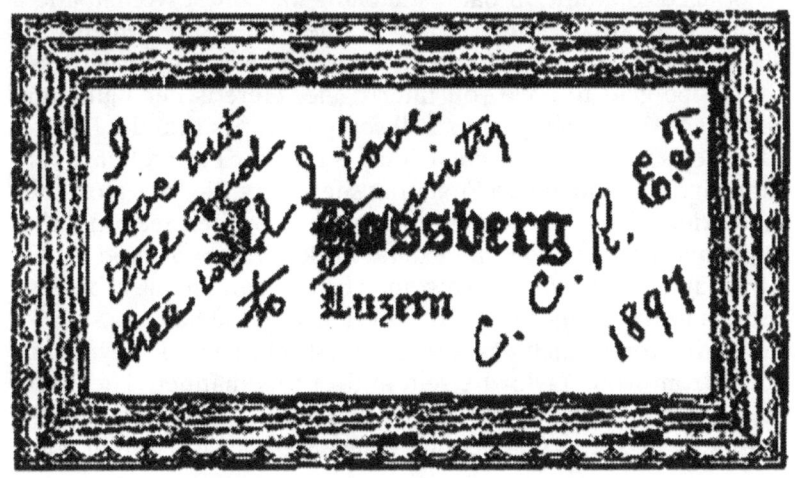

"This, gentlemen," he went on, as he pointed to the following, "is the copy of a label pasted on the back of a certain Swiss clock to be seen at this very moment on the wall of Mr. Roberts' own bedroom in his home in Belport, Long Island. He prizes this clock. He has been heard to say that it goes where he goes and stays where he stays, and as it is far from a valuable one either from intrinsic worth or from any accuracy it displays in keeping time, the reason for this partiality must lie in old associations and the memories they invoke. A love token. Can you not see that it is such from the couplet scrawled across it? If not, just take a look at the initials appended to that couplet. May I ask you to read them?"

The District Attorney stooped, adjusted his glasses and slowly read out:

"C. C. R."

"Carleton Clifton Roberts," explained Mr. Gryce. Then slowly, "The other two if you will be so good."

"E. T."

"Ermentrude Taylor," declared the inexorable voice. "And written by herself. Here is her signature which I have obtained; and here is his. Compare them at your leisure with their initials inscribed according to the date there, sixteen years or more ago. Now where were these two—this man and this woman—at the time just designated? Alone, or together? Let us see if we can find out," pursued the detective with a quiet ignoring of the effect he had produced, which revealed him as the master of a situation probably as difficult and disconcerting as the three officials hanging in manifest anxiety upon his words had ever been called upon to face. "Mr. Roberts was in Switzerland, as his housekeeper will be obliged to admit on oath, she being an honest woman and a domestic in his mother's house at the time. And Ermentrude Taylor! I have a witness to prove where she was also! A witness I should be glad to have you interrogate. Here is her name and address." And he slipped a small scrap of paper into the District Attorney's hand. "What she will say is this, for I think I have very thoroughly sounded her: First, that she is Mrs. Taylor's most intimate friend. This is conceded by all who know her. Secondly, that while her intimacy does not extend back to their girlhood days— Mrs. Taylor being an Englishwoman by birth and remarkably reticent as to her former life and experiences—she has one story to tell of that time which answers the question I have given you. She got it from Mrs. Taylor herself, and in this manner. They were engaged in talking one day about our Western mountains and the grandeur of scenery generally, when Mrs. Taylor let fall some remark about the Alps, which led this friend of hers to ask if she had ever seen them. Mrs. Taylor answered in the affirmative, but with such embarrassment and abrupt change of subject that it was plainly apparent she had no wish to discuss it. Indeed, her abruptness was so marked and her show of trouble so great, she was herself disturbed by what might very easily give offense, and being of a kindly, even loving disposition, took occasion when next they met to explain that it was as a girl she had visited Switzerland, and that her experiences there had been so unfortunate that any allusion which recalled those days distressed her. This is all that ever passed between these two on this subject, but is it not enough when we read this couplet, and mark the combined initials, and recognize them as those of Carleton Roberts and Ermentrude Taylor? But lest you should doubt even this evidence of an old-time friendship so intimate that it has almost the look of a betrothal, I must add one more item of corroborative fact which came to me as late as last night. In a moment of partial consciousness, while the nurse hung over her bed, Mrs. Taylor spoke her first coherent sentence since she fell into a state demanding medical assistance. And what was that sentence? A repetition of this couplet, gentlemen, spoken not once but over and over again, till even the nurse grew tired of listening to it.

'I love but thee,
And thee will I love to eternity.'"

As the last word fell from Mr. Gryce's lips, the District Attorney muttered a quick exclamation, and sat down heavily in his chair.

"No coincidence that," he cried, with forced vivacity. "The couplet is too little known."

"Exactly," came from Mr. Gryce in dry confirmation. "Mrs. Taylor, as well as her friends can judge, is a woman of thirty-five or thirty-eight. If she went to Switzerland as a girl, this would make her visit coincident, so far as we can calculate from our present knowledge, with that of Carleton Roberts. For the surer advancement of our argument, let us say that it was. What follows? Let the inscription of this label speak for us. They met; they loved—as was natural when we remember the youth and good looks of both, and—*they parted*. This we must concede, or how could the experience have been one she could not recall without a heart-break. They parted, and he returned home, to marry within the year, while she—I do not think she married—though I have no doubt she looks upon herself as a wife and forever bound to the man who deserted her. Women of her kind think in this way of such matters, and act upon them too as is shown by the fact that, on following him here, she passed herself off as a woman separated from her husband. Changing the Miss before her name to Mrs., she lived under this assumption for twelve years at her present hotel. In all that time, so far as I can learn, she has never been visited by anyone of an appearance answering to that of her former lover; nor have I any reason to think she ever intruded herself on him, or made herself in any way obnoxious. He was married and settled, and contrary to the usual course of men who step with one stride into affluence, was living a life of usefulness which was rapidly making him a marked man in public esteem. Perhaps she had no right to meddle with what no longer concerned her. At all events, there is no evidence of her having done so in all these fourteen years. Even after Mrs. Roberts' death, all went on as usual; *but*—" Here Mr. Gryce became emphatic—"when he turned his attention to a second marriage and that with a very young girl—(I can name her to you, gentlemen, if you wish) her patient soul may have been roused; she may have troubled him with importunities; may have threatened him with a scandal which would have interfered greatly with his political hopes if it had not ended them at once. I can conceive such an end to her long patience, can't you, gentlemen? And what is more, if this were so, and the gentleman found the situation intolerable, it might account for the flight of that arrow as nothing else ever will."

Both men had started to their feet.

"How! It was not *she*—"

"It was not she who was struck, *but it was she who was aimed at.* The young girl merely got in the way. But before I enlarge upon this point," he continued in lower tones as the two officials slowly reseated themselves, "allow me to admit that any proof of correspondence between these old-time lovers would have added much to my present argument. But while I have no doubt that such an interchange of letters took place, and that in all probability some one or more of them still exist, Mrs. Taylor's illness and Mr. Roberts' high position prevent any substantiation of the same on our part. I must therefore ask you to assume that it was in obedience to some definite agreement between them that she came to the museum on that fatal morning and made her appearance in that especial section of the gallery marked II. If this strikes you as inconceivable and too presumptuous for belief, you must at least concede that we have ample proof of his entire readiness for her coming. The bow brought up so many days before from the cellar was within reach; the arrow under his coat; and his place of concealment so chosen as to make his escape feasible the moment that arrow flew from the bow. Had she entered that section alone—had the arrow found lodgment in her breast instead of in that of another—nay, I will go even further and say that had no cry followed his act, an expectation he had every right to count upon from the lightning-like character of the attack,—he would have reached the Curator's office and been out of the building before quick discovery of the deed made his completion of this attempt impossible."

"But the girl did cry out," remarked the Assistant District Attorney. "How do you account for that, since, as you say, it was not natural for one pierced to the heart without warning?"

"Ah, you see the big mistake we made,—Correy and all the rest of us. Had Miss Willetts, or I should say, Mademoiselle Duclos, been the one to let out that dolorous cry, the man just behind the partition would have been there almost in time to see her fall. Correy, who started up the stairs at the first sound, would have been at the gallery entrance before the man of the arrow could have dropped the hanging over his retreating figure. But it was not from her lips, poor girl, that this gasping shriek went up, but from those of the woman who saw the deed and knew from whom the arrow came and for whom it was meant. How do I know this? Because of the time which elapsed, the few precious minutes which allowed Mr. Roberts to get as far away as the court. For she did not voice her agony immediately. Even she, with her own unwounded heart keeping up its functions, stood benumbed before this horror. Not till the full meaning of it all had penetrated her reluctant brain did she move or cry out. How long this interval was; whether three minutes were consumed by it, or five, we have no means of telling. She, in her despair, would take no note of time, nor would Mr. Travis, reeling in the opposite gallery under the shock of seeing all that he loved taken from him in one awful minute."

Here the detective turned with great earnestness toward the two officials.

"This question of time has been, as I have repeatedly said, the greatest stumbling-block we have encountered in our consideration of this crime. How could the assassin, by any means possible, have got so far away from the pedestal, in the infinitesimal lapse of time between the cry that was heard and the quick alarm which followed. Now we know. Have you anything to say against this conclusion? Any other explanation to give which will account for every fact as this does?"

His answer came in a dubious gesture from the District Attorney and a half-hearted "No" from his Assistant. They were both either too awed by the circumstance or too fearful of mistake, to accept without a struggle an accusation of this grave and momentous character against one of Mr. Roberts' stamp and consequence.

This was no more than Mr. Gryce had expected, and while he realized that his reputation as a detective of extraordinary insight in cases of an unusually baffling nature trembled in the balance, he experienced a sudden distaste of his work which almost drove him into renouncing the whole affair. But the habits of a lifetime are not parted with so easily; and when the Chief Inspector observed—evidently with the idea of goading him on—"This seems to be mainly a matter of conjecture, Gryce," his old self reasserted itself, and he answered boldly:

"I acknowledge that; but conjecture is what in nine cases out of ten smoothes out many of our difficulties. I have here a short statement made by myself, after the most careful inquiries, of all that Mrs. Taylor and the untrapped director did and said in the few difficult moments when they met face to face over the body of his unfortunate victim. I will ask you to listen to a portion of it.

"'She had not moved. After her one cry of horror which had brought a rush of witnesses upon the scene, she remained fixed on her knees in the absorbed introspection common to those brought suddenly face to face with a life and death crisis. He, finding that his own safety demanded action suitable to his position as a director, had entered with the crowd and now stood in her presence, in face of his own diabolical work, in an attitude of cold courage such as certain strong natures are able to assume under the pressure of great emergencies.

"'So long as she was deaf to all appeal to rouse and explain the situation, he stood back, watchful and silent; but when she finally roused and showed a disposition to speak, his desperation drove him into questioning her in order to see how much she understood of an attack which had killed a harmless stranger and let herself go free.

"'He asked her first if she could tell them from which direction came the arrow which ended this young girl's life.

"'She made no reply in words; but glanced significantly at the opposite gallery.

"'This called from him the direct inquiry, "Did you see

anyone over there at the moment this young girl fell?"

"'She shook her head. Afterward she explained the denial by saying that she had been looking down into the court.

"'But he did not cease his inquiries. Turning to the people crowding about him, he put the like question to them; but receiving no answer, a silence followed, during which a woman suggested in tones loud enough for all to hear, that there were no arrows on the other side of the court, but that the gallery where they stood was full of them.

"'This seemed to alarm Mrs. Taylor. Turning to the director, she asked whether he was sure that the opposite gallery held no arrows and no bows; and when he replied that nothing of the kind was to be found along its entire length, she proceeded to inquire whether any such deed could be committed in a place so open to view, without attracting the observation of some one wandering in court or gallery.

"'This, undoubtedly, to ascertain the full extent of his danger, before bestowing a thought upon herself. But at his answer, given with the cold precision of a thoroughly selfish man, that if anyone in the whole building had seen so much as a movement in a spot so under suspicion, that person would have been heard from by this time, she faltered and was heard to ask what he had in mind and why the people about her looked at her so. He did not respond directly, but made some remark about the police, which increased her alarm to the point of an attempted justification. She said that it was true about the arrows, as anyone could see by looking up at the walls. But where was the bow? No one could shoot an arrow without a bow, and when some one shouted that if an arrow was used as a dagger, one wouldn't need a bow, a sort of frenzy seized her and she acted quite insane, falling at the young girl's side and whispering sentence after sentence in her ear.

"'What more was needed to stamp her as a mad woman in the eyes of the ordinary observer? Nothing. But to you and me, with the cue just given, it has another look. She had just seen the man whom she had herself spared from an accusation which would have been his ruin accept in the coldest fashion an explanation which left her own innocence in doubt. What wonder she succumbed to temporary aberration! As will be remembered, she soon became comparatively calm again, and so remained until in an interview I had with her a half hour or so later I urged her, possibly with too much insistence, for some explanation of the extreme agitation she had shown at the time, when she broke forth with the remarkable statement that it was not the child, but her husband, she was mourning, stricken to death, as she would have us believe, simultaneously with the young and innocent victim then lying dead at her feet.

"'Of course, such a coincidence was much too startling not to be regarded by us all as the ravings of delirium; nor has anything occurred since in the way of communication from, or in regard to the absent one, to show that this so-called warning of death has been followed up by fact. But, if you test her action by the theory I have just advanced, viz., that the man she called husband was at that moment in the room with us and that these words were a plea to him—the last appeal of a broken-hearted woman for the support she felt to be her due—how the atmosphere of unreason and mystery clears itself. His suggestion that what was needed there was an alienist, and the pitiful efforts she made to exonerate herself without implicating him in the murderous event, fall naturally into place, as the action of a guilty man and the self-denying conduct of a devoted woman.'"

"Romantic! too romantic!" objected the District Attorney. "I should think we were listening to one of Dumas' tales."

"Dumas got his greatest effects from life, or so I have been told," remarked the Chief Inspector.

Mr. Gryce sat silent.

Suddenly, the District Attorney observed with the slightest tinge of irony edging his tone:

"I presume you would find a like explanation for the messages she professed to be sending to her husband, when engaged in babbling fool words into the dead girl's ear."

"Certainly. He was there, mark you! He stood where he could both see and hear her. All she said and all she did was by way of appeal to him for some token of regret, some sign that he appreciated her reticence; and when she found that it was bringing her nothing, she fainted away."

"Ingenious, very ingenious, Gryce. Had you failed to give us proofs connecting this idol of the Republican party with the actual shooting, it would have been simply ingenious and a quite useless expenditure of talent. But we have these proofs, and while they are mainly circumstantial, they undoubtedly call upon us for some recognition, and so we will hear you out whatever action we may take afterward."

"But first I should like to ask Mr. Gryce one question," interposed his assistant. Then addressing the detective: "Two mysteries are involved in this matter. You have given us a clever explanation of one of them, but how about the other? Will you, before going further, tell us what connection you find between the theory just advanced and the flight and ultimate suicide of Madame Duclos under circumstances which point to a desire to suppress evidence even at the cost of her life? It was not from consideration for Mr. Roberts, whom you have shown she hated. What was it then? Have you an equally ingenious explanation for that too?"

"I have an explanation, but I cannot say that it is altogether satisfactory. She died but yesterday, and my opportunities have been small for any work since. What I have learned was from her sister-in-law, whom I saw this morning. Realizing that she will be obliged to give full testimony at the inevitable inquest, she is at last ready to acknowledge that she has been aware for a long time of a secret in Madame's life. That while she knew nothing of its nature, she had always thought that it was in some manner connected with her prolonged residence abroad. Whether it would also explain the meaning of her return at this time and the seemingly inexplicable change made in her daughter's name while *en route*, must be left to our judgment. Madame had told her nothing. She had simply made use of their home, coming and going, not once, but twice, without giving them the least excuse for her inexplicable conduct. A hundred questions could not elicit more. But to one who like myself has had the opportunity of observing this wretched woman at the moment of her supreme distress an insight is given into her character, which suggests the only plausible explanation of her action. Her sacrifice was one of devotion! She perished in an exaltation of feeling. Love drove her to this desperate act. Not the love of woman for a man, but the love which women of her profound nature sometimes feel for one of their own sex. Mrs. Taylor was her friend—wait, I hope to prove it—and to save her from experiencing the extreme misery of seeing the man who was the joy as well as bane of her life suffer from the consequences of his own misdeeds, Antoinette Duclos felt willing to die and did. You smile, gentlemen. You think the old man is approaching senility. Perhaps I am, but if the contention is raised that no connection has been shown to exist between Mrs. Taylor and this foreign Madame, save such as was made by the death of Madame's child, I must retort by asking who warned Madame Duclos of the fatal occurrence at the museum in time for her to flee before even our telephone messages reached her hotel? Gentlemen, there is but one person who could have done this—our chief witness, Ermentrude Taylor. She alone had not only the incentive, but the necessary opportunity. Coroner Price as well as myself made a great mistake when we allowed Mrs. Taylor to go home alone that day."

"Very likely." This from the Chief Inspector. "But if the information I have received on this point is correct, she seemed at that time to be so entirely dissociated with a deed whose origin had just been located in the opposite gallery, that you have no real cause to blame yourselves in this regard."

"True; our minds were diverted. But you are waiting for me to explain what I mean by opportunity. Since my attention has been drawn to Mrs. Taylor again, I have been making inquiries. The chauffeur who drove her to her hotel has been found, and he admits that she stopped once on her way home, to buy some coffee. He watched her as she went into the store and he watched her as she came out; and he smelled the coffee. Happily, the interest he took in her as a sick woman intrusted to his care was strong enough for him to remember the store. It was one with two entrances, front and back; and next door to it there is a public building with a long row of telephone booths on the ground floor. If I read the incident aright, she bought her coffee, ordered it ground, slipped out at the rear door and into the adjoining building, where, unnoticed and unheard, she called up the Universal and got into communication with Madame Duclos. When she returned it was by the same route. She did not forget her coffee nor give way under the great strain to which she had subjected herself till she reached her own apartment."

"Clever."

"And true, gentlemen; I will stake my reputation on it, unable as I am to explain every circumstance, and close up every gap. Have you any further questions to ask or shall I leave you to your deliberations?"

XXIX

A STRONG MAN

An hour later when the Chief Inspector rose to depart, it was with the understanding that until their way cleared and their duty in this matter had become inevitable, no word of this business should reach the press, or even pass beyond the three officials interested.

Strange to say, they were able to keep this compact, and days elapsed without any public recognition of the new factor which had entered into the consideration of this complicated crime.

Then a hint of what was seething in the official mind was allowed to carry its own shock to the person most interested. Mr. Roberts was summoned to an interview with Coroner Price. No reason was given for this act, but the time was set with an exactness which gave importance to a request which they all felt the director would not venture to disregard.

Nor did he. He came at the time appointed, and Coroner Price in welcoming him with becoming deference could not but notice the great change which had taken place in him since that night they stood together in the museum and saw the Indian make the trial with bow and arrow which located the point of delivery as that of the upper pedestal. In just what this change lay, the Coroner hardly knew, unless it was in the increased grayness of his hair. Mr. Roberts' face, handsome as it was, was not an expressive one. Slight emotions made no impression there; nor did he today present anything but a calm and dignified appearance. Yet he was changed; and anyone who had not seen him since that night must certainly observe it.

The Coroner, who was also a man of a somewhat stolid cut, proffered him a seat and at once opened fire.

"You will pardon me any inconvenience I may have put you to, Mr. Roberts, when I tell you that Coroner D— of Greene County, is anxious to have a few words with you. He would have visited you at your home; but I induced him to see you here."

"Coroner D— of Greene County!" Mr. Roberts was entirely surprised. "And what business can he have with me?"

"It is in regard to the suicide of Madame Antoinette Duclos, committed, as you know, a week since in the Catskills."

"Ah! an extraordinarily sad affair, and of considerable moment I should judge, from its seeming connection with the one previously occurring at our museum. The girls' mother, was she not? Grief evidently unseated her brain. But—" here he changed his position quietly but with evident effort:—"in what manner am I supposed to be in a position to help the Coroner in his inquiry into this case? I was a witness, together with many others, of what happened after the accident which took place at the museum; but I know nothing of Madame Duclos or of her self-inflicted death, beyond what has appeared in the papers."

"The papers! An uncertain guide, Mr. Roberts. You may not believe it," Coroner Price remarked with a strange sort of smile, "but there are secrets known to this office, as well as to Police Headquarters, which never get into the most enterprising journals."

Was this meant to startle the director, and did it succeed in doing so?

It may have startled him, but if so, he made no betrayal of the fact. His manner continued to be perfectly natural and his voice under full control as he replied that it would be strange if in a case like this they should give out all the extraneous facts and possible clues which might be gathered in by their detectives.

This was carrying the offense into the enemy's camp with a vengeance. But the Coroner was saved replying by Mr. Roberts remarking:

"But this is not an answer to my question. Why should the Coroner of Greene County want to see *me*?"

Coroner Price proffered him a cigar, during the lighting of which the former remarked:

"It's certainly very odd. You say that you didn't know Madame Duclos."

"No; how should I? She was a foreigner, was she not?"

"Yes; a Frenchwoman, both by birth and marriage. Her husband, a professor of languages, was located some sixteen years ago, in New Orleans."

"I never knew him. Indeed, I find it hard to understand why I should be expected to show any interest in him or his wife."

"Well, I will tell you. You may not have known the Madame; but it is very certain that she knew you."

"She?" This certainly unexpected blow seemed to make some impression. "Will you give me your reasons for such an assertion? Was the name Duclos a false one? Was her name like that of her daughter, Willetts? If so, allow me to assure you that I never heard of a Willetts any more than I have of a Duclos. That a woman of whatever name and nationality should desert her child fills me with horror. I cannot speak of her, dead though she be, with any equanimity. A mother and act as she did! She herself was to blame, and only she for what happened to that beautiful girl—so young—so sweet—so innocent. I have a weakness for youth. To me a girl of that type is sacred. Had I been blessed with such a child—But there, I am straying again from our point. What makes you say Madame Duclos knew me?"

Before replying, the Coroner rose, and taking a small package from his desk, opened it, and laid out before the astonished eyes of Mr. Roberts the freshly printed photograph of himself with which we are so well acquainted, and then the half-demolished one which for all its imperfections showed that it had been originally struck off from the same negative.

"Do you recognize this portrait of yourself as one taken by Fredericks some dozen years ago?"

"Certainly. But this other? This end and corner of what must have been my picture too, where was *it* found?"

"Ah, that is what I have called you here to learn. This remnant of what you have just admitted to have been your photograph also was found in the very condition in which you see it now, in the wastebasket of the room where Madame Duclos lodged previous to her flight to the Catskills."

"This! with the face—"

"Just that! With the face riddled out of it by bullets! She shot six into it at intervals; waiting for the passing of an elevated train by her windows, in the hope that the bigger noise would drown the lesser."

"It is nothing," was Mr. Roberts' indignant comment, as he brushed the picture aside. "That was never my picture, or she wanted a target for her skill and didn't care what she took. That is all I have to say to you or to the Coroner of Greene County, on a matter in which I have no concern. I am sorry to disappoint both of you, but it is so."

He rose, and the Coroner did not seek to detain him. He merely observed, as the director turned to go:

"Have you heard the latest news about Mrs. Taylor?"

"No."

"She is improving rapidly. Soon she will be able to appear before the jury already chosen to inquire into the cause and manner of Miss Willetts' death."

"A fine woman!" came in a burst from the director's lips as he faced about for a good-bye nod. "I don't know when I have seen one I admired more."

And Coroner Price had nothing to say, he was stupefied.

But it was not so with Mr. Gryce, who entered immediately upon Mr. Roberts' departure.

"Not a jarring note," he remarked. Evidently he had heard the whole conversation. "I never for a moment imagined that he knew Madame Duclos. Any knowledge we gain of her will have to come from Mrs. Taylor."

"He's a strong man. We shall find it difficult to hold our own against him if we are brought to an actual struggle."

"Why did he run the forefinger of his right hand so continuously into his right-hand vest pocket?" was Mr. Gryce's sole comment.

By which it looks as if he had seen as well as heard.

"I didn't notice it. Is the District Attorney prepared to make the next move? Mine has failed."

"Not yet. The game is too hazardous. We should only make ourselves ridiculous in the eyes of the whole world if we should fail in an attack upon a man of such national importance. After the two inquests and a letter I hope to receive from Switzerland, we may be in a position to launch our first bomb. I don't anticipate the act with any pleasure; the explosion will be something frightful."

"If half you think is true, the unexpected confronting of him with Mrs. Taylor should produce some result. That's what I reckon on now, if the business falls first to me."

"I reckon on nothing. Chance is going to take this thing out of our hands."

"Chance! I don't understand you."

"I don't understand myself; but this is a case which will never come into court."

"I differ with you. I almost saw confession in his face when he turned upon me at last with that extravagant expression of admiration for the woman you say he meant to kill."

"Why did his finger go so continuously to his vest pocket? When you answer that, I will give a name to what I just called *chance*."

XXX

THE CREEPING SHADOW

Mrs. Taylor suffered a relapse, and the inquest which had been held back in anticipation of her recovery was again delayed. This led to a like postponement of an inquiry into the death of Madame Duclos; and a consequent let-up in public interest which thus found itself, for the nonce, deprived of further food on which to batten.

Meanwhile, Mr. Gryce was not idle. Anxious to determine just how and where Madame Duclos' story fitted into the deeper and broader one of the museum crime, he made use of his fast waning strength to probe its mysteries and master such of its details as bore upon the serious investigation to which he was so unhappily committed. When he had done this,—when he had penetrated, as it were, into the very heart of the matter to the elimination of all doubt and the full establishment of his own theory, it was felt that the time had come for some sort of positive action on the part of those interested in the cause of justice.

This they decided should take the form of a personal interview between certain officials and Mr. Roberts himself. A lesser man would have been asked to meet the District Attorney in his office; but in a case of such moment where the honor of one so prominent in many ways was involved it was thought best for them to visit him in his own home. To do this without exciting his apprehension while still making sure of his presence required some management. Various plans were discussed with the result that a political exigency was brought into play. The District Attorney asked Mr. Roberts for an interview for the purpose of introducing to him a man whose influence could not fail to play an important part in his future candidacy.

He did not name this man; but we will name him. It was the Chief Inspector.

The appointment was made and the day set. It was the following Monday. On Tuesday, Coroner Price was to open his inquest.

Did Carleton Roberts see any connection between these two events?

Who can tell? The secrets of such a brain are not to be read lightly. If we possessed Sweetwater's interest, and were to follow in secret fashion every action of the director on the evening preceding this date, what conclusion should we draw in this regard? How would we characterize his anticipations, or measure in our own mind the possibilities of the future as felt by him?

He was very quiet. He ate his meal with seeming appetite. Then he took a look over his whole house. From the carefulness with which he noted everything, the changes which he had caused to be made in it were not without their interest for him. Not a young man's interest, but yet an interest as critical and acute as though he had expected it to be shared by one whose comfort he sought and in whose happiness he would fain take part.

This, to Sweetwater, had he our vision, would have been incomprehensible from any point of view; especially, had he seen what followed when the owner of all this luxury returned to his library.

There was a picture there; a small framed photograph which occupied the post of honor on his desk.

It showed a young and pretty face, untouched, as yet, by the cares or troubles of this world. He spent a minute or so in looking at it; then he slowly lifted it, and taking the picture from the frame, gave it another look, during which a smile almost derisive gathered slowly on his lips. Before this smile had altogether vanished, he had torn the picture in two and thrown the fragments into the fire he had kindled early in the evening with his own hands.

If he stopped to watch these fragments burn, it was from abstraction rather than from interest; for his step grew lighter as he left the fireplace. Whatever this young girl's face had meant to him in days gone by was now as completely dissipated as the little puff of smoke which had marked the end of her picture.

If he read the papers afterward it was mechanically. Night, and the one great planet sinking in the West, appeared to appeal to him much more strongly than his books or the more than usually stirring news of the day.

He must have stood an hour in his unlighted window, gazing out at the tumbling waves lapping the shore.

But of his thoughts, God wot, he gave no sign.

Later, he slept.

Slept! with his hand under his pillow! Slept, though there were others in the house awake!—or why this creeping shadow of a man outlined upon the wall wherever the moon shone in, and disappearing from sight whenever the way led through darkness.

It came from above; no noise accompanied it. Where the great window opened upon the sea, lighting up the main staircase, it halted,—halted for several minutes; then passed stealthily down, a shadowy silhouette, descending now quickly, now slowly, as tread after tread is left behind and the great hall is reached.

Here there is no darkness. Open doors admit the light from many windows. A semi-obscurity is all, and through this the figure passes, but hesitatingly still, and with pause after pause, till a certain door is reached—a closed door—the only door which is closed in this part of the house.

Here it stands—stands with profile to the panels, one ear against the wood. One minute—two minutes—five minutes pass. Then a hand goes out and touches the knob. It yields; yields without a sound—and a small gap is seen between the door and its casing. This gap grows. Still no sound to disturb the tragic silence. Stop! What was that? A moan? Yes, from within. Another? Yes. Then all is quiet again. The dream has passed. Sleep has resumed its sway. The gap can safely be made wider. This is done, and the figure halting without, passes in.

XXXI

CONFRONTED

Late in the afternoon of the following day, the expected car entered Mr. Roberts' spacious grounds. It contained, besides the chauffeur, just two persons, the District Attorney and the Chief Inspector. But it was followed by another in which could be seen Mr. Gryce and a stenographer from the District Attorney's office.

The house was finished by this time, and to one approaching through the driveway presented a very attractive appearance. As the last turn was made, the sea burst upon the view—a somewhat tumultuous sea, for the wind was keen that day and whipped the waves into foam and froth from the horizon to the immediate shore-line. To add to the scene, a low black cloud with coppery edges hovered at the meeting of sea and sky, between which and themselves one taut sail could be seen trailing its boom in the water.

To one of them—to Mr. Gryce, in fact, upon whose age Fancy had begun to work, this battling craft presented an ominous appearance. It was doomed. The gale was too much for it. Did he see in this obvious fact a prophecy of what lay before the man upon whose privacy they were on the point of intruding?

The house was so arranged that to reach the main entrance it was necessary to pass a certain window. As they did so, the figure of Mr. Roberts could be seen in the room beyond moving about in an interested survey of its new furnishings and present comfortable arrangement. To these men bent on an errand as far as possible removed from interests of this kind, this evidence of Mr. Roberts' pleasure in the promise of future domesticity gave a painful shock, and raised in the minds of more than one of them a doubt—perhaps the first in days—whether a man so heavily weighted with a burden of unacknowledged guilt could show this pleasurable absorption in his new surroundings.

However, when they came to see him nearer, and marked the stiffening of his body and the slight toss-up of his head, as he noted the number and the exact character of his guests, their spirits fell again, for he was certainly a broken man, however much he might seek to disguise it. Yet there was something in this extraordinary man's personality—a force or a charm wholly dissociated it may be from worth or the sterling qualities which insure respect—which appealed to them in spite of their new-found prejudice, and prevented any dallying with his suspense or the use of any of the common methods usually employed in an encounter of this kind.

The Chief Inspector to whom the first say had been given faced the director squarely, as he saw how the hand which had just welcomed the District Attorney fell at his approach.

"You are surprised, Mr. Roberts, and rightly, to see me here not only in connection with the Prosecuting Attorney of the City of New York, but with a member of my own force. This, you will say, is no political delegation such as you have been led to expect. Nor is it, Mr. Roberts. But let us hope you will pardon this subterfuge when you learn that it was resorted to for the sole purpose of sparing you all unnecessary unpleasantness in an interview which can no longer be avoided or delayed."

"Let us sit."

It was his only answer.

When they had all complied, the District Attorney took the lead by saying:

"I am disposed to omit all preliminaries, Mr. Roberts. We have but one object in this visit and that is to clear up to your satisfaction, as well as to our own, certain difficulties of an unexpected nature which have met us in our investigation into the crime in which you, as a director of the museum in which it occurred, and ourselves as protectors of the public peace, are all vitally concerned."

"Granted," came in the most courteous manner from their involuntary host. "Yet I fail to understand why so many are needed for a purpose so laudable."

"Perhaps this will no longer surprise you, if you will allow me to draw your attention to this chart," was the answer made to this by the District Attorney.

Here he took from a portfolio which he carried a square of paper which he proceeded to lay out on a table standing conveniently near.

Mr. Roberts threw a glance at it and straightened again.

"Explain yourself," said he. "I am quite at your service."

The District Attorney made, perhaps, one of the greatest efforts of his life.

"I see that you recognize this chart, Mr. Roberts. You know when it was made and why. But what you may not know is this: that in serving its original purpose, it has proved to be our guide in another of equal, if not greater, importance. For instance, it shows us quite plainly who of all the persons present at the time of first alarm were near enough to the Curator's office to be in the line of escape from the particularly secluded spot from which the arrow was delivered. Of these persons, only one fulfills all other necessary conditions with an exactness which excuses any special interest we may feel in him. It is he who is tabulated here as number 3."

It was said. Mr. Roberts was well acquainted with his own number. He did not have to follow with his eye the point of the District Attorney's finger to know upon whose name it had settled; and for a moment, surprise, shock,—the greatest which can befall a man,—struggled with countless other emotions in his usually impassive countenance. Then he regained his poise, and with a curiously sarcastic smile such as his lips had seldom shown, he coldly asked:

"And by what stretch of probability do you pick me out for this attack? There were other men and women in this court, some very near me if I remember rightly. In what are their characters superior, or their claims to respect greater, that you should thus single me out as the fool or knave who could not only commit so wild and despicable an act, but go so far in folly—let alone knavery—as to conceal it afterward?"

"No evidence has been found against the others you have named which could in any way connect them with this folly—or shall we say knavery, since you yourself have made use of the word. But hard as it is for me to say this, in a presence so highly esteemed, this is not true of you, Mr. Roberts, however high are our hopes that you will have such explanations ready as will relieve our minds from further doubts, and send us home rejoicing. Shall I be frank in stating the precise reasons which seem to justify our present presumption?"

The director bowed, the same curious smile giving an unnatural expression to his mouth.

"Let me begin then," the other continued, "by reading to you a list of questions made out at Headquarters, as a test by which suspicion might be conscientiously held or summarily dismissed. They are few in number," he added, as he unfolded a slip of paper taken from his vest pocket. "But they are very vital, Mr. Roberts. Here is the first:

"'Whose hand carried the bow from cellar to gallery?'"

The director remained silent; but the oppression of that silence was difficult for them all to endure.

"This the second:

"'Was it the same that carried the arrow from one gallery to another?'"

Still no word; but Mr. Gryce, who was watching Mr. Roberts' every move without apparently looking up from the knob of his own cane, turned resolutely aside; the strain was too great. How long could such superhuman composure endure? And which word of all that were to come would break it?

Meanwhile, the District Attorney was reading the third question.

"'Is it possible for an arrow, shot through the loophole made by the curving in of the vase, to reach the mark set for it by Mr. Travis' testimony?'

"That question was answered when Mr. La Flèche made his experiments from behind the two pedestals. It could not have been done from the one behind which Mr. Travis crouched, but was entirely possible from the rear of the other."

With a wave of his hand, Mr. Roberts dismissed this, and the District Attorney proceeded.

"'Which of the men and women known to be in the museum when this arrow was delivered has enough knowledge of archery to string a bow? A mark can be reached by chance, but only an accustomed hand can string a bow as unyielding as this one.'

"I will pause there, Mr. Roberts. You may judge by our presence here to whose hand and to whose skill we have felt forced to ascribe this wanton shooting of a young and lovely girl. We wish to be undeceived, and stand ready to listen to anything you may have to say in contradiction of these conclusions. That is, if you wish to speak. You know that you will be well within your rights to remain silent. Likewise that if you decide to speak, it will be our painful duty to make record of your words for any use our duty may hereafter suggest."

"I will speak." The words came with difficulty,—but they came. "Ask what you will. Satisfy my curiosity, as well as your own."

"First then, the bow. It was brought up from the cellar a fortnight or more before it was used, and placed on end in the Curator's office, where it was seen more than once by the woman who wipes up the floors. The person who did this cast a shadow on the cellar wall,—that shadow was seen. Need I say more? A man's shadow is himself—sometimes."

"I brought up the bow; but I do not see how that implicates me in the use which was afterward made of it. My reasons for bringing it up were innocent enough—"

He stopped—not even knowing that he stopped. His eyes had

been drawn to a small article which the District Attorney had dropped from his hand onto the table. It looked like an end of black tape; but whether it was this or something quite different, it held the gaze of the man who was speaking, so completely that he forgot to go on.

The hush which followed paled the cheeks of more than one man there. To release the tension, the District Attorney resumed his argument, observing quietly, and as if no interruption had occurred:

"As to the arrow and its means of secret transfer from one side of the building to the other in the face of a large crowd, let me direct your attention to this little strip of folded silk. You have seen it before. Surely, I am quite justified in asking whether indeed you have not handled it both before and after the lamentable occurrence we are discussing?"

"I see it for the first time," came from lips so stiff that the words were with difficulty articulated. "What is its purpose?" he asked after a short pause.

"I hardly think it necessary to tell you," came in chilling response from the now thoroughly disenchanted official. "It looks like a loop, and notwithstanding your assertion that you see it now for the first time, we have ample evidence that it was once attached to the coat you wore on that fatal day and later carefully severed from it and dropped on the museum floor."

The District Attorney waited, they all waited with eyes on the subject of this attack, for some token of shame or indignation at this scarcely veiled insinuation. But beyond a certain stillness of expression, still further masking a countenance naturally cold and irresponsive, no hint was given that any effect had been produced upon him by these words. The coal before it falls apart into ash holds itself intact though its heart of flame has departed; so he—or such was Mr. Gryce's thought as he waited for the District Attorney's next move.

It was of a sort which recalls that soul-harrowing legend of the man hung up in an iron cage above a yawning precipice, from under whose madly shifting feet one plank after another is withdrawn from the cage's bottom, till no spot is left for him to stand on; and he falls.

"I hear that you are an expert with the bow and arrow, Mr. Roberts, or rather were at an earlier stage of your career. You have even taken a prize for the same from an Alpine Club."

Ah! that told. It was such an unexpected blow; and it showed so much knowledge. But the man who thus beheld his own youth brought up in accusation against him quickly recovered; and with an entire change of demeanor, faced them all and spoke up at last quickly and defiantly:

"Gentlemen, I have shown patience up till now, because I saw that you had something on your minds which it might be better for you and possibly for me to be rid of. This affair of Miss Willett's death is, as all must acknowledge, baffling enough to strain even to the point of folly any effort made to explain it. I had sympathy with your difficulties, and have still enough of that sympathy left, not to express too much indignation at what you are pleased to call your suspicions. I will merely halt for the moment your attempts in my direction, by asking, what have you or anybody else ever seen in me to think I would practise my old-time skill on a young and beautiful stranger enjoying herself in a place so dear to my heart as the museum of which I have been a director now these many years? Am I a madman, or a destroyer of youth? I love the young. This inhuman death of one so fair and innocent has whitened my locks and seared my very heart-strings. I shall never get over it; and whatever evidence you may have or think you have, of my having handled bow and arrow in that museum gallery, it must fall before the fact of my natural incapability to do the thing with which you have charged me. No act possible to man is more in contradiction to my instincts, than the wanton or even casual killing of a young girl."

"I believe you."

It was the Inspector who spoke, and the emphasis which he gave to his words lifted the director's head again into its old self-reliant poise. But the silence which followed was so weighted with possibilities of something yet to be said by this portentous holder of secrets, that it caused the nobly lifted head slowly to droop again and the lips which had opened impulsively to close.

Were the words coming—the words which might at a stroke pull down the whole fabric of his life, past, present and to come?

In his excited state of mind he seemed already to hear them. Doom was in their sound, and the world, once so bright, was growing dark about him—dark!

Yet how could these men know? And if they did why did they not speak? And they did not; they did not. There was silence in the air, not words; and life for him was taking on once more its ancient colors, when sharp and merry through the heavy quiet there rang out the five clear calls of a cuckoo clock from some near-by room. One, two, three, four, five! Jolly reminder of old days! But to the men who listened, the voice of doom spoke in its gladsome peal, whether the ears which caught it were those of accuser or accused. Old days were not the days to be rejoiced in at a moment so perilous to the one and so painful to the others.

With the cessation of the last shrill cry, the Inspector repeated the phrase:

"I believe you, Mr. Roberts. But how about the woman who was troubling you with demands you had no wish to grant? Miss Willetts, as you choose to call her, though you must know that her name is Duclos, was not the only person in the line of the arrow shot on that day from one gallery to the other. Perhaps this weapon of destruction was meant for one it failed to reach. Perhaps—but I have gone far enough. I should not have gone so far if it had not been my wish to avoid any misunderstanding with one of such undoubted claims to consideration as yourself. If you have explanations to offer—if you can in any way relieve our minds from the responsibilities which are weighing upon us, pray believe in our honest desire to have you do so. There may be something back of appearances which has escaped our penetration; but it will have to be something startlingly clear, for we know facts in your life which are not open to the world at large, I may even say to your most intimate friends."

"As, for instance?"

"That Mrs. Taylor is no stranger to you, even if Mademoiselle Duclos was. We have evidence you will find it hard to dispute that you knew and—liked each other, fifteen years or so ago."

"Evidence?"

"Incontrovertible, Mr. Roberts."

"Attested to by her? I do not believe it. I never shall believe it, and I deny the charge. The ravings of a sick woman,—if it is such you have listened to—"

"I advise you to stop there, Mr. Roberts," interjected the District Attorney. "Mrs. Taylor has said nothing. Neither has Madame Duclos. What the former may say under oath I do not know. We shall both have an opportunity to hear tomorrow, when Coroner Price opens his inquest. She is in sufficiently good health now, I believe, to give her testimony. Pray, say nothing." Mr. Roberts had started to his feet. "Do nothing. You will be one of the witnesses called—"

There he stopped, meeting with steady gaze the wild eyes of the man who was staring at him, staring at them all in an effort to hold them back, while his finger crept stealthily and ever more stealthily toward his right-hand vest-pocket.

"You would dare," he shouted, then suddenly dropped his

hand and broke into a low, inarticulate murmur, harrowing and dreadful to hear. To some it sounded like a presage to absolute confession, but presently this murmur took on a distinctness, and they heard him say:

"I should be glad to have five minutes' talk with Mrs. Taylor before that time. In your presence, gentlemen, or in anybody's presence, I do not care whose."

Did he know—had he felt whose step was in the hall, whose form was at the door? If he did, then the agitation which in another moment shook his self-possession into ashes was that of hope realized, not of fear surprised. Ermentrude Taylor entered the room and at the sight of her he rose and his arms went out; then he sank back weak and stricken into his chair, gazing as if he could never have his fill at her noble countenance luminous with a boundless pity if not with the tenderness of an unforgotten love.

When she was near enough to speak without effort and had thanked the gentlemen who had made way for her with every evidence of respect, she addressed him in quite a natural tone but with strange depths of feeling in her voice:

"What is it you want to say to me? As I stood at the door, I heard you tell these gentlemen that you would like to have a few minutes' talk with me. I was glad to hear that; and I am ready to listen to—*anything*."

The pause she made before uttering the last word caused it to ring with double force when it fell. All heads drooped at the sound and the lines came out on Mr. Gryce's face till he looked his eighty-five years and more. But what Carleton Roberts had to say at this critical moment of his double life was not at all what they expected to hear.

Rising, for her eyes seemed to draw him to his feet, he cried in the indescribable tone of suppressed feeling:

"Shadows are falling upon me. My interview with these gentlemen may end in a way I cannot now foresee. In my uncertainty as to how and when we may meet again, I should like to make you such amends as opportunity allows me. Ermentrude, will you marry me—now—tonight, before leaving this house?"

A low cry escaped her. She was no more prepared for this astounding offer than were these others. "Carleton!" came in a groan from her lips. "Carleton! Carleton!" the word rising in intensity as thought followed thought and her spirits ran the full gamut of what this proposal on his part meant in past, present and future. Then she fell silent and they saw the great soul of the woman illumine a countenance always noble, with the light of a purpose altogether lofty. When she spoke it was to say:

"I recognize your kindness and the impulse which led to this offer. But I do not wish to add so much as a feather's weight to your difficulties. Let matters remain as they are till after—"

He took a quick step toward her.

"Not if my heart is full of regret?" he cried. "Not if I recognize in you now the one influence left in this world which can help me bear the burden of my own past and the threatening collapse of my whole future?"

"No," she replied, with an access of emotion of so elevated a type it added to rather than detracted from her dignity. "It is too much or it is not enough."

His head drooped and he fell back, throwing a glance to right and left at the two officials who had drawn up on either side of him. It was an expressive glance; it was as if he said, "You see! she knows as well as you for whom the arrow was intended—yet she is kind."

But in an instant later he was before her again, with an aspect so changed that they all marveled.

"I had hoped," he began, then stopped. Passion had supplanted duty in his disturbed mind; a passion so great it swept everything before it and he stood bare to the soul before the woman he had wronged and under the eyes of these men who knew it. "Life is over for us two," said he, "whether your presence here is a trap in which I have been caught and from which it is hopeless for me to extricate myself; or whether it is by chance or an act of Providence that we should meet again with eager ears listening and eager eyes watching for such tokens of guilt as will make their own course clear, true it is that they have got what they sought; and whatever the result, nothing of real comfort or honor is left for either you or me. Our lives have gone down in shipwreck; but before we yield utterly to our fate, will you not grant me my prayer if I precede it by an appeal for forgiveness not only for old wrongs but for my latest and gravest one? Ermentrude, I entreat."

Ah, then, they were witness to the fascination of the man, hidden heretofore, but now visible even to the schooled spectators of this tragedy of human souls. The tone permeated with pathos and charm, the look, the attitude from which all formality had fled and only the natural grace remained, all were of the sort which sways without virtue and rouses in both weak and strong an answering chord of sympathy.

The woman in whom it probably awakened a thousand memories trembled under it. She drew back, but her whole countenance had softened, revealing whatever of native charm she also possessed. Would she heed his prayer? If she did not, they could well be silent. If she did—

But the woman gave no sign of yielding.

"Cease, Carleton," came in stern reply—stern for all the approach to concession in her manner. "If your life and my life are both over, let us talk of other things than marriage. When one faces death, whether of body or spirit, one clings to higher hopes than those of earth or its remaining interests. If my forgiveness will help you to this end, you have it. I have had but one aim in life since we parted, and that was to see your higher self triumph over the material one. If that hour has come or is coming, my life needs no other consolation. In having that, I possess all."

The man who listened—the men who listened—stood for a moment in awe of the nobility with which she thus expressed herself. Then the only person present whom she seemed to see burst forth with a low cry, saying:

"You shall not be disappointed. I—"

But there she hushed him. "No," said she. And he seemed to understand and was silent.

What did this mean?

The District Attorney betrayed his doubt; the Chief his, each in a characteristic way. The former frowned, the latter tapped his breast absently with his forefinger while looking askance at Mr. Gryce, who in his turn took up some little object from the desk beside which he was standing and to it confided whatever surprise he felt at this proof of some uncommunicated secret shared by these two, of which he had not yet become possessed. Then he again looked up and the glances of the three men met. Should they attempt to sound this new mystery of mutual understanding to which as yet they had received no clue? No, the inquest would do that. Neither this man nor this woman could stand a close examination. He would weaken from despair, she from the candor of her soul. They would wait. But ah, the tragedy of it! Even these men hardened by years of contact with every species of human suffering and crime were openly moved. If they needed an excuse, surely they could find it in the superior abilities and attainment of the man upon whom justice was about to wreak its vengeance. And yet, what more despicable crime had they ever encountered in the long line of their duty. The youth and innocence of the real victim and the worth of the intended one only added to its wickedness and shame. It was this thought which again steeled their hearts.

Meantime the two upon whom they now redirected their attention had attempted no further speech and made no further move. She had said No to something he was willing to concede, and he had accepted that no as final. Had this brought him any relief? Possibly. And she? Had it had a like effect on her? Hardly. Though her aspect was one of calm resignation, her physical powers were perceptibly failing. This in itself was alarming, and determined them not to subject her any longer to an interview which might rob her of all strength for the morrow. Accordingly, the District Attorney, addressing Mr. Roberts, suggestively remarked:

"Mrs. Taylor is showing fatigue. Would it not be better for you to say at once while she is yet in a condition to remain with us, whether you prefer to make a public statement of your case or leave it to unfold itself in the ordinary manner through the two impending inquests and the busy pen of the reporter?"

"First, am I under arrest? Am I to leave this house—?"

"Not tonight. An officer will remain here with you. Tomorrow—after the inquest, perhaps."

"I will make a statement. I will make it now. I wish to be left in peace tonight, to think and to regret." Then turning to her, "Ermentrude, a woman who has served me and my family for twenty-five years is at this very moment in the rear of the house. Go to her and let her care for you. I have business here,—business of which I am sure you approve."

"Yes, Carleton. And remember that I shall be put upon my oath tomorrow. The questions I am asked I must answer—and truthfully," she added, with a look as full of anguish as inquiry.

"I shall be truthful myself," he assured her, and again their eyes met.

After a while she gave a stumble backward, which Mr. Gryce perceiving, held out his arm and assisted her from the room.

But once in the hall he felt the clinch of her fingers digging into his arm.

"Is there no hope?" she whispered. "Must I live—"

"Yes," he interrupted kindly, but with the authority given him by his relations to this case. "You have won his heart at last, and he speaks truly when he says that to you and to you alone can he look for comfort, wherever the action of the law may leave him."

She shivered; then glowed again with renewed fire.

"Thank you," she said; and they passed on.

XXXII

"WHY IS THAT HERE?"

They waited while he wrote. A sinister calm quite unlike that which the victim of his ambition had shown under the stress of equal suffering if not equal guilt had subdued his expression to one of unmoved gloom, never to be broken again.

As word after word flowed from the point of his pen upon the paper spread out before him, the two officials sitting aside in the shadow watched for the flicker of an eyelash, or a trembling of the fingers so busy over their task. But no such sign of weakening did they see. Once only did he pause to look away—was it into the past or into futurity?—with a steady, self-forgetful gaze which seemed to make a man of him again. Then he went on with his task with the grimness of one who takes his last step into ignominy.

We will follow his words as he writes, leaving them for the others to read on their completion.

"I, Carleton Roberts, in face of an inquiry which is about to be held on the death of her who called herself Angeline Willetts, but whose real name is as I have since been told Angeline Duclos, wish to make this statement in connection with the same.

"It was at my hand she died. I strung the bow and let fly the arrow which killed this unfortunate child. Not with the intention of finding my mark in her innocent bosom. She simply got in the way of the woman for whom it was intended—if I really was governed by intent, of which I here declare before God I am by no means sure.

"The child was a stranger to me, but the woman in whose stead she inadvertently perished I had known long and well. My wrongs to her had been great, but she had kept silence during my whole married life and in my blind confidence in the exemption this seemed to afford me, I put no curb upon my ambition which had already carried me far beyond my deserts. Those who read these lines may know how majestic were my hopes, how imminent the honor, to attain which I have employed my best energies for years. Life was bright, the future dazzling. Though I had neither wife nor child, the promise of activity on the lines which appeal to every man of political instinct gave me all I seemed to need in the way of compensation. I was happy, arrogantly so, perhaps, when without warning the woman I had not seen in years, who,—if I thought of her at all, I honestly believed to be dead—wrote me a letter recalling her claims and proposing a speedy interview, with a view to their immediate settlement. Though couched in courteous terms, the whole letter was instinct with a confidence which staggered me. She meant to reënter my life, and if I knew her, openly. Nothing short of bearing my name and being introduced to the world as my wife would satisfy her; and this not only threatened a scandal destructive of my hopes, but involved the breaking of a fresh matrimonial engagement into which I had lately entered with more ardor I fear than judgment. What was I to do? Let her have her way—this woman I had not seen in fifteen years,—who if at the age of twenty had seemed to my enthusiastic youth little short of a poet's dream, must be far short of any such perfection now? I rebelled at the very thought. Yet to deny her meant the possible facing of consequences such as the strongest may well shrink from. And the time for choice was short. She had limited her patience to a fortnight, and one day of that fortnight had already passed.

"I have in my arrogant manhood sometimes credited myself with the possession of a mind of more or less superiority; but I have never deceived myself as to the meretricious quality of the goodness with which many have thoughtlessly endowed me. I have always known it was not even up to that of men whose standards fall far short of the highest integrity. But never, till that hour came, had I realized to what depths of evil my nature could sink under a disappointment threatening the fulfillment of my ambitious projects. Had there been any prospect of escape from the impending scandal by means usually employed by men in my position, I might have given my thoughts less rein and been saved at least from crime. But these were not available in my case. She was not a woman who could be bought. She was not even one I could cajole. Death only would rid me of her; kindly death which does not come at call. This is as far as my thoughts went at first. I was a gentleman and had some of a gentleman's feelings. But when my sleep began to be disturbed by dreams, and this was very soon, I could not hide from myself toward what fatal goal my thoughts were tending. To be freed from her! To be freed from her! dinned itself in my ears, sleeping or waking, at home or abroad. But I saw no plain road to this freedom, for our paths never crossed and my honor as well as safety demanded that the coveted result should be without any possible danger to myself. Cold, heartless villain! you say. Well, so I was; no colder nor more heartless villain lives today than I was be-tween the inception of my purpose and its diabolical fulfill-ment in the manner publicly known.

"So true is this that, as time went on, my ideas cleared and the plan for which I was seeking unfolded itself before me from the day I came upon a discarded bow lying open to view in the museum cellar. The dreams of which I have spoken had prepared me for this sudden knowledge. The woman who blocked my way and against whom I meditated this crime was connected in my mind with Alpine scenery and Alpine events. It was at Lucerne I had first met her, young and fresh, but giv-ing no promise of the woman she has since become; and in the visions which came and went before my eyes, it was not her-self I saw so much as the surroundings of those days, and the feats of prowess by which I had hoped to win her approba-tion. Among these was the shooting at a small target with a bow and arrow. I became very proficient in this line. I shot as by instinct. I could never tell whether I really took aim or not, but the arrow infallibly hit the mark. In my dreams I always saw it flying, and when this bow came to hand a thought of what the two might accomplish came with it. Yet even then I had no real idea of putting into practice this fancy of a distem-pered brain. I brought the bow up from the cellar and hid it unstrung in the Curator's closet, more from idle impulse I fondly thought, than from any definite purpose. Another day I saw the Curator's keys lying on his desk and took them to open a passage to the upper floor. But for all that, I felt sure that I would never use the bow even after I had thrust it near to hand behind the tapestry masking the secret entrance to this passage. One dreams of such things but they do not per-petrate them. I might approach the deed, I might even make every preparation for its accomplishment, but that did not mean that the day would ever come when I should actually loose an arrow from this bow against a human breast. More than once I laughed at the mere idea.

"But the devil knew me better than I knew myself. Im-pelled by these same instincts, I answered the letter sent me with the assurance that I would surely see her, but I did not name any day, intuitively knowing that what I dreamed of do-ing but certainly should not do required a certain set of cir-cumstances not easily to be met with. Instead, I bade her show herself in the second section of the southern gallery, every Tuesday and Friday at the exact hour of noon. If at the mo-ment the two hands of the clock came together, she saw me on the lower step of the main staircase, she was to know that I was free to talk and would soon join her. If she did not see me there, she was to return home and come another day. She answered that she would come but once, and set the day. This was startling to my pride, but in a way it brought me a sense of relief. To wait till all was propitious might mean continual delays. The very fact of my uncertainty as to whether or not I should have the courage of my wishes at the critical moment made an indefinite prolongation of my present condition undesirable. Better one straight risk and be done with it.

"I was to wait two weeks. Why she exacted so long and seemingly unnecessary a delay, I do not know. Before I saw her, I thought it was from a sheer desire to make me suffer; now I know it was not for that. However, it did make me suffer, from the alternate weakening and strengthening of my resolve. When the day came, the most trivial of circumstances would have deterred me from what still had the nature of a dream to me. Unhappily, everything worked for its fulfillment. There had never been fewer persons in the building at the noon hour; nor had there been a time during the past two weeks when the Curator was more completely occupied in a spot quite remote from his office. As I tried the door leading up the little winding staircase to the one back of the tapestry where the bow lay, and found it, just as I had left it, unlocked, I had a sense for the first time that the courage concerning which I had had so many doubts would hold. At that moment I was a murderer in heart and purpose, whatever I was after or have been since. As I recognized this fact, I felt my face go pale and my limbs shake from sheer horror of myself. But this weakness was short-lived and I felt my blood flowing evenly again when having slipped into my place behind the upper pedestal I peered through my peep-hole in a search for her figure in the spot where I had bidden her await me.

"She was not there, but then it was not quite twelve, though the noon hour was so near she must be somewhere in the gallery and liable at any minute to cross my line of vision.

"It was fifteen years, as I have already said, since I had seen her; and I had no other picture of her in my mind than the appearance she had made as a girl, coarsened by time and disappointment. Why I should have looked for just this sort of change in her, God knows, but I did expect it and probably would not have recognized her if I had passed her in the court. But I was not worrying about any mistake I might make of this kind. All I seemed to fear was that at the critical moment some one would pass between us on my side of the gallery. I never thought of anyone passing in front of her.

"I had picked out Section II as the place where she was to show herself, because it was in a direct line with the course an arrow would take from a sight behind the vase. I had bade her to look for me in the court, and that would bring her forward to the balustrade in front. A knot of scarlet ribbon at her breast was to distinguish her. But the spot I had thus chosen for her, and the spot I had chosen for myself had this disadvantage; that while I could see straight to my mark from the peep-hole I have mentioned, I could see nothing to right or left of that one line of vision. Why I did not realize the hazard involved in this fact I do not know. Enough that my whole thought was centered on the lookout I was keeping and it was with a shock of surprise I suddenly saw the whole scene blotted from my view by the passing by of some one on my own side of the gallery. This must have been the Englishman who found his vantage-point from behind the other pedestal. He went by quickly, and as the opening cleared once more, I beheld the woman for whom I was waiting appear in the spot selected. For an instant I was dazzled. I had not expected to see so noble a figure; and in that instant a cloud came before my eyes, my resolution failed,—I was almost saved—she was almost saved—when instinct got the better of my judgment, and the arrow flew just as that young creature bounded forward in her delight at seeing her steamer admirer watching her from my side of the court.

"The shock of thus beholding a perfect stranger fall under my hand benumbed me, but only for an instant. In the two weeks of intolerable waiting through which I had just passed, I had so forcibly impressed upon my consciousness the exact course I was to pursue from the instant the arrow left the bow that I went about the same automatically. Pulling out the edge of the tapestry, I slipped behind it, dropping my bow in the doorway left open for my passage. This caused me no thought and awakened no fears. But what took all the nerve I possessed, and gave me in one awful moment a foretaste of the terror and despair awaiting me in days to come, was the opening of the second door—the one leading into the Curator's office.

"What might I not be forced to encounter when the knob to this was turned! Some strolling guest—Correy the attendant—or even the guard who was never where he was needed and always where he was not! For anyone to be there of sufficient intelligence to note my face and the place from which I came meant the end of all things to me. It was not necessary for this imaginary person to be in the room. To be within sight of it was enough. But this fear—this horror of impending retribution—did not make me hesitate or delay my advance a single instant. Everything depended upon my being one of the crowd when the first alarm was raised. So with the daring of one who in escaping a present danger hurls himself knowingly into another equally perilous, I pushed open the door and entered the office.

"It was empty! Fortune had favored me thus far. Nor was there anyone in the court beyond, near enough or interested enough to note my presence or observe any effort I might make at immediate departure. With the hope riding high within my breast that I should yet reach the street before my crime was discovered, I made for the nearest exit. But I was not destined to reach it. When I was only some half a dozen paces from the great door, Correy's cry rang loudly through the building, with the result that all egress was shut off, and I was left, with no other aid than my own assurance, to face my hideous deed with all its appalling consequences.

"How it served me, you have seen. Steeled by a sense of my own danger, I was able to confront the woman whom I had so deeply wronged,—whom I had even endeavored to kill,—and ply her with those questions upon whose answers depended not only my honor, but my very life.

"My cold-blooded absorption in my own security, and her almost superhuman devotedness, must have given the Powers cognizant of mortal lives a new lesson in human nature. Never has a greater contrast been shown between self-seeking man and self-forgetful woman. But deeply as I was impressed by the steadfastness and magnanimity of her spirit, nay by the woman herself, I have been less oppressed by the great debt I owed her than by the thought, growing more intolerable every day, that in my frenzied struggle against fate I had cut short the existence of a young and lovely girl whose right to live was beyond all comparison superior to my own.

"But now, as the shadows fall thickly about me and the last page of my dishonorable existence awaits to be turned, my mortal wound is this: that I must leave to loneliness and unspeakable grief the great-souled woman who has seen into the heart of my crime and yet has forgiven me. All else of anguish or dread is swallowed up in this one over-mastering sorrow. To her my heart's thanks are here given; to her my last word is due. May she find in it all that her soul calls for in this hour of supreme disaster: repentance equal to my sin, and a recognition of her worth, which, late as it is for her comfort, may lead to her acceptance of the consolation yet to be meted out to her from eternal sources."

That was all. The pen dropped from his hand and he sat inert, almost pulseless, in the desolation of a despair known only to those who, at a blow, have sunk from the height of public applause into the depths of irretrievable ignominy.

The District Attorney, who was a man of more feeling than was usually supposed, contemplated him in compassionate silence for a moment, then gently—very gently for him—leaned forward and drew from under the unresisting hands the scattered sheets which lay in disorder before him, and passed them on to his stenographer.

"Read," said he; but immediately changed his mind and took them back. "I will read them myself. Mr. Roberts, I must ask you to listen. It is right for you to know exactly what you have written before you affix your signature to it."

Mr. Roberts bowed mechanically, but he looked very weary.

The District Attorney began to read. It is a matter of doubt whether Mr. Roberts so much as heard him. Yet the reading went on, and when the last word was reached, the District Attorney, after a pause during which his eye had consulted that of the Chief Inspector, remarked in a kindly tone and yet with an emphasis impossible to disregard:

"I see that you have made no mention of Madame Duclos in this relation of the cause and manner of her young daughter's death. Is it possible that you are ignorant of the part she played in your affairs or the reasons she had for the suicide with which she terminated her life?"

"I know nothing of the woman but that she was the mother of the girl who—" he hesitated, then added with a gesture of despair, "fell under my hand."

The District Attorney said nothing in reply, he simply waited. But no denial or further admission came.

"She was a friend of Mrs. Taylor," suggested the Chief Inspector as the silence grew somewhat oppressive. "An old friend; a friend of her early days; do you not remember?"

"I do not."

His tormentors went no further. Why harass him for an item of knowledge which the morrow would certainly bring to light. Instead, they hurried through the remaining formalities, adding to the reading already made a capitulation of such answers as he had given to their questions, and witnessing, while he signed both papers.

This done, he was left for a moment in peace, while the two officials drew aside into the embrasure of the window for a momentary conference.

He seemed to notice the hush, for he roused from the torpor into which he was again about to sink, and glanced cautiously about him. The stenographer was busy with his papers, and the other two stood with their backs to him. If help was to come it must come now. This he realized, with a sudden graying of his face which took from it the last vestige of that youthfulness which had been its distinguishing feature; and the finger which had fumbled from time to time in his vest-pocket stole thither once more, bringing forth a little vial which in another moment he raised to his lips.

Was there no one to see? No one to stop him?

No, the stenographer was closing up his bag; and the two officials deep in conversation. He could drain the last drop unseen.

But the sound of the little vial crashing upon the hearthstone whither he had flung it broke the quiet and startled the District Attorney forward in a doubt bordering upon terror.

"What is that?" he asked, pointing to the fragments that had just missed the ash heap.

"It contained oblivion," was the answer given him in steady tones. "Do you wonder that I sought it? Nothing can save me. I have two minutes before me. I would dedicate them to *her*."

His head fell forward on his hands. The clock on the mantel struck. Could it be that when the second hand had circled its small disc twice—

This was the thought of the District Attorney, but not of the Chief Inspector. He had advanced to the desk where Mr. Roberts was still sitting, and remarked with a gravity exceeding any he had hitherto shown:

"Mr. Roberts, I have a great disappointment for you. This little vial of yours which held poison yesterday contained nothing but a few drops of harmless liquid today. The change was made in the night, by one suspicious of your intention. You will have to face the full consequences of your crime."

Carleton Roberts' arms collapsed and his face fell forward upon them, and they heard a groan. Then in the short silence which followed, another and a very different sound broke upon their ears. Seven clear calls from the cuckoo-clock rang out from the room beyond, followed by a woman's smothered cry.

It was the one ironic touch the situation had lacked. It pierced the heart of Carleton Roberts and started him in anguish to his feet.

"O God!" he cried, "that I should have let that thing of evil shriek out the wicked hours from day to day, only to torment her now with old remembrances! Why did I not crush it to atoms long ago? Why did I leave it hanging on my wall—"

With a dash he was in the hall. In another instant he was at the door of his bedroom, followed by the two officials crowding closely up behind him.

Would they find her there? Yes; where else should she be, she whom this call from the past might almost draw from the grave! She was there, but not in the spot where they had expected to see her, nor in that state of collapse of which her former weakness had given promise. Apart from Mr. Gryce, with her form drawn up to its full height she stood, with her finger pointing not at the cuckoo-clock as would seem most natural, but at a small newspaper print of the dead girl's face pinned up on another wall.

"Why is that here?" she cried in a passionate inquiry which ignored every other presence than that of him who must heed and answer her. "Carleton, Carleton, why have you pinned that young girl's face up opposite your bed where you can see it on waking, where it can look at you and you at it—Or—" here checked by a sudden thought she broke off, and her tone changed to one of doubt, "perhaps you did not put it there yourself? Perhaps its presence on your wall is a trick of the police to startle you into betrayal. Was it? Was it?"

"No, Ermentrude." The words came slowly but firmly. "I put it there myself. I thought it would haunt me less than if left to my imagination."

Then in a low tone which perhaps reached no other ears than hers:

"I do not know what it does to me; or what I see in it. Something besides youth and beauty. Something—"

"Hush!" She had him by the arm. "Forget it; these men are listening—"

But with a convulsive movement, he broke from her hold, and in so doing his eyes fell on a mirror confronting him from the opposite side of the room. Two faces were visible in it, his own and that of his young victim pictured in the print hanging on the wall behind him. They seemed alive. Both of them seemed alive, and as he saw them thus in conjunction, the sweet, pure countenance of the child he had instinctively mourned, peering at him over his guilty shoulder—the sweat started on his forehead and he uttered a great cry. Then he stood still, swaying from side to side, the eyes starting from his head in a horror transcending all that had gone before.

"Take him away!" she cried. "Out of the room! Let him remain anywhere but here. I pray you; I entreat."

But he was not to be moved.

"Ermentrude," he whispered; "they say her name was Duclos. She gave her name as Willetts. What *was* her name? You know the truth and can tell me."

XXXIII

AGAIN THE CUCKOO-CLOCK

Then to the wonder and admiration of all, this extraordinary woman showed her full strength and the inexhaustible power she possessed over her own emotions. With a smile piteous in its triumph over a suffering the depths of which they were just beginning to sound, she held his gaze in hers and quietly said:

"You have driven me to the wall, Carleton. If I answer, nothing remains to us of hope or honor; nothing upon which to stay our souls but a consciousness of truth. Shall we let all go and meet our fate as people should who stand on a desolate shore and see the whole world roll away from before them?"

"What was her name?"

At his look, at this repetition of his question, she straightened up, and addressed herself to Mr. Gryce.

"You were astonished and regarded me curiously when at the sound of that foolish little clock I entered this room. That little clock means everything to me, gentlemen." Here she surveyed them one after the other with her proud and candid eye. "It is the one witness I have—is it not, Carleton?" she asked, turning quickly upon him. "You have not failed me in this?"

He shook his head.

"A witness to what I am still ready to ignore, if such is your will, Carleton."

Terror! terror far beyond anything they had seen in him yet, paled his cheek and made his face almost unrecognizable; but he could still speak, and in the murmur he let fall she heard no word of protest.

"May I ask one of you to take down that clock?"

In a few minutes it lay on the table to which she had pointed. Mr. Gryce who had at that moment in his pocket a copy of the inscription pasted on its back, expected her to turn it over and show them the token of Mr. Roberts' and her united initials.

But it was not this she had in mind. Though she took up the clock, she did not turn it round, only looked at it steadily, her trembling lips and a tear—the first they had seen—testifying to the rush of old memories which this simple little object brought back to her long suffering heart. Then she laid it down again and seemed to hesitate.

"I want to get at the works inside," she appealed to them with a helpless accent. "Can you tear off the back? That would be the quickest way. But no, I know a quicker," and lifting the clock again she turned it upside down and shook it.

They heard—what did they hear? No one could say, but when she again reversed it, there fell out upon the table and rolled to the floor a small gold circlet. Lifting it, Mr. Gryce held it out to her. Taking it, she carried it over to the District Attorney and placed it in his hand.

"Read the inscription inside."

He did so, and looking quickly up, said:

"This is a wedding ring! Yours! You believe yourself to have been married to him."

"I *was* married to him in Switzerland. The marriage was legal; he knows it, he acknowledges it, or why should he keep this ring. I have endured seeing him put another woman in my place. I have kept silence for years; but when he asks the right name of the child shot down in the museum, and asks it in a way which compels answer, then I must make known my rightful claims. For that child was not only mine, but *his*; born after he left me, and reared without his knowledge, first in this country and then in France."

And breaking down now utterly, she fell on her knees sobbing out her soul at the feet of him from whose honor she had torn the last poor, pitiful shred.

As for him, he said nothing; even his lips refused the smallest cry. Only his hand which had hung at his side went to his heart; and thus he stood swaying—swaying, till he finally fell forward into the arms she suddenly threw out to receive him.

"Carleton! Carleton!" she wailed, searching for consciousness in his fast glazing eye. "It was to show you your child that I made the appointment at the museum. Not for myself. Oh, not for myself, but for your sake, that you might have—"

Useless; all useless.

He was dead.

Would she have had it otherwise? Would any of them? When they were quite sure of the fact, she placed the ring in his still warm hand; then she solemnly put it on her finger, and turning, faced them all.

"Do not blame me too much for this final blow I gave him. He had already seen the truth in that mirror over there. His face— look at it and then at this picture of her taken after death, and see the resemblance! It is showing plainer every minute. It was the something which had worried and eluded him. Nothing could have kept back the truth from him after that one glimpse he caught of himself and her in the mirror. I loved him. Mine is the grief; you will let me stay here with him tonight. Tomorrow I will answer all questions."

XXXIV

THE BUD—THEN THE DEADLY FLOWER

You who have read thus far will care little for the legalities which followed the events just related, but you may wish to know to a fuller extent some of the facts in Ermentrude Taylor's life which led to this tragic end of all her hopes.

Her story is twofold, the portion connecting her with Carleton Roberts being entirely dissociated from that which made her the debtor of Antoinette Duclos. Let me tell the latter first, as it preceded the other, and tell it in episodes.

Two girls stood at one end of a long walk of immemorial yews. At the other could be seen the advancing figure of a man, young, alert, English-clad but unmistakably foreign. They were school girls and bosom friends; he their instructor in French; the walk one attached to a well-known seminary. When they had entered this walk, it had been empty. Now it held for one of them—and possibly for the other, too—a world of joy and promise;—the world of seventeen. Innocent and unthinking, neither of them had known her own heart, much less that of her fellow. But when in face of that approach, eye met eye with an askance look of eager question, revelation came, crimsoning the cheeks of both, and marking an epoch in either life.

Noble of heart and tender each toward the other, they were yet human. Arm fell from arm, and with an equally spontaneous movement, they turned to search each the other's countenance, not for betrayal,—for that had already been made—but for those physical charms or marks of mental superiority which might attract the eye or win the heart of a man of the ideality of this one.

Alas! these gifts, for gifts they are, were much too unequally distributed between these two to render the balance at all even.

Ermentrude was handsome; Antoinette was not.

Ermentrude had besides, what even without beauty would have made her conspicuous to the eye, the figure of a goddess and the air of a queen. But Antoinette was small and had to feel secure and in a happy mood to show the excellence of her mind and the airy quality of her wit.

Then, Ermentrude had money and could dress, while Antoinette, who was dependent upon an English uncle for everything she possessed, wore clothes so plain that but for their exquisite neatness, one would never dream that she came from French ancestry, and that ancestry noble.

Yes, she had that advantage; rank was hers, but not the graces which should accompany it. More than that, she had nothing with which to support it. Better be of the yeoman class like Ermentrude, and smile like a duchess granting favors. Or so she thought, poor girl, as her meek regard passed from the friend whose attractions she had thus acknowledged to the man whose approbation would make a goddess of her too.

He was coming—not with his usual indifferent swing, but eagerly, joyously, as though this moment meant something to him too. She knew it did. Small memories rushing upon her, made no doubt of that. But why? Because of Ermentrude or because of herself? Alas! she could recall nothing which would answer that. They were much together; he had scarcely ever seen them separate. It might be either—Hardly alive from suspense, she watched him coming—coming. In a moment he would be upon them. On which would his eyes linger?

That would tell the tale.

In an anguish of ungovernable shyness, she slipped behind the ample figure of her friend till only her fluttering skirt betrayed her presence. Perhaps she was saved something by this move; perhaps not. She did not see the beam of joy sparkling in his eye as he greeted Ermentrude; but she could not but mark the heaviness of his step as he passed them by and wandered away into the shadows.

And that she understood. Ermentrude had not smiled upon him. To him, the moment had brought pain.

It was enough. Now she knew.

But why had not Ermentrude smiled?

A dormitory lighted only by the moon! Two beds close together; in one a form of noble proportions, and in the other the meagre figure of a girl almost buried from sight among pillows and huddled-up blankets. Both are quiet save for an occasional shudder which shakes the bed of the latter. Ermentrude lies like the dead, though the moonlight falls full upon her face blanching it to the aspect of marble. Even her lashes rest moveless on her cheek.

But she is not sleeping; she is listening—listening to the sobs, almost inaudible, which now and then escape from the beloved one at her side. As they grow fainter and fainter and gradually die away altogether till stillness reigns through the whole dormitory, she rouses and bending forward on her elbow, looks long and lovingly at the wet brow of her sleeping mate. She then sinks back again into rigidity, with a low moan, ending in the whispered words:

"He does not love,—not yet. A slight thing will turn him. Did I not see him glance back twice, and both times at her? The look with which she greeted him was so wonderful."

A village street in Britanny; a parish church in the distance; two women bidding each other farewell amid a group of wedding-guests, gay as the heavens are blue.

"*Au revoir!*" was the whisper breathed by the bride into the ear of the other. "*Au revoir*, my Ermentrude. May you have a happy year in Switzerland!"

"*Au revoir*! little Madame. *You* will be happy I know in those United States to which you are going."

And the tears stood in the eyes of both.

"You will write?"

"I will write."

But the bride did not seem quite satisfied. Glancing about and finding her young husband busy with his adieux, she drew her friend apart and softly murmured:

"There is something I must say,—something I must know, before the sea divides us. You remember the day we all left school and you went home and I came to Britanny? Ermentrude, Achille tells me that on that day he sought the whole house over for you till he came upon you in one of the classrooms; and that you whom I had sometimes seen so sad were very gay and told him between laughing and crying that you were bidding a solemn farewell to all the nooks and corners of the old seminary, because your fiancé awaited you at home, and there would be no coming back."

"I meant my music."

"He did not know that, Ermentrude," and here she laid her hands upon the other's shoulders, drawing back as she did so to look earnestly up into her face. "Was that done for me?"

They were too near for anything but the truth to pass from eye to eye. Ermentrude tried to laugh and utter a quick *No, no!* but the little bride was not deceived. Again upon her face there appeared that wonderful look of hers, which made her face for the moment verily beautiful, and unclasping her hands, she threw them about the other's neck, whispering in awed tones:

"Yet you loved him! loved him too!"

Then after a moment of silence dear to both their hearts, she drew back to give her friend one other look, and quietly said:

"His heart is mine now, Ermentrude, wholly and truly mine. And so you would have it be, I am sure. Life looks fair to me and very sweet; but however fair, however sweet, that life is yours if ever you want it and when you want it. The time may come—one never knows—when I can pay you back this debt. Till then, let there be perfect trust and perfect love between us. Give me your hand upon it—not just your lips—for I speak as men speak when they mean to keep their word."

Their eyes met, their hands clasped; then the bridegroom drew away his bride, and Ermentrude turned with bowed head and glistening eyes, to enter upon the new life awaiting her in ways she had yet to tread.

The second series of episodes opens with the meeting of a man and woman on a rustic bridge spanning a Swiss chasm. They are strangers to each other, yet both instinctively pause and a flush of intuitive feeling dyes the cheek of each.

The eternal, ever-recurring miracle has happened. He sees Woman for the first time, though he had thought himself in love before and had wandered thus far in an effort to forget. So, likewise, with her. She had had her fancies, or rather her one fancy; but when in strolling along this road ahead of her party she saw rising between her and the glorious landscape which had hitherto filled her eye the fine masculine head and perfect figure of Carleton Roberts, this fancy floated from her mind like the veriest thistledown, leaving it free to expand in fuller hopes and deeper joys than visit many women even when they think they love.

Alas! why in that instant of mutual revelation had not the further grace been given them of quick catastrophe shutting the door upon a future of which neither could then dream or sense the coming doom.

It was not to be.

He passed, she passed, and for the time the look they gave each other was all; but the world had been glorified for them both—and Destiny waited.

"Good looks? Yes; but nothing else; very ordinary connections, very. A little money, true. Her uncle, whom by the way I judge you have not seen, will leave her a few thousands; but meanwhile he is a fixture—will not leave her or let her leave him, which is a misfortune since in a social way he is simply impossible. No sort of match for you, Roberts. Cut and run while there is time;

that's my advice to you, given in the most friendly spirit."

"Thank you. As I have but just met Miss Taylor, don't you think such advice is a little premature?"

"No, I don't. She is a woman who must be loved or left; that's all. You've heard me."

Did Carleton Roberts heed these words? No. What man in the thrall of his first romance ever did.

"You love me, Ermentrude?"

"I love you, Carleton."

"For a day, for a month or for a year?" he smiled.

"Forever," she answered.

"That's a long time," he murmured, with his eyes on a little clock hanging in the shop window before which they had stopped in one of their infrequent walks together. "A long time! That foolish little clock will beat out the hours of its short life and go the way of all things, before we shall hardly have entered upon the soul's 'forever.'"

"That clock will last our lifetime, Carleton. Afterward, love will not be counted by hours."

As she said this she turned her face his way and he saw it in its full flower with the light of heaven upon it. In later years he may have forgotten the emotions of that moment, but they were the purest, the freest from earthly stain that he was ever destined to know.

"I will love you *forever*," he whispered. "That little clock shall be my witness." And he drew her into the shop.

"Cuckoo!"

Ermentrude glanced up; the clock hung on her wall.

"Oh," she murmured, "each hour it will speak to me of him and his words," then softly, like one adream in Paradise:

> "I love but thee,
> And thee will I love to eternity."

Such was the event to her. What was it to him? Let us see:

A hotel room—a view of Pilatus, but with its top lost in enveloping clouds.

Seated before it with pen in hand above a sheet of paper, Carleton Roberts eyes these clouds but does not see them; he is hunting in his brain for words and they do not come. Why? His mother's name is on the page and he has only to write that she has been quite correct in her judgment as to the unfitness of the marriage he had had in mind:—that youth should mate with youth and that if she could see the glorious young girl whose acquaintance he had made here, she would be satisfied with his new choice which promised him the fullest happiness. Why then a sheet yet blank and a hesitating hand, when all it had to do was to write?

Who can tell? Man knows little of himself or of the conflicting passions which sway him this way or that, even when to the outward eye, and possibly to the inner one as well, action looks easy.

Did he feel, without its reaching the point of knowledge, that this mother of keenest expectation and highest hope would not be satisfied with what this charming but undeveloped girl of middle class parentage would bring him? Or was there, deep down in his own undeveloped nature, a secret nerve alive to ambitions yet unnamed, to hopes not yet formulated, which warned him to think well before he spoke the irrevocable word linking a chain which, though twined with roses, was nevertheless a chain which nothing on earth should have power to break.

He never sounded his soul for an answer to this question; but when he rose, the paper was still blank. The letter had not been written.

"I do not like secrecy."

"Only for a little while, Ermentrude. My mother is difficult. I would prepare her."

"And Uncle!"

"What of Uncle?"

"He made me take an oath today."

"An oath?"

"That I would not leave him while he lived."

"And you could do that?"

"I could do nothing else. He's a sick man, Carleton. The doctors shake their heads when they leave him. He will not live a year."

"A year? But that's an eternity! Can you wait, can I wait a year?"

"He loves me and I owe everything to him. Next week we go to Nice. These are days of parting for you and me, Carleton."

Parting! What word more cruel. She saw that it shook him, and held her breath for his promise that she should not be long alone. But it did not come. He was taking time to think. She hardly understood his doing this. Surely, his mother must be very difficult and he a most considerate son. She knew he loved her; perhaps never with a more controlling passion than at this moment of palpitating silence.

As she smiled, he caught her to his breast.

"We have yet a week," he cried, and left her hurriedly, precipitately.

It was their last ride and they had gone far—too far, Ermentrude thought, for a day so chilly and a sky so threatening. They had entered gorges; they had skirted mountain streams, had passed a village, left a ruined tower behind, and were still facing eastward, as if Lucerne had no further claims upon them and the world was all their own.

As the snows of the higher peaks burst upon their view, she made an attempt to stop this seeming flight.

"My uncle," she said. "He will be counting the hours. Let us go back."

Then Carleton Roberts spoke.

"Another mile," he whispered, not because he feared being overheard by their driver, but because Love's note is instinctively low. "You are cold; we shall find there a fire, and dinner—and—Listen, Ermentrude,—a minister ready to unite us. We are going back, man and wife."

"Carleton!"

"Yes, dear, it is quite understood. Letters are urging my return to New York. Your uncle is holding you here. I cannot face an uncertain separation. I must feel that you are mine beyond all peradventure—must be able to think of you as my wife, and that will hold us both and make it proper for you to come to me if I cannot come to you, the moment you are free to go where you will."

"But why this long ride, this far-away spot? Why couldn't a minister be found in Lucerne? Is our marriage to be as secret as our engagement? Is that what you wish, Carleton?"

"Yes, dear; for a little while, just for a little while, till I have seen my mother, and rid our way of every obstacle to complete happiness. It will be better. When one has promised to love *forever*, what are a few weeks or months. Make me happy, dear. You have it in your power to do so. Happy! When once I can whisper 'wife,' the world will not hold a happier man than I."

Did she yield because of her own great longing? No, it was by that phrase he caught her: *The world will not hold a happier man than I.*

Mountains! Icy peaks, with sides heavy with snow! And so

near! Almost they seemed to meet across the narrow valley. She gave them one quick glance, then her eyes and her heart became absorbed in what she could see of this Alpine village, holding up its head in the eternal snows like an edelweiss on the edge of a glacier.

It was to be the scene of her one great act in life; the spot she was entering as a maiden and would leave as a wife. What other spot would ever be so interesting! To note its every detail of house and church would not take long—it was such a little village, and the streets were so few; and the people—why she could count them.

Afterward, she found that the exact number and the difference in color of the short line of timbered houses stretching between them and the church were imprinted on her brain; but she did not know it at the time for her attention was mainly fixed upon the people when once she had seen them, for there was a strangeness in their looks and actions she did not understand, all the more that it seemed to have nothing to do either with Carleton or herself.

It was not fear they showed, not exactly, though consternation was not lacking in their aspect, so strangely similar in all, whether they were men or women, or whether they stood in groups in the street or came out singly on the doorstep to glance about and listen, though there seemed to be nothing to listen to, for the air was preternaturally still.

"Carleton, Carleton," she asked as he came to lift her to the ground, "see those people how oddly they act. The whole town is in the street. What is the matter?"

"Nothing, except that if we do not hasten we shall have to return unmarried. The minister is waiting for us."

"What, in the church?"

"Yes, dear. We are a little late."

She took his arm, and though they were a fine couple and the event was almost an unprecedented one in that remote village, only a few followed them; the rest hung round their homes or gazed with indecision at the mountains or up and down along the empty roads.

"Wilt thou have this woman...."

The ceremony had proceeded thus far and all seemed well, when with a rush and a cry a dozen people burst into the building.

"The snows are moving!" rang up the aisles in accents of mad terror. "Save yourselves!"

Then came the silence of emptiness. Every soul had left the church save the three before the pulpit.

An avalanche! and the ceremony was as yet incomplete! Ermentrude never forgot Carleton Roberts' look. Doubtless he never forgot hers. Meanwhile the minister spoke.

"There is a chance for escape. Take it; the good God will pardon you."

But the bridegroom stood firm and the bride shook her head.

"Not till the words are said which make us man and wife," declared Carleton Roberts. "Unless"—and here his perfect courtesy manifested itself even in this crisis of life and death—"you feel it your duty to carry what assistance you can to the saving of your frightened flock."

"God must save my flock," said the minister with a solemn glance upward. "I am where my duty places me." And calmly as though the pews were filled with guests and joy attended the ceremony instead of apprehended doom, he proceeded with the rite.

"Wilt thou have this man...."

The glad "I will" leaped bravely from Ermentrude's lips; but it was lost in loud calls and shrieks from without, mingled with that sound—terrible to all who hear—impossible to describe—of the might of the hills made audible in this down-rushing mass, now halting, now gathering fresh momentum, but coming—always coming, till its voice, but now a threat, swells into thunder in which all human cries are lost, and only from the movement of the minister's lips can this couple see that the words which make them one are being spoken.

Then comes the benediction, and with the falling of those holy hands, a headlong rush into the open air—a vision of flying forms here, there, and everywhere—men staggering under foolish burdens—women on their knees with arms lifted to heaven or flung around their babes—hope lost under the bowing mountain; and in the midst of it all, plain to the view of all, the stranger's horse and carriage which, standing there, stamped with undying honor these terrified villagers, who had seen and not touched them though Death had them by the hair.

"Quick! quick! You mother there with the child, get in, get in; there is room here for one more."

But another got the place. The driver, reeling as he ran, sprang for the empty seat and hung there between the wheels as the horses plunged and tore away to safety just as the great mass with its weight of gathered boulders and uprooted forests crashed in final doom upon that devoted village, burying it from sight as though it had never been.

To safety? Yes, for two of them; the other, struck by a flying stone, fell in the road and was covered in a trice. So close were they to destruction's edge at this moment of headlong flight.

Not till the painted towers encircling Lucerne had come again into sight did the newly wedded pair find words or make the least attempt to speak. Then Carleton kissed his bride and for a moment love was triumphant. Was it triumphant enough to lead him to acknowledge their marriage? She looked anxiously in his face to see and finally she asked:

"How much of this are we to tell, Carleton?"

"All about the catastrophe; but nothing more," he answered.

And while her heart retained its homage, the light in her eyes was veiled.

Married but not acknowledged! Would it not have been better if the avalanche had overwhelmed them? She almost thought so, till bending, he murmured in her ear:

"I shall follow you soon. Did you think I could go on living without you?"

"Why so thoughtful, Ermentrude? You are not quite yourself today?"

"Uncle is very ill. The doctors say that he may not live a month."

"And does that grieve you?"

A yes was on her lips, but she did not utter it. Instead, she drew a little ribbon from her breast, on which hung a plain gold ring, and gazing earnestly at this token she remarked very quietly:

"Carleton, have you ever thought that but for this ring no proof remains in all this world of our ever having been married?"

"But our hearts know it. Is that not enough?" he asked.

"For today, yes. But when uncle goes...."

His kisses finished the sentence for her, and love resumed its sway; but when alone and wakeful on her pillow, she recalled his look, the sting of her first doubt darted through her uneasy heart, and feeling eagerly after the ring she tore it from its ribbon and put it on her finger.

"It is my right," she whispered. "Henceforth I shall wear it. He loves me too well to quarrel with my decision. Now am I really his wife."

Did she see a change in him? Did he come less frequently? Did he stay less long? Was there uneasiness in his eye—coolness—languor? No, no. It was her exacting heart which thus interpreted his look—which counted the days—forgot his many engagements—saw impatience in the quickness with which he corrected her faults in manner or language instead of the old indulgence which met each error with a smile. Love cannot always keep at fever-heat. He, the cynosure of the whole foreign element, had the world at his feet here as in Lucerne. It needed no jealous eye to see this; while she—well, she had her attractions too, as had been often proved, and with God's help she would yet be a fit mate for him. What she now lacked, she would acquire. She would watch these fine ladies who blushed with pleasure at his approach, and when her time of mourning was over she would astonish him with her graces and her appearance. For she knew how to dress, yes, with the best of them, and hold her head and walk like the queen she would feel herself to be when once she bore his name. Patience then, till she had stored her mind and learned the ways he was accustomed to in others. She had money enough now that her uncle was dead, and she could do things....

Yes, but something had gone out of her face, and the ring hung loose on her finger.

And he? Had her fears read him aright? Had he grown indifferent or was he simply perplexed? Let us watch him as he paces his hotel room one glorious afternoon, now stopping to re-read a letter he held in his hand, and now to gaze out with unseeing eyes to where the blue of the sea melts into the blue of the sky on the far horizon.

Love had been sweet; but man has other passions, and he is in the grip of the one mightiest in men of his stamp—the all-engrossing, all-demanding one of personal ambition.

Without solicitation, without expectation even, a hand had been held out to him whose least grasp meant success in the one field most to his mind,—a political career under auspices which had never been known to fail. But there were conditions attached—conditions which a year before would have filled him with joy, but which now stood like a barrier between him and his goal, unless.... But he was not yet ready to disavow his wife, trample upon her heart, nay on his own as well;—that is, without a struggle.

For the third time he read the letter which you will see was from his mother.

My Son:—I have an apology to make and a bit of news to give you. When I urged you to give up Lucie and to seek distraction abroad, I felt that I was doing justice to your immaturity and saving you from ties which might very easily jeopardize your future happiness.

But I have lately changed my mind. In seeing more of her I have not only learned her worth but the advantage such a woman would be to one of your tastes and promise. And she loves you more devotedly, perhaps, than you have loved her. How do I know this? Let me tell you of an interview I had with a certain relative of hers last night. I allude to her brother, and for a recognized boss buried out of sight in politics, he has more heart in his breast than I have ever given him credit for. Not having children of his own, he has centered his affections on this choice little sister of his, and finding her far from happy, came to see me yesterday evening with this proposition: If I would consent to your union with Lucie, and withdraw my opposition to your immediate marriage, he would take your future in charge and put you in the way of political advancement only to be limited, as he says, by your talents, which he is good enough to rate very high.

After this, how can I do otherwise than bid you follow your impulses and marry Lucie in spite of the disparity of years to which I have hitherto taken exception. Were she as poor as she is accounted rich, I should say the same, now that I have sounded the depths of her lovely disposition and the rare culture of a mind which those seven years have enriched beyond what is usual even in women of intellect. Her money does not influence me in her favor, nor does it weigh with me in my present opinion of her complete fitness for the position you are so eager to give her. That this will make you happy I know. Let it hasten your return which cannot be too speedy.

This was the bombshell which had disturbed Carleton Roberts' complacency, bared his own soul to his horrified view, and revealed to him the weakness of his moral nature which he had hitherto considered strong. For his first impulse was one of recoil, not only from the secret marriage which shut him off from these new hopes, but from his youthful bride as well. He found himself weary of his flowery bonds and eager for a man's life in his native city. Oh, why had he urged this immature girl to take the ride which had led him into slavery to one who could not advance him in life, however queen-like she moved and talked and smiled upon the world from the heights of her physical perfections. It was brain that was needed—an understanding like Lucie's, tempered, like hers, by years, not months, of culture and refined association.

It was at this point he paused in his restless walk and looked for inspiration to the far-off waters of the bluest of all seas.

Suddenly he resumed his walk; then quickly stopping again sat down at his desk and with an air of desperate haste began a letter to his mother with the announcement:

It is too late. Unfortunately for your scheme, I am already....

He never got any further. A fresh impulse drove him into the street. He could not thus summarily settle his future fate. It meant too much to him. He must take time to think. His heart clamors loudly for its rights; he is only twenty-six—and in a rush of feeling which should have been his salvation, he turned toward that nest among the flowers where help was to be had if help was to come at all in this crisis of conflicting passions.

The hour was noon, one which he had never chosen before for a visit to Ermentrude. Would he find her in? Would she be in spirits to meet him? Would she look beautiful—worthy of his name, worthy of the greatest sacrifice a man can make for a woman? He half hoped that she would; that he would find his chains riveted and secure beyond the power of any force to break.

As his musings faltered, he turned the knob of the little side door and went in. As he did so a shower of rose-leaves fell upon him from the vines enveloping the balcony.

He shuddered slightly and passed down the hall. Everything was very still.

She was asleep. Lying on a couch in utter weariness or pain, she had drifted off into the land of dreams, and he felt that he had a moment of respite. He could look and weigh the question: Love or a quick success? A weakling's paradise or the goal of the strong man?

Meanwhile, she was not as beautiful as he thought. But she was more touching—less robust, less bounteous of aspect, more child-like, more appealing,—a woman who, if he were no more of a man than he appeared to be in this hurly-burly of pleasure and fashion, might in time do him credit and hold him back from follies.

But he was not just the man these casual friends and admirers considered him. There was much more to him than that. He knew this better than Lucie did or her powerful brother, or even his adoring mother. Great opportunities awaited him and a large space in the affairs of men if not of nations. Such confidence did he feel in himself at this fevered moment that he never doubted that eventually he would gain all this, even with the handicap of a good-looking but unsophisticated wife.

But not quickly;... step by step perhaps ... and he was longing to take it all at a bound.

Poor girl! and she lay there under his eyes all unmindful of his conflict or of the fact that her fate as well as his was trembling in the balance; unmindful, though her dreams were far from joyous—or why the tear welling from between her lashes as he gazed.

She was alone in the house; he knew it by the complete silence. He could look and look and study her every feature, without fear of interruption; wait for her waking and be ready to meet her first glance of tender astonishment which might restore him to his better self.

Drawing up a chair, he sat down; then started upright again with dilating eyes and a strange shadow on his brow. One of her arms lay uppermost and on the hand—almost as fine as Lucie's, but not quite,—he saw the ring—his ring, and it hung loosely. The poor child was growing thin, very thin. "If she were to hold her hand downward," he muttered to himself, "I believe that ring would fall off." Did some stray glimpse of his own features, wearing a look never seen on them before, confront him from some near-by mirror that he started so guiltily as this heart murmur rose to his lips? Or was it at a thought, hideous but tempting, which held him, gained upon him and soon absolutely possessed him, till his own hand went out stealthily and with hesitations toward those helpless fingers of hers, now approaching, now withdrawing, and now approaching them again but not touching them, great as his impulse was to do so, for fear she should wake, while yet the devil gripped his arm and lit up baleful fires in his eyes.

He had remembered those words of hers: "Have you ever thought that with the exception of this ring no proof exists in all the world of our ever having been married?" Remember them? He had not remembered them; he had heard them, sounding and resounding in his ears till the whole room seemed to palpitate with them. Then the devil made his final move. Ermentrude shuddered, and her position changing, the hand which had been uppermost fell down at her side and the ring slipped—left her finger—paused on the edge of the couch—then came to rest in his palm held out to receive it.

He had not drawn it from her hand. Fate had restored it. As he forced himself to look at it lying in his grasp, a faintness as of death seized and held him for a moment; then this passed and he slowly rose and step by step with sidelong looks and hair starting upright on his forehead, like one who has walked in blood and sees the trail of guilt following him along the floor, he left her side—he left the room—he left the house—and the rose-leaves fell about him once more, maddening him with their color, maddening him with the memories inseparable from their sweetness—a sweetness which spoke of her, of love, and the attachment of a true heart destined to grieve for a little while at least, for he was never going back, never, never.

There was no eye to see, and no tongue to tell him that the seed, destined to flower into awful crime some dozen or more years later, put forth its first bud at this fatal hour.

He wrote her a letter. He had the grace to do that. Addressing her simply as Ermentrude, he told her that he had been called home to enter upon the serious business of life. That he was not likely to come back, and as she was not really his wife, however pleasing the fiction had been in which they had both indulged, it seemed to him wiser to end their happy romance thus suddenly and while much of its glamour remained, than to linger on and see it decay day by day before their eyes till nothing but bitterness remained. He loved her and felt the wrench more than she did, but duty and his obligations as a man, etc., etc., till it ended in his signature limited to initials like his love.

Despicable! the work of a man without conscience or heart! Yes, and he knew it, and for weeks his sleep was broken by visions and his waking hours rendered dreadful by fears. How had she taken this cool assumption that the ceremony performed in the path of the snow was voided by lack of proof? To whom had she ascribed the loss of her ring, and what must she think of him? He had left Nice almost immediately, but wherever he went, in whatever hotel he stayed, or through whatever street he passed, he was always expecting to see her figure rise up before him in the majesty of innocence and outraged love.

Thus several weeks passed, and seeing nothing of her, hearing nothing from her, a different apprehension darkened his days and despoiled him of rest at night. Grief if not shame had killed her; and the weight of her fancied doom lay heavy on his heart. At last he could bear it no longer, and stealing back to Nice he entered it one dark night and prepared to learn for himself what he feared to trust to the discretion of another. Alone, with hidden face and heavily throbbing heart, he trod the familiar ways and encircled the familiar walls. Had she been there—

But the windows were blank and the place desolate, and he fled the spot and the town, with his questions unasked and his fears unallayed. In two days he had sailed for home. With the ocean between them he might forget; and in time he did. As week followed week, and the silence he had half trusted, half feared, remained unbroken, his equanimity gradually returned, and he prepared to face the prospect of his new marriage much as a man who watches for a dreaded door to open moves with restored confidence about his affairs, when at last convinced that the door is padlocked and the key lost.

One precaution and one only he was wise enough to take. He told his story to Lucie's brother, and left it to him to say whether or not he should marry his sister. And the answer was yes; that if trouble came he would see him through it. A marriage which could not be proved was no marriage, and as for anything else, Lucie's happiness must not be sacrificed to a boy's peccadillos. What were a few wild oats sown by a man of his promise?

And was this the end? Did Ermentrude accept her doom without a struggle?

Let us see.

One afternoon in June, there entered the parlor of the old-fashioned mansion of the Roberts family a lady who had asked to see Mrs. Roberts on business of an important nature. Though plainly clad, her appearance possessed an elegance which insured respect; but when alone and seated in the darkest corner of the great drawing room she put up a trembling hand to thrust back her veil, the countenance thus revealed betrayed an emotion hardly in keeping with the quiet bearing with which she had advanced under the servant's eye.

His home! and these the surroundings amid which he had grown to manhood! Why should the sight of all this rouse emotions she believed eliminated by a treachery most cruel in face of promises most sacred? Why, as she looked about, and noted object after object which must have been there previous to his birth, did she see him as a child and boy and not as the man who had first won and then deserted her? She would not have had it so at this hour when strength was needed rather than tenderness. But she could not help her nature, or still the wild surging of her rebellious heart, as his portrait seen upon the wall challenged her constancy and whispered of the hour when his "forever" echoed her "forever" and the compact for eternity was sealed.

He had broken this compact—broken it soon—broken it before the honeymoon had passed. But she! Was she to show no firmer spirit whose love was of the soul and took no note of time? She was his wife, and acknowledged or unacknowledged, must yet prove to be his blessing though he—he—

But this would not do. The interview before her called for calmness. She would not add to the turbulence of her spirits by another glance at what brought back too much of the past to fortify her for the impending struggle. She had to do credit to his choice, to impress a difficult woman with her dignity as a wife. She must not shake nor weep.

Yet when she heard a step at the door, instinct told her to pull down her veil till the first greetings were over—a precaution for which she was deeply grateful when in another moment a young woman entered instead of her husband's mother for whom she had asked and whom she naturally expected to see.

In the humiliation of the moment, her disappointment took words and she muttered within herself:

"A companion or possibly a relative. I am to be put off with kindly excuses; begged to state my errand—rehearse my claims and my hopes to some gentle go-between! I have not strength for that. I must see the mother—the mother. God give me wisdom and keep me calm—calm."

Meanwhile the young woman she had instinctively called gentle advanced into the center of the room. Mechanically, Ermentrude rose to meet her, and thus stepped into a better light. Tragedy came with her. This it was impossible not to see—not to feel. But the warning which her aspect gave passed as she spoke and said in tones a little tremulous, perhaps, but with an air of perfect courtesy:

"I had hoped to see Mrs. Roberts herself."

The smile with which this was greeted, the flush of pride and the joy of possession which lit the other's pleasing features as she replied, "I am Mrs. Roberts," should have carried the truth to Ermentrude.

But they did not. She looked surprised—baffled, and after the briefest hesitation, observed:

"I am a stranger in this city and have doubtless made some mistake. The Mrs. Roberts I have called to see—and I was told she lived here—is the mother of a gentleman of the name of—"

She could not speak it.

But the other could.

"Carleton?" she asked; and at Ermentrude's agitated nod, added with friendly interest: "This is her home; but she has left it for a while to us. I am Mr. Carleton Roberts' wife."

There are blows which prostrate; there are others which sear but leave the body intact—feet still supporting it—eyes still gazing ahead unmoved—lips moving with mechanical exactness and sometimes still retaining their smile. Only the soul which gave life to all of this is dead. The image is there but the spirit is gone; and if sufficiently preoccupied, the one who struck the blow sees no change. So was it with Ermentrude and Lucie.

"We are looking for mother to return next week," added the latter as Ermentrude stood stark and silent before her. "Would you like to leave a message for her?"

At these words uttered with the sweetness of a rich and sympathetic nature, the soul returned to Ermentrude's body. With a long and earnest look which took in the full measure of the other's personality, radiant with happiness and the consciousness of an assured wifedom, she answered softly:

"No, I will leave no message," and turned as if to go.

"Nor any name?" queried Lucie, eying with admiration the noble lines of a figure with whose perfect proportions her own could never hope to compete.

"Nor any name," came back in indescribable accents from the doorway.

Lucie paused, and gazing in vague trouble after her rapidly disappearing visitor, murmured to herself, "Who is she?"

But the one who could have answered her was gone.

"Carleton, you seldom see such a woman. Younger than I, she had the poise of a woman of thirty. Who could she have been?"

"Describe her."

"I wish I could; I hardly saw her face; it was her figure, her voice, her way of moving and holding herself. I felt as small and quiet as a little mouse beside her. Only I was happy and she was not. That much I feel now that I recall her look in leaving."

"Was she American or—or foreign?" he asked, hiding his trouble, for a great fear had seized him.

"She had an English accent which added very much to her charm."

"Forget her." For a moment his accent was almost fierce, then he laughed the matter off, assuring this bride of a month that she made him cross with her self-depreciation, that there was no one of finer mien and manner than herself, the chosen of his heart upon whom he always looked with pride. Which subtle tribute to what was her greatest charm accomplished its end; she did forget the stranger.

But he did not; he knew what was before him and prepared himself for the inevitable meeting which would be followed by—what?

Not by what he had every right to expect and evidently did. Ermentrude had learned all she would both of this marriage and of the woman who had supplanted her, and had made her resolve. This he saw as they came together in the isolation of a quiet corner of the Park, and so was not greatly surprised, though a little moved, as after the first few words, and with an earnest look, she said:

"I am your wife, I, Ermentrude Roberts, married to you in the sight of God and man. I cannot prove it, but as you once said, our hearts know it and will continue to know it as long as either of us lives. But I am not going to obtrude my claims upon you, Carleton, or stand like a specter in your path. Had this woman you have deceived been weak or foolish or unloving, or indeed anything but what she is, I might have held to my rights and insisted upon a recognition which would have profited you in the end. But I cannot shame that woman—I can neither shame her nor bring her to grief. You have broken one heart, but you shall be saved the remorse of breaking two. I had rather suffer myself. I am alone in the world. I have means. I can ultimately be useful and face good men and women without fear. Why then should I drag down to the dust one as innocent as myself, or take from you what may make you the man I once thought you and hope to see you again. But that I may have strength for this and for all the sacrifices it involves, you must declare here, now, in this open park where we stand, with no one within sight much less within hearing, that I am your wife."

"You are my wife."

"It is enough. Now I can say what otherwise could never have left my lips. I love you, Carleton, love you to eternity as I promised; but I shall never seek you again, and you can go on your way unperturbed. I have consolations here," laying her hand on her breast. "It will no longer be my portion to watch your face for signs of a failing regard. What I have is mine, and that is the undying memory of two months of perfect happiness."

She would have said more, but she saw that he had been greatly shaken. She feared the renewal of a flame not yet altogether extinct in a heart which once beat for her alone, and so contenting herself with a low farewell, she was turning swiftly away, when one last thought made her pause and say:

"I cannot return you your ring. It is lost. I was careless with it and it fell unnoticed from my hand. But tonight I will send you back the little clock which unites our initials. Destroy it if you will, but if some sentiment bids you keep it, let it be this one and no other: 'I recall Ermentrude only that I may be faithful to Lucie.'"

With a low cry his head fell upon his breast in extreme self-abasement, then he slowly lifted his eyes and seeing in her face a full knowledge of his sin, murmured in overwhelming shame and contrition:

"You know me for the wretch I am. I have the ring; it fell from your hand into mine one day while you lay asleep. I do not ask for forgiveness, but this I promise you, Ermentrude:—if the little clock comes back, I will make a place in it for this ring, and neither clock nor ring shall leave me again while I live."

Instinctively her hands went out to him, then they fell back on her breast.

"God will hold you to that promise," she said; and melted away from his sight in the mist which had been gradually enveloping them without being seen by either.

Thus the struggle ended for him, which for her had simply begun.

Not till she found herself in the South with her girl friend, Antoinette Duclos, did she discover that the closest bond which can unite man and woman held her in spite of her late compact with Carleton Roberts. Should she reassert her rights and demand that the father should recognize his child? Her generous heart said No. The old arguments held good. She appealed to Antoinette for advice.

The result we know. When Antoinette's own child died at birth, she took Ermentrude's to her heart and brought it up as her own. There was little difficulty in this, as the Professor had already yielded to a Southern fever and lay at rest in a New Orleans cemetery.

And this brings us to another episode.

The widow in fact and the widow in heart stood face to face above a sleeping infant. They were both dressed for traveling and so was the babe. The dismantled rooms showed why. Young still, for the years of either's romance had been few, each face, as the other contemplated it, told the story of sorrow which Time, for all its kindliness, would never efface. But the charm of either remained—perceptible at this hour as perhaps it would never be again to the same extent. Antoinette basked in the light of Ermentrude's beauty ennobled by renunciation, and Ermentrude in that wonderful look in her friend's plain face which came at great crises and made her for the moment the equal of the best.

They had said little; and they said little now, as is the way of the strong amongst us when an act is to be performed which wrings the heart but satisfies the conscience.

The child was legitimate. It must not grow up under a shadow. To insure its welfare and raise no doubt in its own mind as it grew in knowledge and feeling, the two women must separate. No paltering with this duty, and no delay. A month of baby cries and baby touches might weaken the real mother. It should be now. It should be today.

But first, a final word—a parting question. It was uttered by Ermentrude.

"You will go back to France?"

"Yes. I can easily live there. And you, Ermentrude?"

"To New York. I shall never go far from him. But he and I will never meet. My world will not be his world. I shall make my own place."

"As Ermentrude Taylor?"

"As Mrs. Ermentrude Taylor. I am a wife. I shall never forget that fact."

"And the child? Will you never come to see it?"

Ermentrude's head fell and she stood a long time without answering. Then with a steady look she calmly said:

"I can think of but one contingency which might shake my resolution to leave her yours without the least interruption from me. If *he*—Antoinette, if he were left alone and childless, I might see my duty differently from now. You must be prepared for that."

"Ermentrude, when you send me this little shoe—See, I will leave one on and give you the other, I shall know that you are coming, or that you want the child. My life is yours as I once promised, and do you think I would hold back the child?"

And again their hands met as once before, in that strong clasp, which means:

"Trust me to the death and beyond it."

With Antoinette it was to the death, as we have seen. Warned by Ermentrude of the appalling results of their plan to bring father and child together, and entreated to fly lest her story should imperil the secret upon the preservation of which his very life now hung, she answered to the call as she had promised, and thus acquitted her debt though she failed to save him.

Of her previous act in disfiguring his photograph in her temporary lodging-place, we shall never know the full story. The picture had been hers for years, given her by Ermentrude on their parting, so that the child should not be without some semblance of her father even if she should not know him as such, and it was to secure this clue to their now doubly dangerous secret that Madame Duclos ransacked her baggage previous to her flight from the New York hotel. But whether its destruction in the peculiar manner we know was the result of simple precaution, or of a feeling of antagonism so strong against this destroyer of her beloved's peace, that it had to be expended in some way before she felt strong enough for that supreme sacrifice in his favor toward which events seemed hurrying her, may be known in *Eternity* but will never be told in *Time*.

And Ermentrude? What of her? Alone, robbed of husband and child and friend—where shall we look for her in this world of extreme tribulation? Search the hospitals of France where they press closest to the trenches. There will you find the woman who losing all has found much. Blessing and blest! the angel of the battlefield whom the bullets spare since her work on earth is not yet accomplished!

THE END